THE COMPANY MAN

BOOKS BY EDWARD M. LERNER

Novels

- Probe
- Moonstruck
- Fools' Experiments
- Small Miracles
- Energized
- Dark Secret
- The Company Man
- Déjà Doomed

InterstellarNet series novels

- InterstellarNet: Origins
- InterstellarNet: New Order
- InterstellarNet: Enigma

Fleet of Worlds series novels (with Larry Niven)

- Fleet of Worlds
- Juggler of Worlds
- Destroyer of Worlds
- Betrayer of Worlds
- Fate of Worlds

Collections and nonfiction

- Creative Destruction
- Countdown to Armageddon / A Stranger in Paradise
- Frontiers of Space, Time, and Thought
  (mixed fiction and nonfiction)
- A Time Foreclosed (chapbook)
- Trope-ing the Light Fantastic:
  The Science Behind the Fiction (nonfiction)
- Muses & Musings
- The Sherlock Chronicles & The Paradise Quartet
- The Best of Edward M. Lerner

THE COMPANY MAN

EDWARD M. LERNER

an imprint of

Rockville, Maryland

ISBN: 978-1-64973-129-6

www.PhoenixPick.com

PRIOR PUBLICATION CREDITS

Sections of this novel originally appeared, in substantially different form, in *The Grantville Gazette (Universe Annex)*:

"The Company Man," May 2017 issue
"The Company Dick," September 2017 issue
"The Company Mole" (as a two-part serial), November 2018 and January 2019 issues
"The Company Bane" (as a two-part serial), March 2019 and May 2019 issues

Phoenix Pick Edition, March 2023.

Published by Phoenix Pick
an imprint of Arc Manor
P. O. Box 10339
Rockville, MD 20849-0339
www.ArcManor.com

For that quintessential company man: "The Continental Op,"
Dashiell Hammett's great, nameless detective

CONTENTS

...◆...

THE COMPANY MAN

Working for paranoids isn't the easiest or the safest way to make a living, but it paid well. It even appeared that I had survived another assignment, and I looked forward to enjoying my hard-earned gains.

Afloat in the windowless tin-can cabin of my vessel, three remote rocks visited as planned, bound at last for home, I fantasized about air and water not endlessly recycled, food that had not been freeze-dried and re-hydrated, and gymnastic marathon sex with my wife. Not necessarily in that order.

Till I reached Ceres, my plans consisted of more of the same. There was nothing to do, not even if I wanted. Company vessel 724 (or as I preferred to think of her, the *Bounty*, though whether I channeled Captain Bligh or Mister Christian varied with my frame of mind) flew itself. Only the bridge computer knew where we were or when we'd arrive, and it wasn't telling. Without instruments, without windows, I couldn't as much as guess.

To be fair, the company had come honestly by its paranoia. Registering a mining claim to a rock meant less than squat when the rock regularly wandered millions of kilometers from civilization—and law enforcement. And when the wealth that rock had to offer was more than enough to corrupt anyone. And when to register the claim would have meant disclosing the orbital parameters. How many such rocks did the company exploit? What were their orbits? Apart from the managing partners, I doubt anyone knew.

On my inaugural jaunt for the company, cocky about my own brilliance, I'd suited up en route to my first rock to do some naked-eye astronomy. Only the paranoids had anticipated that ploy: looking outward from within the air lock, even after allowing ten minutes for my eyes to adjust to the dark, I had seen … nada. An arm extended through the open outer hatch caught zero sunlight, meaning autopilot had me oriented away from the Sun—and that the patch of sky before me *must* have been filled with unseen stars.

I'd had to resist the urge to smack myself upside the helmet. Of *course* my employers had insisted upon furnishing my vacuum gear for the flight. Of *course* company ships stocked extra helmets, and never a printer capacious enough to make spares as needed. Clearly, the smartglass visor in my company-provided helmet filtered stars from a black sky. Had I been facing in a suitable direction, doubtless it would have filtered out planets, too. Otherwise every miner with a gram of astronomy sense—not to mention ringers recruited as miners—would try the same exercise I was undertaking. With a sigh, I'd taken the hint, closed the outer hatch, and returned inside. Foiled.

The anticipation of marathon sex was far more pleasant than memories of my past naiveté. It couldn't be long now …

A bridge console chimed: incoming message. I pulled myself into my acceleration couch and tapped to acknowledge. A display lit up and I read: ACCELERATION IN TWO MINUTES. MINE EMERGENCY. RENDER ALL POSSIBLE ASSISTANCE.

Meaning, company commitments notwithstanding, I wasn't going home. Meaning also that, beyond not knowing to where I'd been rerouted, I knew nothing about the emergency. Because the company didn't know? Mining stations, like ships, had no transmission capability. "For security." So how the hell did the company know there *was* an emergency?

All good questions, I thought. And they were all going to go without answers, at least until I got … wherever.

"Columbus managed without a radio," the bored company recruiter had once explained. "And Magellan. And Cook and Drake and pick your explorer."

Not that Magellan or Cook had made it home alive. Was I supposed to like those odds? "Which of them were in vacuum, millions of klicks from help?"

"Hence the hazardous-duty pay," I'd been told. "And most likely, you'll live."

And indeed, so far, I had. But with this undefined emergency, I had to wonder if my luck had run out.

...◆...

Waiting in a hallway, my gaze wandered about the tiny, claustrophobic room to which, almost sooner than I had struggled out of my vacuum gear, I had been delivered by a pair of taciturn miners. (Emphasis on *almost*. The men took the time to give me a full pat down, an ultrasound scan, and to paw through my utility belt and valise. I didn't have any contraband with me, but protocol must be followed—and to the pickiest detail, given that I'd had the temerity, this being an unscheduled stop, to have arrived without a mail bag.) Both men had been edgy, but that was only to be expected. No one's ever pleased with a company auditor showing up. I wasn't too happy myself.

My escorts, without a word, left me. Beyond the hatch, studiously (contrivedly?) ignoring me, my host frowned at his desktop. From time to time he took a sip from a drink bulb. I cleared my throat. Without looking up, he raised a finger. As in the universal annoying gesture for wait a minute. Some emergency.

It could have been the control room of any asteroid mining station anywhere, and I'd visited plenty enough to know. Wall displays cycled from camera to camera to camera, most offering dreary, near-ground-level views of pockmarked, much-churned terrain. Little interrupted the desolation but boot prints, the crab-like sidling of many-tentacled mining bots, and a pressure-suited figure gliding hand over hand along a staked-down guide wire to or from some chore. Sun glinted off the occasional solar reflector chancing to appear over the freakishly close horizon; once I spotted the eldritch blue glow of an ion thruster adjusting a mirror's hover. Other displays offered more panoramic—if no less bleak—vistas: look-downs from the hovering reflectors. As overhead pics flashed past, I twice caught sight of the *Bounty* as it lay tethered to the barren surface and once of the base air lock. The final few wall displays offered interior shots of this underground station: corridors, common areas, the vault (sealed; stacked with lustrous ingots), the arms locker (sealed), even air ducts and cable conduits.

All cartoonish glimpses, of course. Still and vid cameras at company stations were purposefully insensitive and low-res, hence unable to capture any astronomical object other than the Sun. Try as you might, you couldn't repurpose these cams for clandestine astronomy projects. I worked for evil geniuses.

Where display screens *didn't* cover the walls, magnets pinned paper lists, production schedules, hand-scrawled notes, and cartoons to the steel panels. What little of the actual wall I could see glowed in a particularly bilious shade of green. In fine sprinklings, gauzy films, and great, sooty smudges, the ubiquitous dust—you couldn't work an asteroid without tracking more of the stuff inside from every surface foray—tainted everything. In the minutes since I had entered the station, my jumpsuit, clean upon arrival, already gave hints of mimicking a leopard.

The used-gunpowder odor of the dust tickled my nose. I'd get used to that, I knew, and to the bouquet of hardworking men and women in tight quarters, but such olfactory adjustments always took time. To my left, from the room's air duct, came the whirr of a fan. Ventilation and filtration somehow distributed the dust and stench more than removed it.

Finally done with whatever task I was to believe demanded his urgent attention, the station chief glanced up from his desktop. "Welcome to the Rock." Because the smaller asteroids, no matter their official designations, went by either of two more meaningful names: the Rock or (for rubble jumbles loosely held together by their feeble mutual gravity) the Pile. He emerged from behind the desk, shoes zip-zipping on a filthy gripper rug the same sickly hue, beneath ground-in dirt, as the walls, with his right hand extended. "Baxter. Simon Baxter."

I introduced myself. Shaking hands, I felt … paper. A bribe, already? Really? And for the paltry sum a person could palm? I pondered whether to be more amused or insulted—but a momentary narrowing of his eyes and the flicker of a downward glance didn't fit a bribery scenario. Neither did the emergency summons. I found myself closely studying the station chief.

Baxter was a wiry black man, about forty-five, his head clean-shaven and wax-shiny. He had an open, honest face of the sort I associated with saints and con men—and I've never met a saint. Typically enough, Baxter wore a standard company blue jumpsuit, splotched and smudged. He was native-Earth tall, meaning I towered over him. I had studied his HR jacket, of course, along with those of *everyone* assigned to this ass-end-of-nowhere hunk of metal and stone (those files, if not any explanation of the so-called emergency, having accompanied my detour orders), but the hint of a Scottish burr still came as a surprise.

"Come in." Baxter shut the hatch behind me, then gestured at the jump seat affixed to the room's back wall. No matter the hearty greeting, he seemed twitchy. "Take a load off."

"No thanks."

"This may take a while. Sit."

"I'm *fine*." Because in—what? Well under one percent of a gee? Nothing perceptible, in any event—why would I need to sit?

Baxter swallowed. "Suit yourself." Returning behind the desk, *he* sat. It made the difference between eye levels that much more awkward. He took a fat pen from his pocket and began twirling it end over end.

"Suppose you tell me why—"

"Coffee? Tea? A bite to eat?" Baxter's gaze, as he spoke, flicked toward my right hand. Swallowing a second time, still fidgeting with the pen, he glanced up over my shoulder at the room's lone air vent.

Keeping my hand down by my side, I snuck a peek. I didn't find money; the folded scrap of paper looked torn from a ruled notepad. If I were to park myself in the indicated chair, I would be well below the air duct—and *it* wouldn't have a line of sight to me. Unfolding the curved arm rests that would keep me from drifting from the chair at the least little motion, I sat.

If there's anything auditors are taught, it's to put two and two together.

Wondering what was inside the duct, I unfolded the paper. In blocky printing, the hand-written note I found read: ROOM MIGHT BE BUGGED. AFTER I TRIPLE-CLICK MY PEN, WE CAN TALK.

I nodded my understanding. "Nothing for me now, thanks. Maybe some coffee later."

Click-click-click. Baxter slumped in his seat, open-and-honest morphing in an instant to honestly panicked. "Thank *God* you got here."

I didn't suppose He had much to do with it. "Evidently that pen is a bug jammer of some kind." Not that any such item appeared anywhere on the company's *List of Equipment Approved for Use in Mining Facilities.* If something helpful could be printed, it was—and then broken down to feedstock before returning to civilization. Or when an auditor popped by: even as we spoke, the station recyclers were surely molecularizing contraband. "If you actually feel the need for a jammer, didn't turning that on tip off whoever might be listening?"

Baxter managed a wan smile. "I expect that person, or persons, will conclude *you* brought the jammer, the better to negotiate an acceptable cut of whatever goodies I might hope with your help to spirit away. I haven't dared to look, but if there *is* a fiber-optic cable inside that duct above your head, not jammable, they can't see what you did, or didn't, just switch on."

My opinion of the man bumped up a notch. I still didn't know what had him so anxious, but I could venture a guess. When the product is platinum, some pilferage is unavoidable. Beyond that metal's many traditional markets, every settled off-Earth world and habitat—where platinum was a key catalyst for the production of nitric acid, needed to make fertilizer—represented a voracious new demand. The good news was, that kept me in a job—but pilferage didn't add up to an emergency. "Your inventory getting too far out of whack?"

"Nothing so simple." Baxter shivered. "I found a bomb."

A *bomb*? Who the hell would bomb a mining station? Someone planning to make off with a boatload of platinum, that's who. Someone intending to eliminate any witnesses …

I've never claimed nerves of steel—and just then, nerves of wet tissue seemed more descriptive—but focus can be a reasonable substitute. I wondered how long I could sustain it. "You said, 'Thank God you got here.' As if you were expecting me."

Because that was impossible. Okay, evidently not impossible, but mysterious all the same. As mysterious as, apart from somewhere deep within the Belt, *here* was. But by the same token, neither I nor any miner on shore leave could be bribed or coerced into betraying the Rock's location—the mind boggled at how much money *that* treachery could fetch—because the only radios permitted on company rocks were short-range: pressure-suit helmet comms, a similar wattage nav beacon, and the like. It was the beacon that had guided me in once autopilot had gotten me close, and after I'd pulsed out the company authentication code of the month by flashing my ship's attitude thrusters.

Baxter managed a weak smile. "Your confusion is a marvel to behold. It's also a distraction. We need to move past it."

"But you *did* ask for me to be sent here."

"Not you personally. Anyone who could help." Baxter leaned forward, looking hopeful. "You *can* help, right? Company auditors all have law-enforcement experience?"

For a few years, I'd done computer forensics at the Ceres City PD. As a civilian contractor. I grunted noncommittally. Nothing like the bomb squad. That train of thought brought me back to wondering what the *hell* I was doing here. "How, exactly, did you call for help?"

"Hello? Bomb?"

Baxter *hadn't* signaled for a ship large enough to evac everyone. Detonation of the bomb couldn't be too imminent. I waited.

"*How* is something known only to station chiefs. For emergencies."

I waited.

He sighed. "There's a stealthed and silent buoy free-flying somewhere nearby. I don't know where. If I don't reposition a particular retroreflector on the surface at least every second standard day, the buoy beams a Mayday message to headquarters."

"And the company sent *me*?" Because bomb disposal isn't in the job description of a forensic accountant.

Baxter looked away. "Not a lot of information gets conveyed by the repositioning, or not, of the retroreflector. All I could signal was that I needed help."

"So I was on the nearest company ship?" Lucky me.

He shrugged. "That's my guess."

Then we're well and truly screwed, I thought. But all I said was, "Maybe begin at the beginning."

…◆…

Seeing is believing. *Really* seeing, that is. Not the blurry download images from Baxter's pocket comp. And so, now, I believed.

Okay, to the best of my knowledge I had never before seen a bomb. Perhaps I shouldn't have jumped to conclusions from spy and crime vids. But with my head peering gopherlike into the storeroom ceiling duct from which I had carefully removed the grill, what stared back at me at arm's length sure as hell looked like a bomb. Whereas what I'd been shown in Baxter's office, in supposed real-time imagery from a maintenance cam and in many weeks' worth of logged still images alike, was an unobstructed duct.

"Damned storeroom was, is, just too damned musty," the station chief said. His jammer/pen, once again clipped to his pocket, was still active. He had accompanied me to the storage area, latching the hatch behind us. "I would come in here looking for a crate of whatever, and the air in the room always felt, you know, close. Stagnant. Finally, I didn't *care* what the computers had to say. I checked the duct myself."

I imagined Baxter had seen what I saw: a clear-walled bottle (ordinary glass, by the way a penlight beam glinted from it), with hints of dust on the bottom; an off-white, claylike glob (plastique, I inferred); a skinny metallic tube jabbed into the glob (if I were right about plastique, the tube was a blasting cap); and an electronics module with a keypad. Behind and sticking above the rest were batteries. Everywhere, wires. The full assemblage, taped into place, all but blocked the duct. The readout chip on that electronics module was decrementing, its least significant digits changing at the same pace as, I confirmed with a quick downward glance, the seconds on my wrist-clock tattoo. It appeared we had five days till the shit hit the fan—and staring at the bottle, I wondered exactly what that shit was. A neurotoxin? A bioagent?

I asked, "And this is the only bomb?"

"Believe me, I've looked. When people have been on the surface, I've searched their rooms and lockers. This is the only device I found."

Five days till *boom*. Three days, according to Baxter, till a ship was due at the Rock to rotate crews. Two crews alternated here, suggesting the bomb had been planted by someone from the current group. Then again, why deploy the bomb any earlier than, say, a few hours before shift turnover? The longer the bomb sat in the duct, the greater the chances of discovery. As, in fact, it *had* been discovered …

I cogitated some more. Maybe the bomb had been deployed just before the *other* crew had rotated out. It would make a kind of sense, if the bomber wouldn't be coming back and the target were someone in the returning crew. It made yet more sense if the target were the entire remainder of that crew. Had someone recently left that crew, I wondered?

Explosives and blasting caps were common enough in a mining camp, but not bottles of poison. Surely those didn't get past inspection onto a crew ship. So one thing seemed certain: the bottled stuff had been made onsite. Thereafter clearing all traces of bomb-making from the station computer records (as I presumed, and would confirm, must have been done), even for someone with sysadmin privileges, would take serious smarts. *I* could have done it. Happily I'd been elsewhere when Baxter made his discovery, so I could eliminate myself as a suspect.

Ergo: computer smarts was a clue. It would be a place to start, anyway, and I was glad to have one, because about the only other datum I had to go on was a looming deadline. And *deadline* looked to be literal.

But what if the time displayed were padded, to lull anyone discovering the device into the false belief they could safely wait to evacuate on the nearing crew ship rather than attempt to disarm the thing? What if my files about this crew and the incoming crew were disinformation provided by an accomplice at headquarters? What if—?

Stepping off the crate of emergency rations I had set beneath the duct, I shuddered.

"You *did* see it?" Baxter asked anxiously.

"Afraid so."

"Silver lining." Baxter managed a faint smile. "I'm not crazy."

"Silver foil, at best."

"I suppose." With a sigh, he leaned back against the room's closed hatch. "Okay. You can disarm it, right?"

"It's likely booby-trapped."

As if I would know. Still, the blasting cap alone would shatter the glass (although, far more discreetly, tripping the control module might simply open a valve that hadn't been visible to me). What purpose did the explosives serve if not acting as a deterrent?

It wasn't, I decided, a difficult question: the plastique would burst walls all around if the device were discovered, and hatch and duct then sealed to contain the mystery gas. Bottom line—and bottom lines were the sort of thing I was *paid* to be good with—amateur bomb disposal was a Certified Bad Idea.

It all seemed carefully calibrated. A bomb large enough to spread the … whatever across the station. Bomb placement deep enough underground to not compromise the overall integrity of the station, where a bomb near the air lock would plunge everyone, almost instantly, into hard vacuum. Someone had given this a *lot* of thought.

Baxter grimaced. "I was afraid you'd say that."

"Maybe we can ease the device out of the duct, then take it outside before it goes off."

"Did you see a squat tube, about two centimeters long, mounted on the electronics module? Parts code X27C82?"

Maybe I'd seen something like that, but I had no idea about a part number. I stepped back onto the crate. There was such a tube, but the lettering on it was too tiny for me to read. "What is it?"

"An accelerometer. They're standard in most of our robots. It's like the component in your pocket comp that knows when you've changed its orientation—only a lot more sensitive."

Just great. Floor vibrations from climbing on and off my crate apparently weren't enough to trigger the device—I was still here, wasn't I?—but this time I stepped down gingerly, on tiptoe.

"So *can* you disarm it?" he tried again.

"No. I wouldn't have a clue where even to start."

"Well, *that's* unfortunate." He paused. "Okay, we have four suspects. Where do you want to begin?"

Uh-uh, I thought. Five suspects from the other crew. And five from this crew, as well, because how better to deflect suspicion than being the person who called in the bomb threat? If appearances were why I had been summoned here, what did that suggest about *my* odds of getting away alive?

Bottom line: for all I knew, anyone among those ten might aspire to seize the crew ship, disable the autopilot, and fly away (never mind that I'd never figured out how to do it) with a heap of stolen platinum. Leaving behind lots of dead bodies …

Holding in another shudder, I said, "Let me get back to you on that."

My plan, if an idea this simple could be so dignified, was straightforward enough: run a normal audit. Merely doing my job—as every miner knew and resented—authorized me to snoop and pry. How else was I going to ferret out the identity of the bomber? Once we knew who he, she, or they were, we ought to be able to convince or coerce them into disarming it. Making them stay onto the next shift, with the bomb due to go off, seemed like incentive enough … It wasn't much of a plan, but try as I might, I hadn't come up with anything better.

Okay, that wasn't exactly true. I could climb back aboard the good ship *Bounty*, of passenger capacity one, and its autopilot would take me home. It'd be safe and smart, no matter that ("RENDER ALL POSSIBLE ASSISTANCE") fleeing might get me fired. And perhaps futile: Baxter, through the minimal effort of *not* shifting something on the Rock's surface, could get my ship turned right around. Also, who was to say that whoever had set the known bomb wouldn't—or hadn't already—put another example of his handiwork aboard my ship? All that practicality aside, a part of me knew that to abandon these men and women would be wrong.

Cutting out could be Plan B. It would wait a few days.

So: on Day One, I tallied records of ore collected, assayed, and processed; ingots printed; ingots delivered through the one-way valve into the vault; ingots reported stacked and tied down by the robotic arm inside; and an eyeball inspection through the vault's thick Lucite view ports. Just barely within the unofficial bounds of acceptable pilferage, almost a kilo unaccounted for, the data matched. I randomly searched cabinets, bins, equipment consoles, and suchlike for contraband—everywhere but in the air ducts. I spot-checked gear and personal belongings that the departing crew might intend to carry aboard the crew ship. That I saw, no oh-two tanks had, since departing Ceres, magically transmuted from base metals into platinum. Anything that blatant I would have had to deal with. I noticed and ignored some pens and a class ring that were almost surely platinum. Had I cared to check, I doubtless would have found many small items miraculously platinum beneath thin veneers, in everything from jewelry to work-shoe toecaps to jumpsuit zippers. Part of the company's evil genius was letting petty theft succeed. Anyone focused on the penny-ante smuggling had less time to spend, and less inclination to spend it, plotting a grand heist. And I went over security logs. In the process, I spotted the vid loop in digital surveillance feed by which a maintenance cam failed to show the bomb. I didn't immediately find digital fingerprints to reveal how, or by whom, the hack had been pulled off.

All that activity was simply me doing a familiar job, laying the groundwork for my Day Two "interviews." That way the coming questioning would *seem* like the routine/follow-up prying of an auditor. I tried to believe I'd put on a more compelling performance than Baxter's feigned preoccupation with his desktop when I had first arrived.

Going through the motions while I did nothing to identify our mad bomber was at once exhausting and nerve-racking, and I looked forward to a few hours of unconscious respite. In damned near no gravity, the hardest floor is comfier (I'd been told) than the softest mattress on Earth. In theory, I could have slept just fine in the wiring-closet/storeroom I'd been given as temporary quarters.

So much for theory. My mind never stopped churning, fixated on the bomb in the ceiling of the very next room. I couldn't as much as pace for fear a clumsy footfall would trigger the bomb. But I *did* come up, at about oh-dark thirty, with an idea that sent me scurrying to the station chief. I rapped impatiently on his hatch.

"Just a minute." He sounded groggy, as if I'd awakened him. As if dumping the problem on me had lifted all the (nonexistent in this gravity) weight from his shoulders. Must be nice.

"It won't wait," I said, overriding the lock and letting myself in. Auditors had prerogatives.

Baxter was with a friend. From Mariana Kwan's file I knew she was thirty-two and Macau-born. Olive-complected, with a loose halo of wavy black hair and only the merest hint of eyefolds, she looked more Portuguese than Chinese. A mining engineer. As the newbie in a crew that had otherwise labored together for eight years or more, she defaulted to being my chief suspect. And seeing these two together? It recalled my instinct that Baxter "finding" the bomb was an obvious way to deflect suspicion.

Kwan had raised a sheet almost high enough to be not quite decent. She wasn't in the slightest embarrassed by my entrance. *I* was. And from the way Baxter wouldn't meet my eye, he was. She said, "I'm curious, now. What can't wait?"

Baxter cleared his throat. "Give us that minute, please?"

I backed out, closing the hatch behind me.

Kwan emerged soon after, jumpsuit draped over one arm, wearing nothing but grip slippers and a loosely wrapped sheet. Maybe she made it to 155 centimeters tall, the top of her head scarcely reaching my waist. It wasn't the top of her head that drew my eyes.

"Done a full enough audit yet?" Head canted, one bare leg thrust forward, she struck a pose. "Or will you be making a closer examination?"

"I'll get back to you," I mumbled, my face hot. I let myself back into Baxter's quarters.

He had gotten dressed. "It's not what you think."

What did Baxter suppose I thought? That his file showed a wife and three teenaged kids. That boinking an employee he supervised was a firing offense under the best of circumstances—which these weren't. I *did* think all that, and also how I'd been away from hearth, home, and humping—er, honey—for way too fricking long before getting dragged here to save this guy's fornicating bacon. But maybe none of that mattered. Not if the brainstorm I had had paid off…

"About Mariana." Baxter swallowed, hesitated, then swallowed again. "The thing is—"

"Skip it." We had bigger fish to fry. And what passed in me for people skills said the bump-and-grind had been at Mariana's instigation. "You and I need to talk ASAP to someone who understands bombs. The comm buoy you visually signaled to get me summoned? It has a long-range radio or, more likely, a high-power laser for the tight beam. Right? Of course, right. *You* couldn't access that transmitter, because you don't have a ship. But *I* do. If I can—"

"You can't—"

"The hell I can't," I interrupted right back. "I figure the company would've made the buoy physically small and unobtrusive, without any big honking telescope. That means it's got to be fairly close to monitor the exact position of your retroreflector. So: we print some IR sensors, do a sky search."

And also vid cameras and lidar to bond to the hull of my windowless ship, because the *Bounty*'s own nav sensors—and its nav computer—were inaccessible. (It was much debated among my peers how, before departing Ceres, mission data made their way into that sealed computer. From the mid-flight update that had rerouted me, the process involved the ship's likewise hidden and unreachable radio receiver. If I made it home, that breakthrough should get me a free drink or three.) Try to access the built-in sensors or the computer anywhere but in a company dry dock, and protective circuitry would fry them with a power surge.

The rumor mill had it that, early in the company's history, a pilot took a can opener to his sealed console—and *zap*. He was adrift for months (no transmitter aboard but a helmet radio, remember?) before he failed to show up as expected and anyone knew to go looking. The derelict was eventually recovered, still coasting along one of its preprogrammed trajectories—its pilot having long since starved to death. Was that story a company plant, just to discourage clever people like me? If so, it worked.

Anyway, assuming I could print my own sensors, low-res crap that they'd be, I had yet to decide how best to get their readouts onto the bridge. Not wireless comm: that wouldn't penetrate the metal hull. Most likely, I'd run cables through the closed air lock. I'd stay in a pressure suit, because the cables would keep the hatches from seating properly. Even making liberal use of anti-leak patches, chances are the ship would be losing air.

None of which factors constituted a selling point.

Shaking my head, clearing the cobwebs, I continued. "Like any rock, the buoy will soak up sunlight. We spot the buoy by its reradiated IR, work out its orbit. I seat-of-the-pants fly my ship to it"—because, Baxter knew as well as I, autopilot wouldn't do a *thing* but fly to a company-specified destination—"and then I—"

"No!" He wrung his hands. "Okay, here's another thing you're not supposed to know. The buoy carries a comm laser, all right. The onboard computer has orbital parameters for the Rock, to track us, and orbital parameters for more distant relay buoys that in turn hold orbital parameters for other buoys, some shadowing other valuable rocks. To safeguard that data, each buoy in the network also carries a bomb and proximity sensors."

Huh. I'd convinced myself a small buoy would be battery-limited. It couldn't, I had then extrapolated, store enough solar energy for its laser to damage an inbound ship that was bobbing and weaving and spinning. Once again, damn it, the company had me outwitted. An onboard bomb triggered by a magnetometer *was* simpler and more reliable.

I said, "If I get close, it blows?"

He nodded glumly.

"Hold on," I said, "I have a *better* idea. I hack a printer, override its blacklist so I can make a transmitter. Under the circumstances, the company can't get too mad. We broadcast"—in every damned direction, since we couldn't see anything to aim at—"on a public emergency channel. We explain our situation and ask for guidance." I thought some more. "My bosses know they sent me here. I'll encrypt with my private key, and they'll be able to decrypt with my public key. No one overhearing will know this is a company asset."

"You think you're the first person ever to imagine bootlegging a transmitter?" Baxter sighed. "It's been tried. If a printer sees it's being hacked, it fries itself. I've seen it happen. Same thing if you try to print lenses or magnifying mirrors—or IR sensors—anything that might contribute to making an astronomical instrument."

Surely the hack was an acceptable risk. If we *didn't* defuse the bomb in the next few days, we'd evacuate on the inbound ship. Suppose every printer in the station were to go *pfft*. So what? My temporary quarters alone held enough emergency rations to last everyone here for weeks. "For sake of argument, suppose I succeed."

"Won't matter. Remember that buoy shadowing us? The comm laser?"

I nodded.

"A long-range comm laser is a short-range weapon, at least against stationary targets. If the buoy hears us broadcasting, it'll take out any antenna we put up."

"Well, shit," I said, and let myself out.

After a sleepless night contemplating bombs, mystery toxins, and Mariana Kwan's sheet wafting to the floor in micro-gee, Dance of the Seven Veils, slo-mo, I followed the scents of coffee, vanilla, and cinnamon toward breakfast. From the direction of the station mess came the sounds of conversation. The zip-zip of my grip slippers and the rumble of a corridor ventilation fan rendered their voices unintelligible, but tone of voice, if I was any kind of judge, suggested argument.

As I entered, the two miners in the room fell silent. Stony faced, drink bulbs in hand, they stood between me and the nearest printer.

"Morning," I offered in passing.

The woman nodded. The man grunted.

Plugging a memory stick into another printer, I ordered a large pancake rollup and a larger coffee bulb.

"Old family recipe," I explained.

Because I hadn't ordered straight from the printer's menu. Because someone on the Rock had synthed, quite possibly on this very printer, whatever poison the hidden bomb was days from dispersing. I couldn't *prove* that, of course. What purpose could there have been for logging what people synthed to eat? If I got off the Rock in one piece, I'd recommend changing that policy.

My unsolicited explanation didn't rate a grunt.

"Mind if I join you?" I ventured.

Anisha Chatterjee made a desultory, one-handed motion that I chose to take as yes. She was slender and graceful, with dark skin, jet-black hair, and soulful eyes: a classic Indian beauty. Thirty, her file said. Electrical engineer and robot wrangler. Born in Mumbai, but her family had emigrated to the Moon before she turned six. Twice as smart as everyone, Baxter had told me, and apt to let it be known. Otherwise charming enough, also per Baxter, that people seldom took offense.

I was still waiting for the charm. "Ready to head back to Ceres?" I asked her.

"Sure." With the uptick of an eyebrow, she silently added, "That's a stupid question."

I tried again, gesturing with the hand that gripped a rollup. "What's it like, eating flat pancakes? With syrup and butter dripping off the stack? Using a knife and fork?"

It was her companion who answered. Ramon "Buck" Buranek was a Vestan, as spindly, and about as tall, as me. Pallid like me, too. Life-support engineer and medic. A dragon tattoo twined about his right forearm, the beast's head evidently hiding inside his short sleeve. His HR file offered useless speculation about if or how a buck and a dragon related to each another. Personally, I guessed they didn't, and that no explanation for the ink was necessary beyond too much booze or pot or whatever. He said, "It's too early for small talk."

"It's too early for anything but." I took a bite of pancake, and made a face. The printer could use a recalibration.

"So much for being subtle." Buck glowered. "A pre-departure audit doesn't make anyone here feel chatty. And maybe you're the genius who decided the strip search when we reach Ceres is inadequate."

Strip search was a bit of an exaggeration. Noninvasive ultrasound scans more than sufficed. And the scans were kabuki theater, in any event, letting miners—and roving auditors—feel good about sneaking scraps of contraband through. "I go where the company sends me, same as you."

This comment didn't merit even a shrug.

After awhile, Anisha cleared her throat. "'Breaking the awkward silence,' she also says with subtlety, 'pancakes and maple syrup are *not* Indian cuisine.'"

True enough, but flapjacks had to be common enough around the UCLA campus where she had gotten her masters. That knowledge was one more item to keep to myself. Her height, or lack of it, showed she was an Earther. Admitting that auditors had access to HR files wouldn't make us any better loved. "Then egg rolls with the mustard sauce on the outside? Vichyssoise that doesn't clot in and clog the nipple of a drink bulb? A French dip sandwich that a person gets to, you know, actually dip?"

She laughed. "Now you're just teasing me. And yes, I—"

"Buck," the PA speaker in the ceiling called out. I recognized Baxter's voice. "Can you come to the control room?"

The control room was next door, apparently too close to bother responding over the intercom. I called out after Buck as he zipped/stalked to the exit, "We'll talk later." Because who was more likely than the crew medic to gin up and handle whatever evil brew lurked in the duct?

Turning into the hall, maybe he grunted.

"So," Anisha said, "are you ready to explain why you're actually here?"

"What do you mean?"

"Please. There's no logic to an audit days before we rotate out, much less scarcely a month after the last auditor passed through. If someone here has come up with anything clever, smuggling-wise, what are the odds you'll spot it before we go? And if we try the usual tricks—of which, of course, I plead complete ignorance—well, those are surely covered by customary inspections when we get home."

I had to give Baxter credit on the topic of this woman's charm. "Then why *do* you imagine I'm here?"

She canted her head thoughtfully. "Maybe *you* found a way to defeat the system. You and the boss are all buddy-buddy."

I shook my head. "The system is foolproof."

"Do you know Robb's law?"

I shook my head again.

"For every foolproof system devised, a new and approved fool will arise to overcome it."

Long, sleepless night notwithstanding, I had yet to find a line of questioning that wouldn't suggest my awareness of the hidden device. I did have plenty of ideas where not to start. Top of my do-not-ask list was: are you, by any chance, the mad bomber?

I took another bite of pancake rollup, chewing slowly, making it last. "You know, I can't decide. Which of us are you insulting?"

"You can choose." She deposited her drink bulb in a recycle bin. "It's off to work I go."

"I came across some interesting anomalies in some of the more obscure system logs." I hadn't, apart from the vid loop that hid the bomb from routine monitoring, but I wanted to see her reaction. Computer smarts remained the closest I came to having a clue to the bomber.

"And sleuth that you are, you know I'm the sysadmin here." She smiled. "You also ought to know I'm good at my job. Trust me, if I'd done anything inappropriate, I wouldn't have left tracks for you to find. And I'd have seen anyone else's 'anomalies' if they existed to be found. Hence: you're fishing. For what, I wonder."

Anisha wasn't quite as good as she would have me believe. Either she had failed to spot the vid loop—or she had failed at hiding it from me. Wouldn't it be nice to know which?

I said, "Maybe you don't *want* to see what I'm seeing?"

"Still fishing," she said, starting for the hatch.

"So," I said. She stopped and turned. "Are you friends with the other crew?"

Her eyes narrowed. "Why ask that?"

Because I wonder if you're planning to kill them off. "Idle curiosity."

"I don't know about friends. There's some friendly rivalry, sure."

Because the company pitted crews against each another, basing bonuses in part on which team brought back the most ingots. Demonstrably the competition *was* motivational, but—and it was a rare instance of the company being too smart by half—that incentive sometimes led to sabotage. Like the background level of theft, this pattern was inferred more than proven, but—to an auditor, in any event—statistics don't lie. Productivity dipped right before crew changeover, and bumped back up soon after the same crew returned. It was just as if end-of-shift effort were being diverted into hiding the richest ore veins. To obscure that sort of subversion took serious computer legerdemain, too.

I asked, "And how does that rivalry play out?"

"Side bets and testosterone displays," she said. "Are we done here?" Once more she headed out.

"What were you and Buck arguing about?"

"Worlds affairs," she called over her shoulder. And then she was gone.

Cornering Buck near the air lock as he suited up, we had a short chat to which his contributions were monosyllabic. Or nonsyllabic, when I included the scowls, shrugs, and squinty-eyed stares most often elicited by my conversational gambits. As for fresh insight into our present situation, that amounted to squat until my final question. "So, you and Anisha. What were you arguing about?"

"Sports," he bit out while sealing his helmet. Then, magnetic boots clunking, he stomped into the air lock and started it cycling.

One of them—at least—was lying. Because they were involved with the bomb? Or garden-variety theft? Maybe I just pissed them off. That last, for sure, could be problematical, because the reason for having humans here in the first place wasn't to do mining. Robots alone did an acceptable job of that, with none of the larceny hazards inherent with any human crew. But absent autonomous missile batteries and military-grade warbots, both thankfully difficult to come by, automation *couldn't* protect against a failure in the company's secrecy measures—a lesson the company had once learned the hard way. Hence, just in case, the onsite armory. Hence, everyone in the crew, petite Mariana Kwan included, was a combat vet. Any one of them was more than capable of snapping me like a twig. (But none of them had had any special training with explosives. I'd checked their files.)

I set aside for later consideration Buck and Anisha's inconsistent stories, then went looking for another member of the crew. Les

Hodges was a biotech/nanotech engineer; in terms of capability for poison crafting, he was as plausible as anyone here. (The situation was getting as muddled as any Brit cozy mystery, Agatha Christie and such, wherein everyone is a suspect.)

I found Hodges—his hands inside a glove box, brow furrowed in concentration—in the station's tiny machine shop, reassembling a battered prospecting bot. A few shiny pieces inside the box looked fresh from a printer. (Among those parts I spotted a squat tube. I told myself Baxter said accelerometers were standard in their bots. I told myself a lot of things.) At the least nudge, parts went airborne. He hummed along with something orchestral and baroque-sounding playing softly in the background. With only the briefest of glances away from his work as I entered, he ordered, "Gimme a minute."

I spent that minute, and the next several, considering the man. He was another Earther, and fairly tall as that breed went. Balding, pale (or was sallow the more accurate term?), with a slot face, cleft chin, and close-set eyes of cloudy blue. Two years a widower; one son at university back on Earth. Maybe it was the stooped shoulders that gave a weary impression of age, or the hang-dog expression, but he struck me as older than the fifty-four years shown in his HR file. I didn't foresee a lot more mining tours in his future—and that might be another reason to suspect him. After awhile, I switched my focus to someone's pet hamster, caroming and somersaulting about its cage. Short of gluing zip strips to the little guy's feet, I guess an exercise wheel was out of the question.

"Done." With an efficiency doubtless acquired from long practice, he extracted his hands from the elbow-length gloves, opened the box, and removed the reassembled bot. He turned, finally, to face me. "Whatever it is, I didn't do it. Is there anything else?"

"Well, as long as you didn't do it." I smiled. "Ready for the crew rotation?"

"Anyone ever not?"

"Good point." I tried the tack that had set Anisha on edge. "Do you have friends among the other crew?"

A long pause and an odd look preceded the one-word answer. "No."

After a bit more such snappy repartee I wandered off, none the wiser, to speak with the delectable Mariana Kwan. Apart from the flirting, that session, too, proved equally useless. I was out of ideas, even as the clock kept ticking.

…◆…

Like the proverbial drunk hunting for his keys near where the light is best and not where he'd last seen them, I fell back upon routine. Auditing was something to do while—I had to hope—my subconscious exhumed an idea more useful than fleeing like a bat out of hell. Because only a day remained till the crew ship was due, and only three days till the bomb released … whatever.

Long story short, someone, and I took Anisha Chatterjee at her word, *was* good at what she did.

But so am I, and routine offered an excuse for putting my skills to work.

No significant piece of software, never mind how extensively tested, is ever one hundred percent bug free. That's why, every few weeks, vendors distribute updates. Company rocks, being off the net, don't get updates except at crew rotation or when someone like me passes through. And on a mass spectrometer that in every other way seemed copasetic, an update I'd had with me refused to install into the instrument's embedded software.

Intrusion-detection software and device diagnostics alike compare a stored checksum for any given app against a checksum value newly calculated for the same app. For the mass spec, old and new checksums matched. But the app's update installer made its own check for the integrity of the software it would patch—and *that* test failed. I'd installed this update on my three planned stops this trip, suggesting the glitch was somehow specific to this particular mass spec.

And with some digging, I discovered the root cause. Device diagnostics and intrusion-detection software alike examine the memory allocated to each app. The update software made a slightly more expansive check, extending its scope over the unallocated memory the as-yet uninstalled patch would occupy. I found a program in what should have been such unallocated memory. Then, doing a painful, line-by-line comparison, I found the small modification to the app that accessed the unauthorized patch.

Ordinarily, overwriting an executable with a jump to patch space alters the calculated checksum. *This* overwrite included a weird embedded constant that, I proved to myself, hid the change as far as the routine checksum calculations were concerned.

Still, I didn't yet see how intrusion detection had been bypassed to make the unauthorized changes, or to keep that activity out of the security log. Those were brain teasers best left for another day. Assuming I got one.

The unauthorized patch itself was simple enough to reverse-engineer. It underreported by a tenth of a percent the concentration of platinum within an ore sample. That didn't sound like much, but doing the math, and depending on when the hack had been made, the inventory discrepancy could reach ten kilos of ultra-refined platinum. In round numbers, a quarter-million Belt bucks.

Someday, maybe, I'd figure out how the crook(s) expected to sneak that much platinum off the Rock. Right then more important matters held my interest. Someone, and I still assumed Anisha, was damned good at covering her digital tracks. That someone, and anyone working with her, wouldn't be involved with the bomb. Why work this hard at stealing a few kilos when the bomber, I had to believe, had the entire inventory in their sights? Once more dealing in round numbers, the vault presently held ten *tonnes* of ingots. My second realization—entirely unrelated, apart from any scrap of progress being inspirational—was that, at last, I understood how to proceed.

…◆…

My brilliant idea, with sleuthing having gotten me nowhere, was entrapment. Baxter let it be known that the scheduled crew rotation had been postponed by at least a week—breaking bad news that he, of course, attributed to me. The announcement didn't make me any more popular, but it did give whoever had placed the bomb, now due to go *boom* in three short days, the motivation to reset the timer. Or so, anyway, I hoped.

While Baxter kept his crew outside for various tasks, I borrowed a drill from the machine shop to make a peephole in the wall between my quarters and the bomb room. I disconnected power from the actuator of a nearby HVAC damper; the automated controls could no longer reposition the damper, and no robot creeping through the duct could get past the damper to the bomb.

Hours later, in the face of crew hostility, I retired early to my room with a covered dinner tray and waited. And waited. And *waited.* Thanks to chemical assistance, I waited the entire night shift awake and alert—and no one showed up.

That's not to say the time had been uneventful.

The next morning, Anisha was nowhere to be found.

…◆…

Her room looked stirred. For all I knew she liked it that way, but everyone assured me she was a neatnik (indeed, the walls were comparatively free of the ubiquitous dust), and also that several small personal items were missing. Likewise gone, from its locker near the air lock: her pressure suit. No one said this looked exactly like Anisha had sneaked out by dark of night shift. No one had to. And if such stealing away seemed odd, well, neither could I understand why anyone able to arrange for a ship to retrieve her from a clandestine platinum mine would settle for a mere ten-kilo heist.

Baxter sent Buck, Mariana, and Les outside to scour the surface for any sign of Anisha, while he and I did a more thorough inside sweep. We didn't find her, of course. We fast-forwarded through surveillance vids for the preceding twelve hours. Once people went into their rooms for the night—personal spaces didn't have cameras—we had nada. Well, I'd seen surveillance feeds hacked before.

The outside search was still underway when the crew ship came within range to flash out the month's authentication code, and Baxter summoned his crewmates back inside.

…◆…

The relief crew crowded into the station, likely anticipating the customary changeover festivities. Neither incoming nor outgoing crew can expect to see any new faces for awhile; rivalries notwithstanding, rotation was ordinarily the occasion for a party. But not this trip.

Mustafa Gilfoyle, station chief of the new crew, was the first to shed his vacuum gear and emerge into the Rock's main corridor. He was a second-generation Loonie; an easy-going guy I knew slightly from years ago on another company rock. In seconds he processed the glum faces and the peculiarity of an auditor onsite at shift rotation. "What's the problem here?"

"Let's wait for the rest of your team," Baxter said. Four more joined us, and he turned to me. "Okay. Your show."

I caught Mustafa's eye. "Let's you, Baxter, and me go for a walk." I led them into the side corridor that held crew quarters, detouring to the mess to dispense a special recipe into a drink bulb. If either man noticed that this bulb had a misting attachment, what spacers use to water potted plants, he didn't comment. Still, the stopover earned me quizzical looks. We paused outside Anisha's room.

"I'll ask again," Mustafa said. "What's going on?"

Baxter cleared his throat. "One of my crew … disappeared this morning. She and her pressure suit are gone."

"More specifically," I corrected, "she was murdered this morning."

Baxter twitched. "Why would you *say* that?"

"To start, the too-clean walls in her room." I raised the drink bulb. "This is luminol."

Evidently I wasn't the only one here who watched crime vids. Mustafa said, "The forensic stuff. Right?"

I nodded. "We three will go into the room, shut the hatch, and I'll turn out the lights. Then I'll prove what I already know."

"It's pretty snug quarters for three," Baxter said.

"Uh-huh," I said. "You're welcome to wait out here."

All "night" I'd expected Baxter to come after me while my attention, or so I'd intended him to believe, remained fixed on the peephole. (I'd delegated that task to my comp, its webcam taped against the opening.) Only nothing had transpired in either room.

My thinking had been this: Baxter or an accomplice deployed the bomb with its load of mystery toxins to take out Mustafa's crew. Dead station chiefs move no retroreflectors. The ship with Baxter's crew, having just departed the Rock for Ceres, would still be nearby when the failsafe "uh-oh, no one moved the retroreflector" Mayday message was received on Ceres.

So: the ship would automagically return to the Rock. Baxter (and his cuddly new friend?) would send the unsuspecting, non-accomplice members of his crew into the station for a look-see, at which point the toxin would take *them* out. He'd have bots dispose of the bodies, leaving behind blood spatters from everyone in both crews—a few cc's of his own blood being a small sacrifice. The conspirators would fly away leaving the company to infer pirates (a) killed Mustafa's crew and then (b) killed Baxter and crew, when they returned, and finally (c) took away the crew ship and its cargo.

Where did I fit in? Before Baxter pulled the trigger (as it were) on his scheme, he would have needed to confirm what he'd been told about the retroreflector and Mayday signaling. That might have been pure company BS, a tall tale to mollify station chiefs putting up a fuss about their lack of comms. Unless someone—in this case, lucky me—showed up, I figured Baxter would have called off the caper. He likely *had* been on the verge of aborting when, finally, I did arrive. My eleven-day detour had delivered me to the Rock a mere three days before the scheduled crew rotation. But that long, surely nerve-racking, wait would also have meant very good odds Baxter would be in the closest ship when the next "emergency" was inferred.

Once someone like me *was* onsite, Baxter would need to explain the summons. The partial truth, "There's a bomb here," served perfectly well—as long no one else was told—and with everyone a suspect, naturally I hadn't breathed a word. I also couldn't be allowed to warn Mustafa's crew about the bomb and their need to evacuate. Hence, in this twisted conspiracy I had so tortuously concocted, Baxter would come after me during the night. He'd disappear my body and the *Bounty*. A bot placed aboard could easily be made to boost the *Bounty* off the Rock, using only attitude jets, the autopilot disengaged. Odds were the ship would never be seen again. His crew would be told I'd slinked away in the night shift, avoiding more of their disdain.

That was the theory. Instead, after an interminable night spent with my back pressed against the wall beside the hatch, ready to brain Baxter with a wrench when he skulked in … he hadn't.

It had bugged me no end that someone might have found a way to hijack a company ship. I considered myself pretty savvy, and *I* hadn't figured out a way. Injured pride, to be honest, is why, more than anything, I hadn't—entirely—bought into any of this.

Had I mentioned two nights without sleep, the second on uppers and in fear for my life?

"You want me to wait here in the hallway?" With furrowed brow, Baxter studied me. Incredulous, or posing as such? "Because I might have killed Anisha. If anything like that happened, that is."

"It happened," I assured him. And innocent of setting the bomb—for which, once again, I was without suspects—wasn't nearly the same as innocent.

Anisha could have been behind the excess pilferage I'd noticed. If so an accomplice, who might be anyone among her crew, could've gotten greedy. But maybe—and part of me wanted dearly to believe this, because, damn it, the woman *was* charming—she had just been doing her job. She'd seen something amiss, brought her suspicions to someone's attention, and *that* had gotten her killed. The most likely someone for her to have approached being her boss …

"Perhaps so," Baxter said, "but *I* had nothing to do with it."

Mustafa opened the hatch and stepped into Anisha's room.

Baxter and I followed. I oriented us toward the cleanest wall, wondering if I smelled chlorine beneath the pervasive used-gunpowder stench, or if that was my imagination. With bulb firmly grasped in one hand, I flicked off the lights. I spritzed the wall, and glowing blotches appeared.

"Oh, shit," Mustafa said. "Blood spatter."

I spritzed all around that first, lucky hit. Lots more spatter. When I'd read from the wiki in my pocket comp that the fluorescence lasted only about thirty seconds, it had seemed worrisomely short. Just then, by the damning blue glow, a half minute felt interminable. That turned out to be fortunate, because I almost forgot to take pictures. As darkness finally returned, I flicked on the overhead lights.

"And the body?" Mustafa asked. "Chucked off-world?"

In the hunt for Anisha, no one had admitted to hearing the air lock cycle since before dinner. *I* certainly hadn't, and I'd been keyed up even aside from the amphetamines. (As for the station air-lock controls, those gave no indication of having been operated during the recent sleep shift—but I trusted its records about as much as I did the surveillance feeds.) Not to mention it would have taken nerves of steel to tote a dead body through the halls. Sleep shift, and everyone asleep, are quite different concepts. Not to mention that, plastered against the wall for hours, interminably waiting, I'd given considerable thought to how I would dispose of a body.

I said, "I'm pretty sure not. Come with me, and I'll show you."

Our next stop was the main printing/recycling room. Digital readouts showed more or less middling levels of everything. Eyeball the physical reservoirs, however, and the picture changed. Metals and plastics—pressure suit (and murder weapon?) materials—had both jumped. Most stood noticeably above the time-stamped inventory I'd printed the day previous. (No foresight or intuition involved: auditors routinely monitor stocks of metal and plastic. Feedstock increases in either category often suggest mundane personal items getting remade in platinum.) At my level of engineering sophistication, nanotech was indistinguishable from magic, but even I knew that disassembling physical objects into chemical feedstock consumed lots of energy. It was more than a little suggestive that the main battery bank—as characterized from a voltmeter measurement, not by its computerized readout—had all but drained overnight. And the stomach-turning clincher: the organics supply was nearly sixty kilos increased from the day before. About what Anisha must have massed.

"Luminol showed blood spatter in this room, too," I offered to break the silence.

Mustafa muttered under his breath. Curse? Prayer? It hardly mattered. He turned to Baxter. "Someone in your crew is a murderer."

"The news gets worse." Baxter gestured toward the hatch. With a quick visit to a certain nearby storeroom he made his case.

...◆...

Shocker: no one admitted to having a disarm code for the bomb.

That left no options but evacuation. In the best of circumstances, shoehorning two crews onto a one-crew ship would be unpleasant. But with an unidentified murderer aboard? That I wouldn't be along for the ride almost reconciled me to my immediate future. *I'd* be staying to observe events two days hence, and what, if anything, remained afterward of the station.

With two crews loudly venting about the situation, I cleared my throat. No one heard, and I resorted to a piercing whistle. "Another thing, people. I'll be collecting everyone's computers. Preserving evidence for the authorities."

"The *hell* you will," a newcomer snapped.

"From Baxter's crew? Damn straight," another said. "One of them is a killer."

"From everyone," Mustafa said firmly. "We don't know how long the bomb's been here, or if for some reason one of us is the target." Shaken, his crew confronted the possibility of a would-be murderer among their number. "Cough 'em up, people."

Baxter handed over his pocket comp for me to bag and tag. "Now the rest of you," he told his folks. Most, grumbling, complied. "C'mon, Les. Give it up."

Hodges's eyes darted about nervously. Everyone had good cause to be agitated, and I didn't read anything into his reticence. Personal comps are *personal*; experts can glean our most private secrets and embarrassing moments from the devices.

"Back on Ceres, the cops will need it," Baxter said.

Still, Les hesitated.

"It's not a request," Baxter barked. Like a ship's captain, at sea or in space, a station chief's word was law.

"The authentication and encryption are biometric," I reminded. Of course, forensic accountants, like cops, had ways to crack open locked comps. There was nothing to be gained in volunteering that little detail.

But maybe Les knew or, at the least, suspected as much. Maybe he was racked with guilt, about the bomb, or Anisha, or both. Maybe he was plain crazy. Whatever his reason, with no more explanation than a soft-spoken "Sorry," he collapsed, convulsing. Seconds later, his mouth giving off a faint smell of bitter almonds, Lester Hodges was dead.

…◆…

Every crew ship arrived carrying an empty modular vault. The departing crew used a crane to hoist the vault they had spent months filling, replace it with the empty, then load the filled vault aboard the ship. Not even a vault full of platinum had much weight on the Rock—but full or empty, that sucker had plenty of mass and inertia.

Ticking time bomb notwithstanding, no one even considered abandoning ten tonnes of platinum ingots. I spared a moment from my preparations to watch, channeling a toon from my youth of dancing hippos in tutus. Ponderous vault or lumbering hippo: you wouldn't want either bumping into you.

Minutes later, with not quite thirty-six hours remaining on the bomb's timer, I watched the ship launch. Who, I wondered, would still be alive when she got to Ceres?

…◆…

I glued cameras, chemical sensors, and pressure gauges to walls, floors, ceilings, and air ducts throughout the station. The printer catalog included wireless versions (radiating, of course, at very low power levels), any subset within radio range of one another able to self-organize into *ad hoc* networks. I couldn't begin to guess what havoc an explosion or pressure breach might wreak on cabling or even wireless routers, so fault-tolerant and reconfigurable networking seemed the way to go.

The hamster I'd seen had been Les's, and no one objected to my claiming it. Mustafa had had to order his people to leave behind *their* pets, a ferret and a parakeet. I didn't expect to return them. I positioned the animals in their respective cages, with plenty of food and water, in three widely separated rooms.

I sent a recall to the smaller mining bots, lashed magnets to tentacle tips on some of them, and shuttled two dozen bots inside. I tested and retested the Rock's low-wattage primary and backup transmitters, and the fiber-optic cables linking those surface transmitters with the underground station, confirming I had end-to-end connectivity to everything through my helmet radio. Remaining suited up, I took a final pass through the station, harvesting data backups from every automated system capable of dumping its files into portable storage. I printed and then scattered yet more wireless sensors, this time on the surface directly above the underground station, half-expecting the coming shockwave would send them careening clear off this tiny world.

With not quite seven hours to go, I retreated to my ship—surely I'd be safe there, a quarter klick from the station—setting an alarm for thirty minutes until *boom.* Apart from popping my helmet, I remained prepped for vacuum.

Then, for the first time in days, I slept. Fitfully.

…◆…

The explosion came right on time.

I didn't feel a thing. Monitored from the safety of the *Bounty*, events were strangely anticlimactic. The duct with the bomb ruptured, of course. The nearby damper I'd positioned to keep out robots impaled itself in a nearby wall, itself buckled. The storeroom hatch came off its hinges, shredding the gasket. A pressure wave propagated back and forth several times through the station, in the process warping open a few more interior hatches and generally making a mess—but never compromising the integrity of the overall facility. Enough of the ventilation system survived to quickly clear the smoke and dust.

The parakeet happened to be airborne when the blast wave hit; the poor critter was thrown across its cage and clearly broke *something*. Ferret and hamster, as best I could tell, came through spitting mad but unscathed.

An hour later, the animals were *still* okay; even the bird had somewhat perked up. Had the glass bottle, somehow, *not* broken?

The blast had taken out the camera I'd set into the duct. To walk a mining bot up the wall on magneted tentacles took finesse and patience, neither of which I possessed just then, but finally I got a bot to where it could peer into the burst ceiling duct. What little of the bomb's bottle remained had been reduced to grit and slivers. The bottle's content, whatever that might have been, was well and truly dispersed. My sensors hadn't reported anything scary, which likely only meant the catalog for the station's printers hadn't anticipated exotic chemical attacks. Why would it?

For fifty-five hours straight, apart from nodding off once or twice, I cycled among cameras across the station. I directed robots into remote corners for yet more views. I pored over sensor readouts. I monitored the nearby surface for anything out of the ordinary. Nothing. Except for bots and the three animals in their cages, nothing stirred. I was seriously considering a trip inside for a more personal examination when, inside the hamster cage, the plastic water bottle … dissolved.

…◆…

Over the next two days, in more and more of the station, things crumbled. Furniture. The wrappers on emergency rations. Drink bulbs. All manner of everyday items, large and small. Interior hatch seals, and the gaskets inside equipment I hadn't even realized used gaskets. Scariest of all: spare vacuum gear as they hung in their lockers.

It did my mood no damned good to have only crappy views of this slo-mo nightmare. Company printers just wouldn't make sensors with decent resolution or light sensitivity—I might as well have watched through layers of gauze. The webcams on company-approved comps were no better. This was another of those rare instances when, in hindsight, the genius paranoia was too clever by half.

While I didn't know what the bomb had dispersed, it was all too clear what that crap did. It attacked things composed of rubber, plastic, or synthetic fibers. As the damage spread, I speculated it had to involve a bacterium or virus or nanite. Something that replicated and spread. Something *nasty*. I didn't dare go inside for a sample lest the stuff attack my suit. I didn't dare have a robot carry out a sample, for the same fear of contamination.

Throughout, the station maintained atmosphere. I'd never given much thought to types of air-lock hatch seals, but a dive into station schematics revealed an all-metal hatch design. Like springs, properly shaped metal surfaces would press together. That technology, it appeared, was maintaining the station's airtight seal. But many off-Earth facilities—including ships—used rubber gaskets in their hatches. The ship in which I huddled, for one.

Through it all, the animals were fine. They might stay fine for as long as robots could keep delivering food and water—and while recyclers, printers, and life support still ran. I had no idea how long that might be. And I had the greater good to consider.

From the presumed (whistling through the graveyard?) safety of the *Bounty*, I remotely experimented. I doused the station's lights for twenty-four hours. With the lights restored, I could discern little effect upon the pace of destruction. I switched off the heat and let the temperature plummet as low as I dared. I didn't relent for the animals' sake, although I would have regretted their deaths—and, indeed, the parakeet didn't make it. Sustained temperatures below freezing would destroy both hydroponic crops and the bacterial mats in main life support; I had my doubts how accepting the company would have been of that. For what it was worth, lowered temps *did* slow the … whatever, if only by a little.

Might truly deep and prolonged cold—the interior temperature on Belt rocks averages about -70 °C—stop the mystery plague? I had no idea, nor dare I remain, incommunicado, for long enough to find out. There was likely a murderer, or a mad bomber, or both on the crew ship I'd recently seen off, and *I* held key evidence. And anyway, if I were to undertake such an experiment, how long would I stay? Bacteria have been revived from dormancy after millennia frozen in ice.

Would vacuum kill the stuff? I saw no way to do that test without spurting contagion right out of the station. The crud might contaminate the surface, or my ship, or even get blown clean off this tiny world to drift to others. So: no. Make that: hell, no.

I'd been using a mining bot every day to shift the hush-hush retroreflector, lest the unseen Mayday buoy signal Ceres to send out another ship. In preparation for leaving, I reprogrammed the bot to continue those moves in my absence. The last thing anyone needed was another ship and its unsuspecting crew diverted here before I got back to Ceres to explain the situation. For good measure, along with a warning note duct-taped to the outer air-lock hatch, I stomped skull and crossbones into the dust.

With that, there was nothing more here for me to do. I untethered the *Bounty*, then eased her away from the Rock with the gentlest possible puffs from her attitude jets. I did not activate autopilot until we were *way* too distant for the main drive's exhaust to stir up any contaminated dust.

…◆…

It would've been nice to have an inkling when I'd get back home. How long would I be left obsessing about sabotage, murder, and pressure-suit-chomping bacteria? Days? Weeks? Months? As days ceased to be a possibility, I thought about home and hearth. I listened to my music library, watched vids from that library, read, did what little in the way of exercise was possible in the *Bounty*'s tiny cabin. All the while, trying to ignore the siren song of the bagged personal comps …

The longer I stewed in my own juices, the more confused I became. Among the miners were a thief, a murderer, and a bomber. Just possibly, someone took on more than one of those roles. The simplest theory now consistent with what I (thought I) knew: Anisha and a confederate had diverted several kilos of platinum. The confederate killed her, whether from greed or for fear she would confess to me. Someone else made and set the bomb. Les Hodges was guilty of *something*, but I couldn't decide of what.

The interminable flight had given me ample time to imagine other scenarios. Maybe Anisha, rather than being a thief, had discovered the thief, tried to blackmail him or her, and gotten killed for her trouble. Maybe Anisha found something suspicious that led to her asking the wrong questions of the bomber, and *that* got her killed. Maybe—

Enough navel-gazing! Okay, I'd never seen an elephant, but I understood metaphor. I'd been ignoring the giant pachyderm in the cabin. For any merely vindictive or larcenous purpose, simple explosives would have sufficed. Massive, without-warning decompression would, comparatively speaking, have killed everyone at the station *quickly*. Setting loose that weird contagion within the station? Trapping everyone inside, and making their rescue perilous at best and impossible at worst? That had to be someone sending a message. The nasty truth I had been loath to confront was this: the Rock had been targeted by terrorists—or nut jobs.

"Screw it," I declared to untold kiloklicks of vacuum all around. "I *know* Les was up to something. Let's see what's on his comp."

...◆...

Biometric authentication and encryption algorithms are no more secure than the software that realizes them—or any other software on which those algorithms rely. I had a half-dozen patches for operating-system bugs found after Baxter and his crew set out for the Rock. I had only to connect a comp of mine into the PC I'd taken from Les's pocket and exploit any of the unpatched vulnerabilities. Simple.

It wasn't.

I hadn't offered PC updates to anyone on the Rock, and yet, it turned out, Les's comp had all the patches I'd brought. But hadn't Anisha mentioned another auditor had been at the Rock shortly before me? Yes, she had. He must have had with him at least some of the patches I had.

But I *also* had, still unused, a copy of the latest patch set Mustafa's crew had brought directly from Ceres. That patch set was newer than mine—and, I found, included a fix for a very recently discovered operating-system bug. Reverse engineering that patch, I characterized the underlying bug and found my way into Les's comp—

Wherein a couple terabytes of personal stuff needed wading through.

...◆...

The company didn't give miners—or auditors—much in the way of personal space. No strip searches, Buck Buranek's complaints notwithstanding, but to call the company's security measures intrusive remained an industrial-strength understatement. The encrypted data on your personal comp and a camera-free room were pretty much the extent of any privacy. And, because the law required the company to respect the confidentiality of medical records, and hence, of people's pharmaceutical needs, printers accepted personalized inputs for pretty much anything organic. That's how, back on the Rock, I'd been able to fill a bulb with $C_8H_7N_3O_2$: luminol.

Food printers also made intact cells, everything from live-culture yogurt to yeast for fresh breads (and beer) to bleu cheese and steak tartare. Printers were how—shudder—(some) Belters got their "sushi." And that, I suspected, was how *Les* had concocted the contagion I'd seen digesting everything plastic on the Rock. But what did I know?

Income statements and computer code, I could reverse engineer with the best of them. But genomes (*if* the unknown crud were even biological)? I wouldn't know one if it bit me, much less how it would be transcribed for a printer to synth. Still, I (thought I) knew that genomes were *big*, which drew my attention to an email, date-stamped about three months earlier, that had come with several attachments, two quite large. That email could only have reached the Rock in a hand-delivered data cube when a previous auditor visited. The largest attachment—given its file-name extension, a printer recipe—had since been deleted. But the message's second oversized attachment remained. It was a vid.

"Dad, I'm in trouble," a frightened and bedraggled young man, maybe twenty-five, began without preamble. He had a black eye, a split lip, and had been handcuffed to a sturdy chair. No matter the bruising, I needn't have seen the holo in Les's room; the family resemblance was unmistakable. "They've got me. If you don't do as th-they say, they'll k-kill me."

Who *they* might be wasn't clear, apart from someone in a ski mask who strode into view to slap duct tape across the kid's mouth. (The few, non-bouncy steps suggested the vid had been shot on Earth. In standard gravity, for sure, and nothing in the background looked like a spacecraft.) "A slow death, I might add, unless you do as we say. We'll know in due time whether you've cooperated. And we're *very* serious."

Most of the vid, with Les's son quavering in the background, consisted of an admonition to tell no one, a bomb-building lesson, a timetable, and instructions on deploying the final attachment: a trojan. Among its tricks, that malware could splice loops into camera feeds, exactly as I'd encountered on the Rock.

The vid attachment ended on a close-up of the young man's terrified eyes. I wondered how many times Les had watched it.

…◆…

"There you have it. You now know what I do."

With nothing more to add, I stopped recording. The vid was for insurance, for the record. For—were anything even remotely akin to the plague on the Rock also loose on Ceres—the possibility I wouldn't get to report personally on all I'd encountered. Pressure suit, ground vehicles, maybe air locks ... even after I touched down, there would be a plastic-and-rubber gauntlet to be run.

I'd never been as relieved as when a console LED lit to report Ceres had come into range. Autopilot put me into a parking orbit, from which a short-range company tug—with, you know, radar, lidar, and two-way radio with traffic control—would deliver me for inspection to a company facility. And *then* I'd never been as relieved as when the bored-sounding human pilot aboard the approaching tug commented, yawning, "Folks kinda wondered when you'd get here." Her complacency meant Ceres was safe. My honey was safe. I was safe.

Caveat to those rosy sentiments: safe for *now*. The overcrowded crew ship left the Rock a few days ahead of me; that hamster's plastic water bottle took a few days to dissolve.

I was trying my best, with limited success, to focus on a joyous homecoming. The company had suffered one employee killed and another driven to suicide. They'd had an epic security breach and a platinum mine taken indefinitely out of commission. Just to be clear, that was my priority order, not likely to be theirs.

Whether or not, in a moment of humane weakness, the company would care that the son of an employee remained kidnapped and imperiled, the clues to this disaster all appeared to be on Earth. Clues that someone *will* follow up: it surely must be untenable not knowing who drove Hodges to set the bomb, and why, and if they planned to attack again somewhere else. For all I knew, they already had! And when the company *does* investigate, they'll want to disclose as little about the fiasco (including the location of the crime scene!) as possible, and to as few people as possible.

I foresaw my joyous homecoming being cut short by a trip Earthward.

THE COMPANY DICK

In a drug-induced fog, my head pounding, I woke flat on my back in an unfamiliar, windowless place. With a herculean effort, I managed to lift my head. The room was without furniture except for the mildewy, armless, too-short sofa across which I had been dumped, and off an end of which, like dead weights, my calves and feet hung. The walls were dirty white; the floor much scuffed, of pale wood of some kind; the ceiling, aside from its single dim light panel, was dingy and water-stained beige acoustic tiles. A hard rubber wastebasket sat in a corner. From the ceiling-mounted camera, slowly panning from side to side, a red LED glowed balefully. A storeroom, by the look of things, and I being stored.

I went to sit up—and failed. Miserably. The fuel cell had been removed from my exoskeleton and its little reserve battery had run out. Between my own ridiculous Earth weight and that of the inert exoskeleton, I was restrained as effectively as if by the sturdiest of chains. Helpless as a bug pinned to a display board.

Exhausted, I let my head flop back onto the sofa. As I struggled to reconstruct *what* and *why* had brought me here—wherever here was—two words echoed and reechoed in my brain.

Two dead. Two dead. Two dead …

…◆…

Two dead.

I had reminded myself of the toll—never mind how close I had been to becoming the third victim—so often that the words had become a mantra. I dared not forget that this business was serious. Deadly serious.

The pudgy guy ahead of me in line took a step forward. I plodded after. We'd been at this for awhile and, best guess, I had at least an hour to go until the Security checkpoint. All passengers are screened before boarding, of course. But who knows? I might have printed a gun or knife or nunchucks during the flight. As I waited, interspersed with my subvocalized mantra, I gave silent thanks to whoever had designed the mobility exoskeleton I wore over my clothes. Earth was the gravitational hellhole of human space.

Interplanetary Arrivals was too damn big, a harbinger of all that I dreaded about Earth. Floor-to-ceiling wall displays cycled among agoraphobia-inducing panoramas: dizzyingly deep canyons; rank upon rank of snow-capped mountains, each ridgeline taller than the last; undulating plains stretching to an impossibly distant horizon; seascapes manic with crashing waves. The hall echoed with the footsteps and chatter of several hundred people. Ceres in its orbit then being nearly as distant as possible from Earth, the ticket prices had been, well, astronomical, and I'd shared my flight with fewer than a dozen passengers. I took encouragement in having disembarked during peak hours, no matter that, even wearing the exoskeleton, standing in queue had within minutes become torture. The less attention came my way, the better.

Even with the exoskeleton I struggled to stay upright, lurching with each step, learning to hate the hardware. The feeble twitching of Belter muscles sometimes conveyed my intentions to the exoskeleton, but as often miscommunicated. Then a leg would kick out to the side, or a knee would lock, or a foot would stomp, or *something*. After half an hour in the Security line and not even five meters of progress, admitting defeat, I tapped a command (and this task, too, was a struggle) into the tiny virtual keypad of the exoskeleton's back-of-the-left-forearm control panel. Thereafter, lurching like Frankenstein's monster, the hardware marched me forward one step with each tap of the virtual star key. The lone remaining shred of my dignity was that I hadn't—yet—been tempted to slap the big, red, physical, "I've fallen and I can't get up" PANIC button.

It did not improve my mood that two lines to the left, another passenger from my ship glided along in her exoskeleton. Similar grace could have been mine—if I'd agreed before this trip to surgery. An implanted neural controller might even have been the wise choice, but I'm particular about having holes drilled in my head.

At long last, dripping sweat from stress and exertion, I reached the checkpoint. The exoskeleton caught the screeners' eyes, of course. I was prepared for the wanding and the pat down that inevitably followed. But *not* the demand that I surrender the exoskeleton's fuel cell for inspection.

"Without power, I can't stand." That was *maybe* an exaggeration, because sans motorized assistance I could remain in place with the exolegs mechanically locked. Unless someone bumped into me. Then, I'd go over like a sack of potatoes. Surface gravity on Ceres is under three percent of standard.

"We need to check the fuel cell," one of the Security screeners insisted.

"Then *I* need to sit."

While in the serpentine line behind me other weary travelers fumed, one of the screeners retrieved a chair. I sat. By the time they returned my fuel cell (shocker! It *wasn't* a bomb) I had become a statue. The exoskeleton's power reserve—the tiny, built-in, rechargeable battery sized only to run things during a quick, old-for-new, fuel-cell swap—had fully drained. Looking disgusted at my helplessness, a screener snapped the fuel cell back into its socket on the exoskeleton's left thigh. Then it was on to Baggage, and then to another line. Finally, I reached the Customs counter.

"Welcome to the USNA," the Customs officer offered in a bored monotone. The badge pinned to her blouse read CARRUTHERS. Even by Earther standards, she was petite. With her neck craned and head tipped up to meet my gaze, she evoked an image I'd once seen of a baby robin anticipating a juicy worm. I took a passport chip from its shielded sleeve and handed it over. "Mr. …"

For an instant I froze. As secretive as the company was, being one of the Belt's major employers meant it could not hide the identities of its many employees. So, if I were to have any hope of success, I had to be someone other than myself. "Donovan," I completed, recalling my current alias.

Carruthers busied herself for awhile with mating the proffered passport chip to an authenticator, giving the counter's sensor pad only the most perfunctory of swipes with a sanitizing tissue. Inwardly, I shrugged. State-of-the-art med nanites had been the least of my preparations. I pressed my thumb against the sensor pad until the device bleated its constipated approval. (As expected: the company had paid plenty for that ID. Ditto for the other ID chips nestled in dummy sockets of my exoskeleton. Bogus Cerian IDs were not exactly illegal—at least not on this world—but attempting entry with forged credentials surely was.)

"What brings you to Earth, Mr. Donovan?"

"Business," I said. Preventing economic ruin across the Belt must surely qualify as business, and her voice-stress analyzer shone a steady green. That I also hoped to rescue the kidnapped son of a company employee? That was a complication best not contemplated anywhere near a voice-stress analyzer. "Well, not just business. I've never been to Earth before. I'm taking time while I'm here to look around."

"Your computer, please. Logged in."

Since landing, I had struggled merely to stumble about in my exoskeleton. I had had *no* opportunity to practice fine-motor control. The tremor in my hands (damned gravity!) as I typed my pass code confounded the keystroke-dynamics recognition. Four times, to Carruthers's annoyance. Finally, the biometrics module authenticated me. I handed over the comp.

While reading out the balance from my digital wallet, an invasion of privacy the USNA somehow justified as an impediment to money laundering, she added absently, "What sort of business are you in, Mr. Donovan?"

"Management consulting." That was vague enough to encompass, well, almost anything. If there were follow-up questions, I was prepared to discuss forensic accounting for as long as necessary. In any event, she didn't ask, and the LED remained green.

"Business must be good."

"You have no idea," I said, defying any lie detector to object.

With furrowed brow, Carruthers studied my face, comparing it to the holo projected from my passport by her chip reader. "See what?"

"Pardon me?"

"What kind of sightseeing do you have in mind?"

"I've heard about some interesting museums. Historical sites. Natural wonders."

"Yeah, we've got those." An icon began flashing on her screen, and she frowned. "This chip doesn't encode your DNA."

I nodded. "Not done on Ceres. As far as I know, not anywhere in the Belt."

"Yeah, well, that's there. I'll need a sample."

"But visitors to Earth aren't legally required to—"

"Earth? Maybe so. Maybe you could enter that way at, say, Timbuktu. You want to enter the USNA? Then you *will* authorize me to update your passport and file a DNA sample. Or ..."

"Or?" I prompted hopefully.

"Or you can turn around and fly back to whatever rock you came from."

Had I taken as much umbrage as any upright Belter citizen? Not yet griped enough to invite a deep dive through my every digital gadget? It was a balancing act, because I *really* did not want to invite any extra scrutiny.

I shrugged. "Sample away."

"Already done." She pointed at the sensor pad. "Everyone's DNA is collected at entry and compared against a terrorism database. You only needed to authorize filing today's sample."

Crushing gravity *and* fastidious fascism. I couldn't finish my business here soon enough. "Will there be anything else?"

She keyed away at her terminal. Finally, it chirped. She removed and handed back the passport chip, then my comp. "Enjoy your visit, Mr. Donovan."

"Thank you," I answered. Because *I will* was a lie I could never have slipped past the voice-stress analyzer.

...◆...

Exhausted well before I had cleared Customs, I Ubered to a midtown Manhattan hotel. No matter that by local time I had landed in the early afternoon; according to ship and body clocks, it had been the middle of the night. Then, fortified with twelve hours of sleep and an epic, room-service, breakfast, I got down to business.

I spent three days ostensibly enjoying some of the many famous museums, landmarks, and eateries in Manhattan. (As for the restaurants, well, strike *ostensibly*. In the Belt, synthed food was almost all I ever ate. Was all anyone—apart from senior partners of the company, or the few folks equally rich—could routinely afford. I could get used to natural ingredients and actual cooking.) After unfashionably early dinners I returned to my hotel suite, bone weary, to rest and to take in Earther news feeds: a litany of border wars, refugee swarms, climate disasters, health crises, anti-Spacer rage (apparently, as some would have it, we were despoiling a pristine Solar System), and spiraling crime and civil violence. In the abstract, I'd always known the mother world was a mess. Long hours immersed in that madness made it *real*.

And in truth? Those days were all work and no play. I mastered walking in my exoskeleton—and, "thanks" to all its metal, also stoic acceptance of a security pat down at damn near every building I chose to enter. Internalized, after several painful conks, that I had to duck to get through almost every doorway. Came to terms with there being more people here in a single city block than the population of entire Belter *cities*. Proved to myself that I could survive modest exertion, that five liters of synthetic corpuscles and their super-efficient artificial hemoglobin took up the slack for my Spacer-flabby heart. Shuffled around Central Park, away from the worst signal reflections off the zillion nearby skyscrapers, until my comp obtained enough satellite ephemeris data for the GPS chip to locate me. (Freaked out my entire time in the park, I might add, by wind. What a weird phenomenon! Wished I had the time and the agility to try kite flying. To judge by the many gleefully shrieking kids, kites must be great fun.)

I spent an entire evening in battle with downloads from the exoskeleton manufacturer's website. Almost before the ship landed, the UPDATES WAITING LED on the control panel had blazed red to herald a discouragingly large number of critical patches, all new since I'd departed Ceres. Half those updates took it upon themselves to re-enable a factory default setting of "Help us improve by sharing your experience." With growing impatience, I kept re-disabling that. Two updates simply hung, grinding away mid-installation, till I found the obscure operating-system setting that needed tweaking. One update activated the "I've fallen and I can't get up" feature, never asking if I wanted to accept the first-month free trial offer; I undid that, too. When the patch-notification feature proved to have no OFF switch, I disabled the comm entirely. There was no telling what, if anything, the manufacturer's servers recorded from such communications with the exo—and I did not plan to leave behind a trail of digital breadcrumbs. That was the night I found a way (plenty of French wine!) to sleep through the recurring nightmare of falling *splat.*

What else? Practiced dining with a knife, fork, and spoon, and *not* slopping liquids from an open cup or glass. Acquired a small wardrobe of Earther style: men's shirts and trousers were as ubiquitous in the USNA as in the Belt, and likewise of programmable fabrics, but the *cuts* differed. Here, pant cuffs and long, pointy shirt collars had come back. I couldn't disguise my height or exoskeleton, but I didn't need to appear fresh off the ship. And so, I prided myself, I didn't—

As long as I remembered never to look up.

The vast blueness wasn't my problem. An infinite sky is the birthright of *every* Spacer. Buildings, per se, were not the issue, either. Space settlements, by their nature, are large, complex structures. But office towers of five hundred meters and more looming overhead? In *this* gravity? And no matter that I knew clouds to be mere aerosol accumulations, every glimpse of one, even of the white-and-fluffy variety, sent my reflexes into panic and set my overtaxed heart racing.

After three exhausting days—still less than prepared, but with the foreboding sense of time running out—I took the next step on my mission.

…◆…

I had practiced one additional skill in New York and again at every stop along my superficial sightseeing excursion down the East Coast: picking up women. Had my repartee, as the conversational rust wore off, led anywhere, I hadn't the inclination, much less the stamina in this gravitational hellhole, to act on it. Still, no matter that I had yet to notice a tail, I did not dare risk that I didn't have one. Flirting as I went was part of the show—because as of lunchtime on my second day in Washington, DC, the flirting became my cover.

I had lied to my wife, and then argued with her, about my short-notice trip. A once-in-a-lifetime training opportunity in advanced forensic accounting? That was less than compelling, especially on the heels of a long company assignment away from home. Oh, I trusted Bea not to blab—but not *not* to worry. Any scrap of the truth about why the company was sending me to Earth, of all godforsaken places, would have terrified her.

And the hazardous-duty pay I'd extracted? The reward, whether or not I made it home? The company was welcome to send someone else to investigate, I'd said. Of course they wouldn't: the fewer people they brought into this mess, the less likely their vulnerability was to leak out. As for involving any Earther authorities, it was out of the question. Any proper investigation must entail a visit to the crime scene—and *that* (even had it been physically possible) the company would never allow. I kept all that, too, to myself. Bea's uninformed, misdirected anxiety weighed heavily enough.

Lying. Keeping secrets. Hitting on other women. It all made me feel like a dick, and not the investigative sort that circumstances so desperately called for.

Eyes cast downward, I made my way, as the appointed hour approached, to the designated bistro just off the National Mall. I folded myself into the revolving door. Beyond that rotary torture chamber I encountered dim lighting, tinkling jazz piano, and tiny tables. Maybe half the tables were occupied.

I plodded to the brass-and-stained-wood bar. Only a few of the stools were occupied. From one of those, the blonde in a thigh-high pink dress avoided my gaze. Courtesy of the antiqued mirror wall behind the bar, I took in her tanned oval face, pouty lips, and flowing blond hair. By Earther standards, she was an Amazon and a knockout. Give her another half meter and get those breasts out of this cruel gravity, and she would have been my type.

"Hey there," I began.

Glancing my way, she said, "Not interested, sailor."

Her voice was low and throaty. Sexy as hell. To my tabulation of her attributes I added come-hither eyes. I went thither. "Spacer."

"Same thing. The type with a girl in every port."

"I happen to have an opening for *this* port." She ignored me, but I persisted. "Nice place. I'm surprised it's not more crowded."

"Clearly, you haven't eaten here."

"How are the buffalo wings?" Notwithstanding recent utensil practice, I preferred finger food, though that wasn't why I asked.

"Greasier than, and almost as insipid as, the egg rolls." Finally turning my way, she saluted with her glass. "I recommend sticking with these."

I caught the bartender's eye. "Two more of what the beautiful lady is having."

"Two double scotch rocks," he acknowledged. "Single malt."

"You're pretty cocky," she told me.

I waggled an eyebrow. "You don't know the half of it."

A few more lines exchanged from the cheesy script, her eye-popping outfit, and my mismatched socks, and we had established each other's bona fides. Drinks in hand, we reconvened at a nearby table. With a deft pat of the hand, my lovely companion set the privacy screen shimmering. White noise hissed all around us.

"Maureen Rogers," she said, suddenly all business.

"Bernie Fredericks." Not that it mattered, I wondered if her name were any more real than mine. "You're with the company?"

She shook her head. "PI. I sometimes do work for one of their law firms."

While I savored my scotch (unbelievably smooth: the distilled, aged in oaken barrel kind, and nothing like the synthed stuff I got in the Belt), she found a contact-lens case in her capacious purse. "These are for you." She tipped her head questioningly.

As in: why hadn't I just brought my own? Or printed my own once I'd disembarked?

Because getting caught at the border with fake IDs was one thing. A common criminal might arrive with those; if caught, I could hope merely to be shipped back home. But if I'd been caught at Customs with spy gear, or the digital recipe for same? No way was that going to end well.

Maybe she just wondered what I was up to.

Whatever the nature of her curiosity, the company expected me not to share. "Who knows about this meeting?"

"On my side, as far as I know, only one of the law firm's senior partners. We know each other, but I don't ordinarily work with him."

Meaning, I took it, *he* did work for the company, and that he had picked *her* because she didn't. I palmed the lens case. "Good. And who knows about these?"

"Just me. It's my spare set. The thing is, I work the occasional divorce case."

Honey trap, did they call it? "And no one will know I have them?"

"I'll report them lost and expense a replacement pair. Not to worry."

When accountants play detective, they had *better* worry. "How do these work?"

"Slip them on." As the lenses molded themselves to my eyes, Maureen took a comp from her purse. "And I'll need your comp."

I authenticated, and she mated the smart lenses to my comp. She taught me the blink sequences that started and stopped scene capture. Once I'd mastered those, I practiced the squint that downloaded imagery from the lenses to my comp. Then we established and tested a direct link between our comps. Between quantum crypto and routing over the Dark Net, the connection was as secure as either of us knew to make it.

For good measure, she threw in several apps ("Tools of the trade," she called them. "More Dark Net goodies.") I had no reason to believe I had any use for. That those came encrypted and disguised as segments of unallocated spare memory ("Not anything you would want to be found carrying") made me more than a little queasy. Or maybe it was the buffalo wings on which, despite her warning, I'd been chowing down.

She tried again, dispensing with subtlety. "I could be of more assistance if I knew what you were after ..."

Eventually, she shrugged. "What more do you need?"

"Working capital. I believe an amount has been arranged?"

Maureen transferred a large, untraceable wad of cryptocash to my comp. Unlike the money I had had to disclose at spaceport Customs, this was not anything government could tax or trace. Merely confiscate, if they found it. "Anything else?"

Good luck? Given the woman's sometime line of work, getting lucky could be taken the wrong way. And had the company been willing to inform anyone on Earth of their dilemma, I continued to believe, I wouldn't even be here.

I said, "Dialing down the gravity would be appreciated."

…◆…

Had Maureen worn another pair of super-spy contacts to the meet? Back in my hotel room, studying my reflection, I couldn't make out the pair still in *my* eyes until (having to crouch to do so) I'd brought my face to within scant centimeters of the bathroom mirror. So, I had to assume, yes.

I could envision lens imagery capturing my pass code *and* the nuances of me typing it, then bypassing the keyboard via a thumb-drive port. I was pretty sure I could code that hack myself. The possibility would seem academic while the comp remained in my possession, but I don't roll that way. (Two dead. Two dead.) Once I'd ascertained that the (supposedly) inert-till-I-decrypted-them apps didn't include a hidden keystroke logger, I began the switchover to a new authentication sequence. I entered a new pass code, over and over, until keystroke-dynamics recognition trilled completion.

No key logger (that I'd found, anyway) did not mean the unsolicited gifts were otherwise innocuous. After disabling a concealed tracker, I changed names and hotels. Had Maureen *not* tried to tail a secretive company agent, *not* tried to discover something exploitable, I'd have been disappointed. Who didn't hunt for some advantage over the company? *I* had, although my ink-not-yet-dry status as a very junior partner wasn't the sole reason for me being here.

I played around for an hour with Maureen's toys, the wireless skeleton key for electronic locks seeming the most handy. I tweaked the code of several of her apps. Remembering her offhanded *Not anything you would want to be found carrying*, I downloaded two backup sets of everything into spare memory in the exoskeleton controller and deleted the originals from my comp.

Then, bone weary, I ordered room service and went to bed early.

...◆...

I spent another two days in Washington—watching for, but not noticing, any surveillance—while I mastered the art of blink/snapping pictures. The museums were diverting, the monuments inspirational. Even the National Mall, as long as I kept my eyes downcast, was pleasant enough. But once darkness fell? Even after, never mind expense-account wine, a healthy three-fingers slug of single-malt scotch?

Horror.

It always began with the scariest sound in space: the warbling wail of a decompression siren. The roar of escaping atmosphere punctuated the klaxon's periodic lulls. Papers and pens, drink bulbs and food wrappers, hand tools and clipboards, *everything* not secured was sucked up into a maelstrom. My ears popped. My flesh bloated.

As quickly as humanly possible I slapped up emergency patches. So did everyone around me. People I knew. People I *loved.*

Fresh wall cracks gaped even faster.

With air pressure plummeting, as the keening of alarms eerily trailed off, I was in agony. My gut distended from end to end as trapped gases expanded and expanded and *expanded*, spewing puke and shit. I screamed, silently, into the near vacuum—when I could, when the puking eased up—to squeeze out air before the pressure differential destroyed my lungs. Ankles, knees, shoulders, knuckles ... *every* joint was aflame. My eardrums burst. The world turned red as the blood from ruptured vessels seeped into my eyes and as hypoxia took hold.

I could *feel* my eyeballs bulge.

In nightmarish slo-mo, frenetic commotion morphed into the yet more ominous *absence* of activity. People slumping to the floor. Others adrift, launched by involuntary spasms or tugged by the final wisps of escaping air. A floating body nudged me. Long, chestnut-brown hair: a woman. Slowly, she turned. A delicate ear came into sight. The graceful curve of a cheek. The cupid's-bow shape of her lips.

Bea!

I'd jerk awake, gasping for breath, sodden with sweat, trembling. And repeat.

The third morning, done in—but as acclimated as I would ever be—I moved on.

...◆...

Chicago's main museum complex sat alongside a freakishly huge lake. There, on Day One, I observed (*admired* would have been an overstatement; these things had all begun to look alike) yet more artwork and fossils. Traveling inland, I whiled away Day Two gawking at wondrous beasts at the Brookfield Zoo. I wasted far too much time both evenings streaming local news feeds and surfing Earther social media, incredulous that anyone could believe the overpopulated home world would be better off without lunar He-3 or Belt rare earths and precious metals—and somehow unable to look away.

And louder than ever, the words echoed in my brain—

Two dead. Two dead. Two dead. Two dead ...

On my third day in Chicago the tourism act ended. Either no one was surveilling me, or I lacked the skill to notice them. Regardless, the clock was ticking.

Two dead. Two dead. Two dead ...

I began with the last address I had for Darin Hodges: a name conspicuously absent from the collection of lobby buzzers. "I'm a friend of Darin's father," I told the apartment manager, a glum, elderly fellow with the droopy jowls of a St. Bernard. "I promised the old man I'd take Darin out to dinner."

Only Darin hadn't lived there in months. Skipped out owing rent, the manager said, chatty after I paid the young man's arrears. Everything Darin had left behind—no inventory had been taken, of course—had long since been disposed of through a consignment shop (which kept no records of its customers) or recycled.

No clues to be had then, from his possessions, to the young man's whereabouts.

The University of Chicago online directory did not list Darin Hodges, but a snapshot of that directory from the Wayback Machine confirmed that, in the previous semester, he had been a student. I roamed the echoing corridors of Watson and Crick Hall, asking about him, until a young woman with blue-and-mahogany-striped hair and gold hoop earrings pointed me to what had been Darin's office as a research assistant. Former officemates there and, once I tracked down the professor, Darin's erstwhile dissertation adviser, claimed they hadn't been surprised at Darin's dropping out. He had been distracted for months, they said, doing more coffeehouse BS-ing than research. BS-ing about what? Economics. Or politics. Maybe tree-hugging. Labeling his hobby horse didn't seem worth the effort. More discouraging, no two of them agreed when they had last seen him.

If anyone as much as suspected Darin had been abducted, they kept it to themselves. Clearly, no missing person report had been filed. Chicago PD would have found these same acquaintances as readily as had I.

Mentions of coffee were, if not productive, at least timely. I got a recommendation for a nearby coffee bar where, over a double espresso, battling exhaustion, for the umpteenth time I considered more technological methods of investigation. If I hadn't had the skill set, I'd never have gotten into Les Hodges's computer. I wouldn't even be on this quest. I wouldn't be achy and bruised inside the damned exoskeleton, without which I could not as much as get out of bed on this damned planet.

If I accessed the younger Hodges's financial accounts, I'd have a better idea when he had been snatched. The latest transaction might even suggest *where* he had been snatched. Then, by hacking the city's archive of public-safety surveillance, with facial rec I might spot the actual kidnapping. Maybe, even, the kidnappers. But the prospect, however unlikely, of getting caught and serving *years* in this barbarous gravity once again deterred me.

We'd call hacking Plan B.

Darin's father was in biotech, the professor had offered confidentially. Was I aware of that? (Yes.) Perhaps an advanced degree in biotech had never been Darin's idea. He certainly had some kind of issue with his father. (Okay, I hadn't known that. Not for certain. To be sure, the paucity of messages from Darin on his father's computer had implied as much.)

And maybe the young man's adviser was onto something. Somewhere along the way I heard that Darin had volunteered as a docent at the nearby Oriental Institute. Showing ancient Middle Eastern artifacts? That was not exactly a typical hobby for a budding biotech engineer. I plodded the few blocks to the museum, passing a line of posters on utility poles proclaiming a week-earlier protest over Spacer imperialism. All that the arduous trek got me was three more sorry-haven't-seen-hims.

Outside the museum, with evening falling, a car with heavily tinted windows pulled up. The Uber to return me to my hotel, I thought, till the rear curbside window slid down a few centimeters. From within the vehicle, a decidedly non-synthesized voice said, "I hear you've been asking about me."

...◆...

I struggled to contain my shock.

"Darin Hodges?" I said. This was, without a doubt, the "missing" son. It wasn't just that he took after his old man, with the same slot face, cleft chin, and close-set blue eyes. More times than I cared to remember, I had watched Darin in the vid from his father's hacked comp. I saw the same thin lips, the same slight leftward bend to the nose, and the same—if a lot more—curly black hair.

"Yes." I heard the click-thunk of a door unlocking. "Get in, please."

I did. And as the car sat at the curb, my mind raced.

The terrified young man in the vid, handcuffed to a metal-frame chair, pleading for his father's help, had had a black eye and a split lip. Had cringed from a ski-masked, voice-disguised *someone* threatening his slow death unless the elder Hodges did as directed. The passage of time might explain the fading of bruises, but not the young man's freedom—much less why, to protect his son, Les Hodges had … done what he had. Apart from a few people within the company, no one knew *that*.

I hadn't anticipated *Darin* finding *me*. That left me winging it. I temporized, "How did you know it was me asking around?"

"We don't see a lot of middle-aged Spacers around here."

"Your father is a middle-aged Spacer," I reminded. (Earthborn, and so a shorter-than-two-meter pipsqueak, but a Spacer nonetheless. *Belters* crazy or driven enough to visit must be in short supply, though. I sure as hell looked forward to going home.)

"Uh-huh. And how often do I ever see *him*?"

"Let's start over." I introduced myself, my spiel basically what I'd used with the apartment manager. I concluded, "When your dad heard I'd be in Chicago, he made me promise to take you to dinner."

Sarcastically: "So how is dear old Dad?"

"Fine, the last I saw him," I lied. "So, dinner?"

"Why not? A man's gotta eat."

The address Darin told the car turned out to be for a just-off-campus hole-in-the-wall. It struck me as unbusy, even for not quite six on a Thursday evening. Then again, what did I know of Earth collegian dining habits? The hostess, an Earth-tall, perky brunette whom Darin seemed to know—I speculated that she, not the food here, was the main draw—escorted us to a booth in the rear. Her perfume, a floral scent I recognized but could not have named, started my nose running.

Serapes, piñatas, and mariachi music announced that dinner would be Mexican. When our stoop-shouldered waiter brought chips and salsa, water, and menus to the table, I ordered margaritas and nachos, thereby exhausting my knowledge of the cuisine. The menu covers proclaimed PROUDLY VEGAN, and my expectations for the meal ebbed further—not that my dining experience was what mattered.

"Make them frozen," Darin appended. The waiter nodded.

"So," I began.

"So," Darin repeated. "Tell me. Are there many hu … Earthers in the Belt, or is it just my father?"

Humans? Implying I was not? "Quite a few, as it happens. Lots of opportunity out there. The pay is good. That's why your dad went. To provide for his family."

"To abandon his family, you mean." Darin peeled the adhesive paper strip from his paper-napkin-wrapped silverware. Rolled the strip into a tight cylinder. Unrolled it. Coiled the band again, even tighter.

Even I could read that body language. How deep did the resentment go? Changing the subject, I tapped my menu. "So, vegan?"

"Do you know what three animals are the top contributors to Earth's biomass? Do you?"

"No idea."

"Guess."

"Elephants? Then whales?" I'd started us down this rabbit hole by commenting on the meatless menu. "And cattle."

"Cattle first, then humans. And a very distant third? Every other kind of animal on the planet, *combined*. Elephants are massive individually, but together they still comprise only a fraction of one percent of the biomass of just cattle. *That's* how few elephants remain. And how many cattle we keep. And what a blight humanity has made of itself."

"Oh," I offered quietly. It did not placate him.

"And do you know why so many cattle?"

Because, as I'd been learning, there was nothing like a good steak. Synthed meat—synthed *any* food—was a poor imitation of the real thing. "No, why?"

"Because there are so many people. And do you know why?"

From doing what came naturally? "No, why?"

"Spacers," he snapped. "For awhile, it looked like humanity, finally, had come to its collective senses. Had realized our world has its limits. Had realized that too many of us can only mean too little of everything else in nature. There was hope, at the brink of the precipice, that the human population would stabilize. Then the goodies began arriving from off-world, and people—the fools—forgot all about restraint. It doesn't matter if *we* tell ourselves the sky's the limit. The *planet* knows better."

In other words, *more* anger at his father. Shrinks had a term for that kind of misdirected emotion. Displacement, was it? I preferred his officemates' description: coffeehouse BS.

By any label, Darin had no idea the sacrifice his father had made. For *him*. "Les was very proud of you. You know that, don't you?"

"Was?"

Oops! "Was and is. I haven't seen him in months. I'm sure he's still proud of you."

"Not proud enough ever to show up at a Little League game. Or attend an award ceremony. Not proud enough to come to my *graduation.*" Darin plowed, scowling, through a litany of grievances. Les footing the tuition bill at an Ivy League college, and then for three years of grad school, did not merit a mention. Nor did pleading for his father to save his life enter into the diatribe. Finally, the young man shook it off. "How is it you know Dad, anyway?"

"I'm his accountant." I wasn't, of course, but access to Les's company HR file let me improvise. "He talked about you a lot. And about your mother, of course. He misses her." It seemed like a safe bet. Sally Hodges had passed away two years earlier. A half-billion kilometers away at the time, Les had missed the funeral. Doubtless his absence was another black mark. "Anyway, Les made me promise to look you up if I made it to Chicago."

"So you said."

Did he look skeptical? I couldn't decide. Then again, I hadn't gone into accounting for my people skills. I mean, does anyone?

The waiter finally returned with our drinks.

Darin downed a healthy swig. "Miners need accountants?"

"Everyone needs an accountant."

"That's what's wrong with the world. No offense."

I sampled my own margarita, and found salt crystals along the glass rim off-putting. Where I come from, we mix in a pinch of salt, because drink bulbs don't *have* rims. And a Belt margarita never came slushy, because ice chips would clog the nipple. Also, maybe there was too much Triple Sec? All in all, a disappointment. "No, what's wrong with the world is that everyone needs a lawyer."

Darin managed a laugh. "I'm sorry to hear that that pestilence has even gotten to the Belt. What's it like out there?"

Here, at last, was a topic about which I could discourse on autopilot. I kept looking for a segue, but what *is* the proper transition to, "How did you get away from your brutal captors?"

Because, by rights, the kidnappers should not have let him go. Not yet.

...◆...

Well before completing my freshman, months-long excursion aboard one of the company's windowless, instrumentless, fusion-drive-propelled cans, I'd concluded I had gone to work for evil geniuses.

Geniuses? Absolutely! But not until my last Belt outing had I encountered true evil.

And that wasn't the *company's* malevolence ...

...◆...

"All very nice," Darin interrupted my paeans to humanity's space frontier. He leaned across the table, studying me. "But oddly persistent, considering. I mean, how often can you get to the home world? You could've just explained that I'd left the university and you couldn't find me, then spent the day sightseeing."

"When I make a promise, I—"

"You've let your ice melt," he interrupted. "We can't have that." Our waiter was nowhere in sight, and Darin called out to the hostess. "Another round. *Especial, por favor.*"

"Special, how?" I asked.

Darin grinned. "You'll see."

I took a new tack. "Why *did* you drop out of school?"

"Not important."

Waiting him out led only to an awkward silence. "What are you doing now instead?"

The hostess bustled up to our table with fresh margaritas. The *especial* variety added paper cocktail umbrellas. I got the glass with the tiny red parasol. Darin's was blue. She said, "Enjoy."

"Well, Darin, what have you been up to?" I tried again.

He raised his glass, waiting till I did the same. "Bottoms up."

I took a healthy swallow, then waited.

"You know," he smirked, "someone else came around, a couple months back, likewise curious about me."

"Oh?"

"A bill collector, or so he asserted. He also put a disproportionate amount of effort into finding me."

"To collect the rent you had, well, forgotten to tend to before moving on?"

"Drink up, Dad's friend." Darin downed more of his margarita, then waited till I followed suit. "For my back rent? That's a good one. No, the guy worked for the company."

"What company?" I asked, with the sinking feeling that I knew. *The* company. Two months ago I had returned to Ceres. Two months ago, my employers first saw the coercive vid on Les's hacked computer.

If the company *had* hired an investigator Dirtside, why hadn't they said so? And what else hadn't they told me?

Toppling onto the table, spilling what remained of the drugged margarita, as awareness faded, I intuited an explanation. Or maybe it was Darin's smirk that suggested the answer.

That first investigator had never reported back.

...◆...

Two dead. Two dead. Two dead ...

Coming out of my drug-induced fog, I took solace from not having become number three. Yet. Or perhaps the bullet I'd dodged was becoming number four, the fate of the Earther "bill collector" remaining ambiguous. Either way, I silently chewed myself out for having so thoroughly scrubbed my comp of Maureen's spyware. Damn my obsessive-compulsive thoroughness anyway! Never mind the company's penchant for secrecy, right about then I could have used a competent someone tracking me. Not that I had any idea where my comp was, other than gone from my pocket. Ditto, the passport sleeve for my current ID. I would have felt their lumps under my ass.

I'd awakened at least once before into this dismal, windowless storeroom. Apart from a clearer—if still throbbing—head, nothing had changed. I remained immobile, helpless. The cyclopean red eye of a camera still guarded me.

Just maybe I remembered Darin and the pretty hostess maneuvering me from the booth. Either way, I'd lost consciousness before exiting the vegan restaurant. At least I assumed we had left. The indistinct murmurs (argument? pontification?) that penetrated the walls and closed door did nothing to suggest I was in the back room of a restaurant.

Unable to move, I ransacked my memories. Speculated. Analyzed. Cursed myself out. Regretted. Cursed myself out some more.

My chief regret? How *blind* I had been. I had never considered the possibility—at this point, the near certainty—that Darin was a coconspirator. The one ambiguity remaining was whether he had conspired all along, or begun as a victim and been turned. I thought I remembered some famous case involving an abducted Hearst family heiress become a terrorist. The Stockholm syndrome, was that called? Whatever Stockholm was.

Unable to kick myself except figuratively, it was just as well that, soon after my second(?) awakening, the door to my cell opened with a soft squeak. Letting gravity do most of the work, I turned my head. I caught a glimpse of knapsacks, flight bags, and other satchels, all piled against the far wall in the next room. A poster with a woodland scene hung above the luggage. I heard snippets of conversation about ... birthrates? ... and laughter. Darin walked in, carrying a folding chair.

There popped into my mind an ancient cartoon of two filthy, bedraggled prisoners dangling by wrist manacles from a dungeon wall. *Now, here's my plan ...*, one of them was saying. Blinking, I snapped an image of the other room before Darin closed the door behind himself. The hinges protested in this direction, too.

I said, "I still owe you dinner. Or you can treat."

"I'm good," he said. "But you, funny man? You might want to take matters seriously."

"I am. In hindsight, I should never have paid your back rent." Was that a ghost of a smile? Or an expression more predatory? The look, whatever it signified, vanished before I could decide. "So what did happen to that bill collector you mentioned?" And am I going to end up like him?

Darin unfolded the chair and set it facing the sofa. He sat, glaring down on me. "Do you even know my father?"

"I told you. I'm his accountant."

"Uh-huh."

Okay, that had sounded dubious, even to me. "But personal accounting isn't why I'm here. I came to network. Representing Earther companies in the Belt will be a big career step."

"Not with the company? Then"—he intoned ominously—"you're of no use to me."

Sharing or stonewalling? Which offered the better chance of keeping me alive? I wouldn't get a do-over. "Okay, you got me. I'm a lowly accountant for the company. They send me from rock to rock, my job being to audit physical stockpiles and onsite records for evidence of any pilfering. Your dad was among the miners at the most recent rock I visited." When Darin didn't comment, I added, "And I know why you've been in hiding."

"Uh-huh. Why is that?"

"Because as soon as Les got back to civilization and long-range comm, he was certain to try to contact you. It wouldn't have fit the storyline for you to be reachable. You had to have disappeared months ago, when you were kidnapped, and still be gone."

"Do tell," Darin smirked.

"The thing is, your abductors"—and not that I could lift my arms, I wondered if that last word deserved air quotes—"wouldn't have let you go till they knew whether Les had complied. Whether, as per your recorded heartfelt plea, your father had constructed and deployed an aerosol-dispersing device at the mining base. Oh, he might have reported that he'd done so, but no one would know for many months. Not till the relief ship with your dad's crew returned for their *next* tour of duty. And that shouldn't happen till months from now."

The smirk had not quite vanished, but I had the young man's attention. Darin said, "He showed you the vid, then. While you were onsite auditing. Why?"

"No, I came upon the vid after. The thing is, Darin …" Almost despite himself, he leaned closer. It made no difference that he had put himself within arm's length of me, because my arms were also dead weights. "Your father is dead."

"Bullshit."

"No, really. Haven't you wondered why he hasn't tried to make contact? Even in hiding, you'd have gotten an email."

Darin shrugged. "Everyone in his crew went straight from the rock to company jail, whatever the euphemism the company uses for detention. I guess the strip searches to discourage smuggling of platinum scraps weren't invasive enough."

The crew—what remained of it, anyway—*was* in confinement. But not over any mundane pilferage. Not directly. The company cover story was holding. (Two dead. Two dead …) I shook off *my* guilt with outrage at *Darin's* hypocrisy. It's not like I was his guest here.

"He built and hid the device, just as your people ordered." The young man ignored *your people*, reinforcing my suspicions. "It wasn't his fault another miner found it tucked into a ventilation duct. You can imagine the concerns *that* discovery raised. And the questions …"

"Then what happened?"

"I think Les was terrified at what might happen to you if he gave out any information. Because he believed the vid, you know? He believed you'd been kidnapped and abused. He believed that, to save your life, he had to do exactly as ordered. As much as possible, he had. When the device was discovered, he was desperate to show your captors he had done everything he could to cooperate. Protecting you was more important to him than … anything."

"You can't know that."

"You tell me." I stared at him. "Besides whatever nasty stuff the device was meant to disperse, your father *also* synthed a cyanide pill."

The blood drained from Darin's face. Too little. Too late. "Dad took *cyanide*? But he wasn't supposed to …"

Les was not supposed to die. The vid had directed him to set the timer for two days after his crew was scheduled to rotate out. As for the men and women of the alternating crew, they were expendable. And while I had my suspicions, I had no actual clue as to why they were to have been expended.

Words, if I could find the right ones, were the only tools available. "Yes, your dad took cyanide. In front of his crew. In front of his friends. Because once that device had been found—and no one, of course, admitted to any knowledge of it—everyone was made to turn over their personal comps as possible evidence. Your dad must've figured that if he weren't forced to unlock his comp, the encrypted coercive message to him might go unseen. That protecting those secrets with his life might mollify your abductors.

"Of course, an expert at the company *did* unlock everything." That expert being me, a fact whose disclosure I doubted would improve my situation. "We saw the vid. We saw how Les had been put into an impossible situation, how he had been forced to build that device."

I strained to lift my head, the better to stare at my captor. "And the people who coerced your father? *They* are responsible for his death."

Exhausted, closing my eyes and letting my head flop back onto the sofa, I hoped Darin would chew on that.

...◆...

With no timepiece beyond a growing thirst, unsure even if I had nodded off, I had no idea how much time had passed before Darin reappeared. Behind him, past the open door, a woman in dark slacks and a tan sweater strode by. Her head was turned, but though I saw only the back of her head I blink-snapped an image anyway. This wasn't the hostess from the Mexican restaurant. Vegan Woman had been taller, her hair straighter and darker. But, I suspected, my co-abductor *was* in the next room. The whiff of her perfume, and the start of my nose dripping, were unmistakable.

"Time to continue our chat," Darin announced.

Chat had not come out sounding friendly. Perhaps it didn't matter, but I wondered whether he'd already come to terms with his father's death—plainly, they had had issues—or if he had convinced himself I had lied about it to rattle him.

"Unless you like things messy," I countered, "first you'll return my fuel cell and point me to a bathroom."

He pointed, instead, at the wastebasket in the corner.

"I can't stand without power for the exoskeleton, much less walk."

He canted his head, considering, then turned toward the door. "Back in a minute."

"I'll be here," I called after him. I snapped more images through the doorway as he exited, and again when he returned with a brown paper sack.

With a roll of duct tape from the bag, he bound my ankles. Around and around he wound the tape, a good ten times. "Hands together now." I couldn't lift my arms and so, grumbling, he maneuvered them together and bound my wrists just as securely. *Then*, he snapped a fuel cell taken from his bag into the exoskeleton. "I'll be back in a couple of minutes."

"I'll need at least five. And will the camera be turned off?"

He left, not deigning to answer.

It took me more or less forever to maneuver bound legs off the sofa and to sit up. (Seated, I saw that the PANIC button had gone missing from the exoskeleton's forearm control panel. Two of the chips visible through the ragged hole bore sooty scorch marks. I pictured the flat blade of a screwdriver prying out the button, in the process shorting the chips immediately beneath. The joke was on them: I hadn't enrolled in the service.) It took me as long to stand, to the accompaniment through the wall of faint sniggers. It took longer—toppling twice, struggling laboriously back to my feet—to shuffle to and from the chamber pot. It's not as if I'd had reason to train the exoskeleton to interpret muscles twitches made while restrained hand and foot. Some hopefully discreet experimental flexing as I shuffled convinced me that even at full exertion, the hardware could not snap my bonds. As for unzipping myself? Doing my business with bound wrists? Those were about as much fun.

Finally, gasping for breath, I plopped onto the sofa, but sitting. I hoped the voyeurs watching through the webcam had found the exhibition compelling.

When Darin returned, he'd brought a water bottle. Just to see condensation beads dotting the plastic, a few drops running down onto his hand, made me realize how thirsty I had become. Ice cubes softly clinked within as he held out the reusable container.

I raised my arms, wrists still bound. "Open it, please?"

He pulled up the spout, and handed over the bottle. As I drank, clumsily, managing somehow to slosh some of the water onto my shirt, he asked, "What was that?"

On my left forearm, in a corner of the control panel, the CHARGING LED glowed yellow. Accepting the water might already have sunk my plan. Such as it was. "What's what?"

He pointed. "That lamp."

"Status indicator of some kind? Not happy with having a button pried out?" As he extended an arm to reclaim my fuel cell, I dipped my head to indicate the bottle. "Let me finish this first. I can't lift my arms without power."

"Be quick about it."

I chugged the bottle, and he plucked it empty from my hands. I had barely rested my arms in my lap when he popped out the fuel cell.

Darin settled into his chair. "You've had your fluid-adjustment break. Now, we talk."

I talked, he meant.

He had sought *me* out. Why? I assumed, to stop me from continuing to look for him. To stop me drawing attention to him. Had my explanation for the search been credible, I imagined we'd have had dinner and gone our separate ways.

Then there was the so-called bill collector. However expendable the company considered me, they wanted—no, they *needed*—to get to the bottom of things. If they had retained, and then lost contact with, an Earther investigator, almost certainly they would have told me, if only to tip the odds for my success. By that line of reasoning the bill collector was a fiction invented to rattle me, his indeterminate fate intended to encourage my cooperation.

Almost certainly.

Like a particularly dimwitted rat in a maze, my thoughts thereafter darted every which way and ended up getting nowhere. I'd been drugged, kidnapped, and imprisoned. If I lived to implicate Darin, he could implicate everyone in the cabal. Short of rescue or escape, was there any way back from that?

Two dead. Two dead. I very much wanted *not* to be number three.

I licked my lips. "Tell me what you want to know." Not that I cared, beyond construing from his answer which lies I could get away with while still earning his trust.

"Why are you here?"

"Because you drugged me and brought me here," I blurted out.

While that crack imparted nothing he didn't already know, what could needless antagonism accomplish? What was wrong with me?

He seemed not to take offense. "Understood. But why did you come to Earth?"

Company business. This time, I caught myself before volunteering more needless truth. What was it Mark Twain had said? If you tell the truth, you don't have to remember anything. Maybe the epigram applied as well to selective truths. "To find you. I told you so upfront."

"To buy me a dinner, as you promised my father. Only you *also* told me he's dead. Which is it?"

"Both, except for the promise part."

Darin frowned. "So Dad *is* dead? How?"

"I told you earlier. He took cyanide."

"Tell me about this device you say he made, and what happened with it."

I saw no harm in answering. Darin and his associates knew what they had ordered built. "A clear glass bottle. An electronics module of some sort, lots of wires, and a slab of stuff like clay. Stuck into the clay was a metal tube that one of the miners told me was a blasting cap. Everyone was afraid to touch the thing."

"Sounds like a bomb," Darin suggested.

"It looked like a bomb," I agreed. "Apart from the glass bottle part. Logically, that held a gas or chemical or something."

"Logically. Did you or anyone see anything in the bottle?"

Had I? I thought back. "Dust speckles on the bottom of the container."

My mention of dust made him smile. "What else? What did you think about the bottle?"

"That the explosion or a control valve would release whatever …"

I froze mid-sentence. What the *hell* was I doing, rattling on this way? I did a quick mental rewind and replay of the past few exchanges. It was as if I'd forgotten the danger. It was as if I wanted my answers to please.

What the *hell* was in the water I'd chugged?

"You were saying?" Darin urged.

The Belt is *big*. Flying from rock to rock on company business, I read a lot. I watched vid after vid. I'd done plenty more of both during the long flight to Earth, mostly detective and spy stories: my homework. (Also, the entire run of the second reboot of *Buffy the Vampire Slayer*. The flights were boring. Don't judge me.) Several plots had involved someone compelled to talk under truth serum. And before dropping out, Darin had been a graduate student in biotech. How hard would it have been for him to have synthed a drug? Make that two drugs. He had likely also synthed whatever had knocked me out at the restaurant.

"Umm," I continued, mumbling, "something would release whatever was in the bottle."

But *truth serum*, like *lie detector*, was a misnomer. Wasn't it? At least, what I recalled from police-procedural stories was that sodium pentothal and its ilk were basically anti-anxiety meds. They lowered inhibitions. Reduced or eliminated fears. Suppressed higher cortical functions, in theory making it harder to sustain a lie. (Good one, Mr. Twain.) They could be disorienting. They did not so much force truth-telling as make a person want to please. At one time, psychiatrists had used the meds to treat PTSD and the like. Under the guidance of a skilled practitioner, a drugged subject would confirm what the questioner already knew.

And when the questioner didn't know the truth? Drugged subjects in the main *still* answered with whatever a questioner signaled, intentionally or not, he expected. And so, shrinks wielding sodium pentothal, persistently probing and hinting about abuse to *otherwise* traumatized child patients, had once gotten a bunch of innocent parents and daycare workers thrown into prison as abusers.

Good thing I didn't read only fiction.

"What was in the glass bottle?" Darin asked.

"The bottle with the bomb? I don't know."

"Why a bomb *and* a bottle?"

Were my arms not impossibly heavy, I'd have shrugged. "My guess? The explosives were to discourage any attempt, if the thing were found, to move or disable it. If so, the plan worked."

"And the company? Do they know what was in the bottle?"

"I don't see how. The device hadn't gone off when the crew-rotation ship arrived. Everyone abandoned the base."

That was truthful—as far as it went. But auditors flew from rock to rock in single-person ships. I had remained behind in my ship after the miners evacuated, remotely monitoring the deserted base through cameras left inside. Within a few days of the device going off, every sort of plastic, rubber, and synthetic fiber … dissolved. Including the nylon layer of backup pressure suits that had been left behind. The base itself retained atmosphere—the air lock was gasket-free, its shaped-metal hatches pressing like springs against the metal frame—but anyone who had stayed behind, or who entered the base afterward, would have been trapped.

Bottom line, and that's what we accountants deal in, I knew what the stuff dispersed by the bomb *did*. But was it a potent, if selective, corrosive gas? Plastic-loving, fast-reproducing bacteria? Plastic-hating, self-replicating nanites? Did anyone know what, precisely (beyond, perhaps, more of Darin's biotech handiwork), it *was*? No.

What I did know was that determining what had been set loose was impossible absent venturing inside the stricken base—and that, no simple undertaking. During the hasty preparations for my trip to Earth I'd overheard chatter at company headquarters about how they hoped, someday, to regain use of the mine. The thinking had yet to advance beyond generalities, involving a custom-built robot cum mobile laboratory and a hermetic barrier to encase both bot and the mine's air lock. Remotely operated by techies—outside the barrier on the asteroid's barren surface—the robot would enter the base. Unless and until testing identified the contagion and someone crafted a way to neutralize it, the robot would remain sealed within. And short of constructing a new base from scratch, all the precious platinum on that rock would remain in the ground.

"I don't see how," I repeated.

Darin shook his head. "If the company had Dad's computer, they must know what was inside the bottle."

For once in this interrogation, I got to speak the unvarnished truth. "The vid ordered Les to digitally shred everything after he'd deployed the device. He *did* destroy the recipe used to print it and whatever was in it. I suppose he couldn't bring himself to delete the vid, because that might have been the last he ever saw of you." As, in fact, it had been.

"You must have a theory," Darin pressed.

Drugs and lowered inhibitions be damned, I had to out-and-out lie. "Knockout gas of some kind?"

"And you say there was something like dust at the bottom of the jar?"

My confirmation again pleased him. That dust, somehow, was a clue. Though its meaning eluded me, I knew I needed to get the information out to the company.

"So, what's the company's reaction to all this? I mean, beyond so recklessly sending you to nose about?"

"They're *pissed*."

Darin laughed. "Why was the device put there to begin with?"

"You must already know."

"Why do *you* think the device was put there? Why does the company?"

"Well ..." With the exoskeleton inert I couldn't even squirm. "Do my uninformed speculations matter?"

"You must have some theory," he coaxed.

"Extortion." Suppressed inhibitions be damned, I had to chose my next words with special care. At least if I hoped to get out of here alive. "The company is incredibly, obscenely rich. I understand wanting a piece of that. Honest, I do. After tax evasion, the Belter national pastime is trying to put one over on the company.

"Knocking a platinum mine out of production blew a huge gaping hole in their forecasted cash flow. I'm an accountant. I *know* how that hurts them. I assume the plan was to incapacitate the miners on the one rock, demonstrating that something worse could have been done. And having shown it could be done once? Then other crew members, on other asteroids, could likely be coerced to take down even more production. I expect your people will demand a payoff to ensure that doesn't happen on any company rock."

He sat silently for awhile, smugly stroking his chin. Was that confirmation?

In the next room, people argued. Oh, the words were often indistinct; the depth of emotion was clear enough. Such unintelligible polemics had become all too familiar.

What I didn't get was why the conspirators had been so cold-blooded. Knockout gas would have made their point. But the vile stuff that *had* been released? If the device had gone undiscovered until it went off, the men and women of the relief crew would have been trapped. For the short term, perhaps, they would have been fine (Les's gerbil in its cage had seemed unaffected—at least till its water bottle dissolved). But they could forget about the long term. Once the contagion found its way into the synthesizers, dissolving an internal gasket or two, food production would have ceased.

"That's why ..." I trailed off, mid-blurt. *Damn* whatever inhibition-lowering drug he had given me.

His eyes narrowed. "Why what?"

Why he was so interested in the dust settled to the bottom of the bomb bottle? Until Darin had asked, the dust had made zero impression on me. I'd never mentioned it to company debriefers. Anyway, *dust* was my term. Darin had said, "something like dust."

How had the rubber-eating stuff been synthed? Or, rather, how had it been synthed without revealing itself by eating gaskets inside one of the base printers? Before I'd headed Earthward, these questions had been driving company engineers *nuts*.

For lack of any answer, a witch-hunt had been ongoing as I left. Never mind that smuggling contraband aboard a company ship would have involved bypassing two independent automated surveillance systems *and* corrupting an entire four-person team hand-inspecting everything. No matter that company Security in the main searched outbound ships for disguised radio transmitters, or components thereof, a seemingly empty but sealed glass bottle would surely have merited a closer look.

And if inspectors had opened a plague bottle on Ceres? I shuddered, just to think of the devastation ...

"Why *what*?" Darin repeated.

"I don't know," I answered shakily. "You know how an idea will just pop into your head? And be gone even before you can grasp it?"

"We'll just have to bring that thought back, won't we?" He took a deep breath. "Once more then, from the top ..."

Slumped against the sofa back, struggling for breath, I wheezed, "I've *got* to have a break."

"No, you don't," Darin said. "You're just sitting there."

Conveying exhaustion took no great acting skill. Or any. "I weigh like thirty times what I'm used to, jaw included. Talking is hard. Just breathing is wearing me out."

From astride his chair, its back still toward me, he watched my chest heave. "I suppose we could take five."

"No," I insisted, panting. "Not 'take five.' I need another bathroom break. I need something to eat"—about then, even soy-cheese nachos would do—"and more to drink. And I need sleep."

"And if *I* say no?"

Beats me, I almost said, but a beating wasn't the notion to put into his head. I let my eyes fall shut, my head tip forward.

"Fine," Darin said.

"Steak, medium rare, and a loaded baked potato would be nice."

"Beef?" he barked. "You want *beef*?"

I couldn't stop myself flinching. "Just trying to lighten the mood. Except the part about needing something to eat."

"Fine." He stood and strode from the room. In the short while he left the door ajar, I heard the pretentious tones of a 3V talking head—and a man with a nasal voice yelling back at it. Who gets worked up over some local zoning board approving a high-rise complex? The man was still ranting ("Packing them in like cattle!") when Darin returned with a couple sandwiches on a chipped plate, a wrinkled apple past its sell-by year, a refilled water bottle—and my fuel cell.

Pathetic weakness, or perhaps it was the PBJ mess my first clumsy bite squeezed onto my shirt, got the tape around my wrists snipped and a rickety folding table to support the snack. Carrying in the table (was that bamboo?) required both hands, and Darin didn't close the door behind him. After he sat, I got my first unobstructed pictures of the room beyond, in which the luggage pile seemed to have grown, and, twice, profile shots of bearded men walking past the doorway. Good data about my captors. A bad omen for my prospects. After maybe two minutes, responding to a complaint from that adjoining room, Darin closed the door.

Mid-meal, I dropped my left hand into my lap, below the tabletop. Soon after, the CHARGING LED flipped from yellow to green: I had approximated the reserve-battery charging time about right.

Beneath the table, the tiny lamp was not in sight of Darin or the unblinking webcam, but the table might not be staying. I turned that arm to palm up, control panel and its status LEDs down.

Either my yawning was contagious, or Darin was also tired. He stood, mouth briefly agape. "Get settled. I'll be back soon to unplug you. We'll finish in the morning."

I did not much care for the sound of *finish*. "How about some kind of blanket?"

He paused by the exit, a hand on the knob. The camera, in its motorized mount above the door, continued to sweep from side to side. "What else, Princess? Silk jammies? Hot cocoa? Shall I send for a masseuse?"

"The blanket is to put over my head, so I can get some sleep. Unless you care to turn off the lights?"

"Or, you could close your eyes."

By the time he returned with a blanket, I had maneuvered myself into a sleeping position: lying on my left side, knees raised until the short sofa supported my feet. My left arm rested palm-side up—putting the exoskeleton control panel, with its glowing LEDs, *down*. My face was to the back of the sofa, and my back to the ceiling camera. Darin dropped the folded blanket, stinking of mothballs and stale sweat, on my head and shoulder. As he groped for and removed the fuel cell on my exoleg, I managed with my right hand to tug an edge of the blanket down to waist level.

I heard the soft pad of Darin striding away, hinges squeaking, the *click* of a door latch, and the thud of a deadbolt slamming into place. I heard a man with a gravelly voice greet Darin, and then, at an almost imperceptible level, indistinguishable conversation. The occasional word or phrase I might have made out—midway, pizza, socks, plastic, carrying capacity, starve the beast—told me nothing. Unless that had been Sox, not socks, which could mean I remained on the south side of Chicago. Somehow, I promised myself, I'd live to make it to a ballgame. And have another pizza.

I rotated my left arm to palm down. Cautiously, so as not to dislodge the tented blanket, I slid my right hand to the control panel. I had scarcely roused the virtual keypad when the CHARGING LED reverted to yellow. Type fast, I told myself. But lest I run out of time,

I used a few precious seconds of panel glow to smear the status LEDs with PBJ drippings scraped from my shirtfront.

Plan A was to restore the exo's comm and then activate the "I'm fallen and I can't get up" service. I'd get an operator online, and he, she, or it could connect me to 9-1-1. In theory, Plan A was easy to put into effect. No matter that the PANIC button itself had been ripped out, whatever software the button invoked should still be available. Tapping feverishly, working by the soft glow of the control panel, I enrolled in the emergency service—and found I still couldn't trigger a distress call. Those scorches I'd noticed? A critical chip or two had indeed fried.

On to Plan B, and the tracking software Maureen Rogers had tried to plant on me. I'd deleted it and all her other shady software from my comp—not that I had my comp anymore. But I *did* have the disabled copies I'd saved, just in case, in spare memory of the exoskeleton controller. With a few hurried taps I installed Maureen's tracker, spliced HELP! PRISONER! into the app's output format, and linked the program to the exo's wireless capability.

Alas, the restored app would not give Maureen much to go on—even assuming she hadn't given up on tracking me. It turned out that by disabling the exo's "I've fallen" service, back in New York, I had *also* disabled the exo's underlying GPS service. Without GPS, the spyware could only locate me to the vicinity of the nearest cell tower. That wasn't nothing. It should suffice to get Maureen on her way here from DC. Better yet, it might get her to start some associate or hireling already in Chicago to hunting for me.

If she hadn't given up.

Poking around deep within the menu system, in a race against the rapidly draining battery, I found and re-enabled the exo's embedded GPS service. It, of course, had no idea where I was. Yet.

Back in Manhattan, meandering about Central Park, my comp had taken about twenty minutes to find enough satellites and download enough detailed orbital data to initialize its own GPS service. The exo's little reserve battery was only sized for five, and I guestimated I'd already burned through at least three of those. I might eke out a few extra seconds by lying still—the motors must draw more power than did the electronics—and maybe I'd be lucky.

Maybe, before the battery ran dry, I'd get a precise lat-long readout. Then, so would Maureen's spyware.

It was a nice idea, anyway. The exoskeleton's GPS chip was still initializing when, beneath the blanket, everything went dark. My right forearm and hand flopped to the sofa, dragging my elbow from my side.

Eventually, somehow, I drifted off to sleep …

…◆…

Somewhere among the impaling stakes, torture racks, thumbscrews, red-hot pincers, and trays of glittering surgical instruments, in one of the rare moments when I wasn't plummeting, or suffocating beneath my own gargantuan weight, or wilting beneath the penetrating gaze of dead miners, my wife came to me.

Bea starring in my dreams was in no way unusual, especially when I was far from home. Black attire was common enough, too—but of the peek-a-boo, lacy variety. Not in black from head to toe. Not veiled. Not (when she lifted the veil) with tear-stained cheeks. Not, once she met my eyes, so *angry*.

"You went away for the damned company," she said. "For the crumbs they condescended to throw your way. So, you got them to name you a junior assistant deputy associate minion. What good will that stake do you now?"

"Do *us*," I corrected. "Worst case, do you. However this turns out."

"Did you honestly think I'd want their damned *blood money*?"

"It's not like that." My voice trailed off even as Bea's image morphed into … an iron maiden. Forever, side by side, it and I fell. As it faded away, I came down, *splat*, in a deep oubliette. The walls began to dissolve, and I realized they weren't stone and mortar, but plastic. The floor gave way beneath me—

Once more, I was falling …

…◆…

I shuddered awake, blinking at the sudden bright light, as my blanket went flying.

"Rise and shine, Princess." I couldn't *see* Darin, but I knew the voice. Grabbing my shoulder, he rolled me onto my back, then slapped a fuel cell into its socket on the exoskeleton's left thigh.

That was the moment, as he crouched over my legs, to knee him in the head. To make a run for it. For a nanosecond, I even considered it. The three, maybe four, loud voices in the next room (did these people ever *not* argue?) dissuaded me. They would have been upon me faster than I could unbind my ankles or hobble to the door.

Darin stood. The opportunity, such as it was, had passed. "Hands," he commanded. I raised them, and he wrapped my wrists with layer upon layer of fresh tape. I was glad to see a peanut-butter smear still masked the controller LEDs. "Five minutes for your morning ablutions."

I took my time. With power restored, the exo's GPS would be trying to initialize.

Eventually, I was back on the sofa, behind the restored rickety table, gnawing on a gravel-and-twigs energy bar. Maybe my morning water bottle was also drugged; I was too parched to leave it untouched and too keyed up to judge. We went through everything *again*. My arrival at the rock where his father worked. Discovery of the device. Evacuation. What the company thought, and I thought, of all this. The rehash took more than enough time for GPS to have initialized. To have localized me. More than long enough for my reserve battery to have finished recharging.

No sign yet of the cavalry.

Through the closed door, I heard a flurry of footsteps. Thumping. Rustling. "Time to wrap it up," a woman called out.

I can't say I cared for the sound of that.

"I'll be right along," Darin yelled back.

"Hurry it *up*," the same woman shouted.

"In a *minute*." In a lower voice, Darin continued, "And Dad dead."

"Two dead." I'd gotten careless, or worn down, or there *had* been drugs in the latest water, and I'd succumbed to them. Maybe all three. Whatever the reason, the words just popped out.

"*Two* people took cyanide?"

I hadn't killed anyone, but there was no disguising my guilty shiver. "If I could identify the bomber, or so I reasoned back there on the Rock, I could get him or her to disarm the device. Auditing gave me an excuse to interview everyone—not asking about the bomb, of course, but in general. What I did uncover was an inventory discrepancy, somebody having diverted several kilos of platinum. More likely *two* somebodies, one distrusting the other to keep quiet. Soon after I'd begun poking around, one of the crew vanished." Pretty little Anisha Chatterjee, turned to …

"The morning after her disappearance, I spotted an unexplained spike in organic feedstock for the printers." Also, after I'd synthed and eaten breakfast. My gorge rising at the memory, I forced myself to continue. "An increase that came to about her body mass."

Darin chewed on his lower lip. "You don't suppose Dad …?"

More thumping and stomping noises from the next room. Doors, each fainter than the last, slamming. And then, silence. If the unseen among my captors had left, what did that bode for me?

Nothing good, especially if I didn't keep my wits about me.

I said, "Les didn't seem like the homicidal type. Anyway, what with the vid of you, he had plenty else on his mind." Then more truth slipped out. "But if I hadn't gone digging, hadn't been trying to identify the bomber, I wouldn't have rattled whoever did kill Anisha. Who gives a good goddamn if she planned to rip off the company for a little?"

"Who gives a good goddamn if someone rips off the company for a *lot*?" Glancing at his wrist-clock tattoo, then at me, Darin stood. He managed to look apologetic. "The thing is …"

The thing was, he and his cronies had planned to trap and kill off a crew of five. Why would he balk at eliminating the witness already bound hand and foot? The extent just then of my offensive potential was leaping to my (bound) feet—while somehow not falling—and lunging across the table to head-butt him. After which, without doubt, I *would* crash to the floor.

What good is money to you now? Bea chided. Of course, she wasn't here. Besides, I'd never shared with her my deal with the company. If this was guilt, well, then fair enough. But maybe it was my subconscious making a suggestion …

"You know," I whispered, leaning over the table, "you can get a bit extra out of the company. And in return, I get to walk out of here. What do you say?"

"Go on."

I dropped my hands into my lap. "The company set me up with a slush fund. For expenses."

"How much are we talking about?"

What I had left didn't strike me as all that bribe-worthy. I lied.

He whistled.

"Do we have a deal?" I pressed.

He laughed unpleasantly. "So you can use a duress code, or so the funds you transfer can be traced? I don't think so."

"No. Cryptocash. Anonymous. Untraceable. Untaxable." Also, for those reasons, beloved of organized crime and money launderers. Illegal for decades in the USNA, of course, and most other Earther jurisdictions. Kidnappers and extortionists would not quibble over that detail.

Darin was silent, but clearly tempted.

I said, "The funds are in a standard wallet on my comp. I'll transfer it all. Just promise you'll let me go."

"Uh-huh. I power up your comp, and it broadcasts your location. Oh, I'd still walk away before anyone got here, but I don't need anyone to come looking for me. Pass."

He wasn't wrong. To make a transfer required being online. A cryptocash transaction was a bookkeeping entry, no more and no less, in a digital ledger distributed, and replicated, on computers across the planet. That had been the basic architecture going back to the mother of all cryptocurrencies, bitcoin. No communication with that ledger? No transfer. For this to work, my comp *had* to go onto the net.

"Hear me out," I said. "Open up my comp. Pull the GPS chip before turning it on. It can't reveal where I am when it doesn't know." I didn't volunteer the presence of an active GPS chip in my exoskeleton.

He mulled it over. Went into the next room, returning with what looked like my comp. (Also with a bulge in his pants, and I doubted he had become happy to see me.) Sat. Unfolded the comp face down on the table, and exposed the guts of it. Surfed for awhile on his own comp, I presumed to identify the GPS chip used in mine. Finally, he pried loose a chip, closed my comp, turned it over, powered it up, and slid it toward me across the wobbly table. "Do it."

I rested my hands, still taped together, on the comp. "Can't, not this way. Keystroke-dynamics recognition."

He swore, demanded I try authenticating anyway. Authentication failed twice.

I raised my hands. "Remove the tape. It's the only way this will work."

He did. I shook my hands, flapped my fingers all about. "Give me a couple of minutes. I won't type normally till the hands get normal circulation back in them and they wake up." I rubbed one wrist, then the other. I dropped the hands back into my lap, still massaging.

Just maybe, I heard a soft scuffing noise from beyond the door.

"Get to it," Darin said.

I interlaced my fingers, turned my palms toward him. I straightened my arms, flexing fingers till the knuckles cracked. "Almost there," I announced.

The gun came out of his pocket, though not yet pointed at me. "Hurry it up. I have things to do."

"Really?" Somehow, I held my voice steady. "You would shoot me?"

"I have my father's death on my conscience. What do I care about you? So quit stalling and *type*."

Indeed, I was stalling. I typed. Mistyped. "Umm, a gun in my face does nothing to steady my hands."

"I'm losing my patience," he snapped.

Ever so cautiously, the door behind Darin opened a crack. Sans squeak: as though the hinges had been oiled. Something (I could not make out quite what. A small mirror, perhaps?) peeked into the room.

I logged onto the comp and opened my wallet app. "Almost there," I declared. "No need to shoot."

I'd intended that suggestion for the cavalry, evidently preparing to breach. Darin must have grokked it, too, or heard a suspicious noise behind him, or seen an unexpected shadow or a reflection from the mirror. However he intuited the danger, whatever he thought was going on—he raised his gun.

And all hell broke loose—too many things, too quickly, to process, much less for their order to register:

—I hurled myself down and to the side, off the sofa.

—Shouted orders to "Drop the gun."

—Maureen burst into the room.

—Shots rang out.

—Sadness at everything I was leaving behind, Bea most of all. Sorrow and guilt for the children Bea and I had always wanted, but for whom I had never quite been ready.

—With eyes wide, and a bright red splotch spreading across his shirtfront, Darin crumpled to the floor.

—And excruciating pain, burning, in my shoulder …

The next several … minutes? … were a blur. Pressure—and agony!—on/in/throughout my shoulder. Ululating sirens. Urgent ministrations of EMTs. (When had they arrived? I must have blacked out.) Being sped from my cell, feet dangling off the end of an Earther-sized gurney. In the next room, where I'd seen bags and knapsacks piled, one lonely tote remained: Darin's, I assumed. The gurney jolting over an uneven surface, and me gasping with each bump. Cops swarming. An interminable ambulance ride, with Maureen at my side, squeezing my hand. The ambulance drove with its siren off; apparently, I was stable.

"It's okay, Bernie," she said. "Try to relax, Bernie."

Parsing *Bernie* took a second. That was me, as far as Maureen knew. Smart cookie that she was, she figured I was apt to be using aliases. Hence, she was reminding me of the name she had given to the authorities. Because she would've known some moniker for me, even if I were the kind of jerk who gave out fake names to women in bars. (Which the cops *would* decide, because I *had* been using a different name in Chicago. Likewise fake.) Just happening to be in the neighborhood from Washington to rescue a total stranger from his kidnapper would never pass the smell test. Especially not with a dead body involved.

I had just about finished puzzling through all that when she leaned close, brushing the hair from my eyes. To kiss my forehead, I supposed. For show. I didn't see why she would bother when the EMTs were ignoring us, one tapping notes into her comp, the other poking around inside an ambulance supplies cabinet: inattention

I chose to take as further confirmation I'd pull through. The next thing I knew, Maureen had a *finger* in my eye, removing one of my spyware lenses. The second lens quickly followed. She whispered urgently into my ear, "Where are you staying? Under what name?"

I answered, wondering why she'd asked.

An EMT glanced our way.

"A little privacy, please," Maureen snapped, and the EMT's head whipped back around to her supplies cabinet. Maureen continued, in a yet softer whisper, "Keep your voice down. I'm guessing the snatch involved company business, and you want as many details as possible kept close."

I nodded.

"Here's our story. We met in a DC bar. We planned to hook up again when I came to Chicago on my own business. I'll refuse to identify the client. That bit of noncooperation may cause me some grief till my lawyer arrives, but no big deal. Before you and I could meet up, you were grabbed, told it was for ransom from the company. But you managed to get out a quick note to me, just 'help.' How I found you is my problem to explain. Do *not* mention the tracker. And from the moment I came through the door, tell everything *just* as it happened. Okay?"

I whispered back. "They'll want to confirm my note, won't they?"

"You're married, so we were using self-destructing messaging. Um, Snapchat. No record anywhere. Okay?"

As one more tiny bit of misdirection, my wedding band had been in a suitcase since Ceres, and I had never mentioned a wife, but Maureen had read me right. Whatever the EMTs had put into my IV finally began kicking in and, my mind beginning to wander, I wondered what being able to understand people would be like.

"Okay?" she prompted.

Was it? "Maybe not. GPS on my comp is disabled."

"Then how did … no, that can wait. I grabbed two comps from that room before the cops got there. Was one of those yours?"

I managed to nod.

"If it comes up, your captors took your comp. You have no idea where it went."

"Okay." But through the ever-thickening drug stupor, yet another complication tried to assert itself. The cops would discover soon enough that I'd been asking around for Darin Hodges. I'd lost track of time, but that could not have been longer than a day or two ago. As I struggled to put my apprehension into words, the meds took over. Everything faded away …

…◆…

"Dear Bea, I am *so* sorry that … " I stopped recording. Hit erase. Such an overwrought apology was no way to begin. Reconfirmed that I was in a tight close-up, that the odd position at which the exoskeleton held my arm immobilized was outside the camera's view, that no hint of wound dressing peeked through the fabric of my shirt. Switched mindsets to banter. "Hey, kiddo. It's yours truly, from the Land of Too Damned Heavy. I miss you bunches." Hit pause while I considered *that* opening. Good enough, I decided. "You have no idea how much I miss you, beyond even how abstinence makes the heart grow fonder. But the class is good. The food here is terrific. We"—while I lied through my teeth, what did some of the Royal We matter?—"even had the opportunity to play tourist. And check out the accommodations they gave us."

I could feel my composure slipping. Panning the camera across the sitting area of the hotel suite, then showing the vertiginous view from the glassed-in balcony, got my face off the vid. "Here's the thing, hon. There was a bit of a mishap on a sightseeing excursion. Kids out joyriding, which means, I discovered, disabling automatics and controlling a ground vehicle manually. Primitive, right? Anyway, it was a minor accident, what folks here call a fender-bender." I finished panning, put on my best sincere face, and put that face back onto the camera. "The thing is, in the collision my safety harness did a number on my arm and shoulder. Belter bones, ya know? Not the sturdiest.

"So, hon, as much as I hate to say this, I'll be staying awhile after the class ends. Being on Earth is tough enough. *Launching* from here before those bones fully knit, before PT? I could ruin that arm for good, or so the docs tell me."

That prognosis, at least, was honest. The bullet that inbound had so inconsiderately missed my exoskeleton had struck metal when trying to exit my shoulder. Titanium is a lot harder than lead; ricocheting bullet fragments made mincemeat of muscle and bone.

No matter my happy pills, I wasn't.

I was feeling sorry for myself, again, knew I had to wrap things up before the self-pity slipped out. "So keep the home fires burning. I'll let you know when I know more. Love you."

Off the recording went before I could add anything mawkish. I was again feeling like the wrong type of dick. Also, trapped, and not just by stern doctors and my duty. The Chicago PD expected me to hang around while they cleared up "a few details." After the surgery on my shoulder, that had meant questioning most every day. And if the cops decided to run my DNA against the Customs database? That would add another alias to those the police knew, and bring on unwanted attention from the feds.

"Done," I called out.

With only one possible shooter, the cops had taken Maureen into custody. Once the cops released her, she had shown up at my door. By then I understood: the cover story required that we seem hooked up. And it explained her questions in the ambulance about my latest name and hotel. I used the waterbed; she took the couch.

"She's a lucky woman." Maureen emerged from the kitchenette with steaming mugs of coffee. She handed me a mug, then settled with the other into one of the overstuffed chairs overlooking the balcony. "Let's see about getting you home to her."

Home, like clarity, seemed remote. Okay, I had survived. That mattered to *me*, but it didn't rise to the level of success. My one lead, my only reason for coming to this hellhole, had been Darin Hodges—and he was dead. "That will take actually accomplishing something."

"Haven't you?" she asked. Because by then I'd shared some of what I'd been through, some of what this mess was all about. She had earned it, not to mention that I needed the help.

"Precious little."

Oh, I'd concluded Darin had been in on the conspiracy all along, never—till he forced Maureen's hand—its victim. If coercing his father to plant the bomb wasn't his idea, he had gone along, starred in the vid to make it all happen. He had, almost certainly, designed the whatever-it-was plague, and I'd messaged the company that the dust in the bottle was somehow relevant. We knew Darin had had accomplices and, courtesy of the nifty spy lenses, I even had some pictures—but not a full face shot of any of them. My snaps (once I got the opportunity to download them) of the gear pile—"go bags," Maureen called them—turned out to be just as useless: the single luggage tag in view had been edgewise to my line of sight. From an address and menu I could remember only in part, Maureen had even identified the vegan restaurant. Which she had pursued into yet another dead end. The hostess—who had not shown up at her job since my abortive dinner—worked off the books and, it turned out, under a false name. For whatever it was worth, I spotted her in Maureen's picture of a staff-picnic picture found decorating a restaurant wall.

"It was never about extorting money from the company, was it?" Maureen continued. Prompted? Goaded? Insinuated? Intuited?

Because it turned out that detectives, like accountants, tend to follow the money. Go figure. And there had been no ransom demand for me.

"I can't yet say that." From the start, I'd expected a demand for a payoff in return for some method to decontaminate the base. Within the company, everyone aware of the true situation did. But not for awhile. "Remember that, apart from low-power helmet comms, company rocks don't have radio transmitters. Darin and friends hadn't expected the release of their nasty stuff to be discovered till the *next* crew rotation. That's months from now."

Sun was streaming through the glass doors that opened onto the balcony. Maureen got up and drew the sheers. "Okay, maybe that was the original plan. But you admitted to Darin, and he must have told his accomplices, that the company already knows about the device. That his father's crew, what remains of it, evacuated with the incoming crew. The bad guys gain nothing by waiting. So why haven't they made their demands?"

I shook my head. First thing after my release from the hospital, I'd checked back in with a managing partner at the home office, the messages encrypted both coming and going. Still no demands.

Maureen frowned. "So what are Darin's friends up to? What's their endgame?"

"You're asking me?" Because I was a clear failure as a detective.

"Well, you're who's here. Also, I don't accept for a moment that the cops have lost interest in me. So, yeah, there *will* be questions."

Did she suppose I wasn't already asking myself these things? Not already driving myself crazy with them?

Being privately owned, the company was not subject to securities law. They were not required to disclose disasters like the loss of the mine. The partners could hope to sustain the secret for awhile, but their (and in the tiniest sliver, also my) stockpile of platinum had its bounds. Absent new production, there *would* be market turmoil and industrial disruptions. In habitats large and small, and on every settled off-Earth world, platinum was *the* essential catalyst for the production of nitric acid for fertilizer. When prices spiked at the prospect of shortages—and more so once actual shortages started to bite—entire ecologies would be endangered. I figured the company had maybe two years to reclaim or replace the abandoned mine before the sky fell.

So okay, metaphor isn't my thing. Perhaps not irony, either. Or detecting. Maybe I should stick with accounting.

"You all right?" Maureen asked. "You zoned out there."

"Just tired."

"I know you don't want to hear it, but we have work to do. So whenever you're ready for a few questions ..."

That morning, a Chicago PD homicide detective had grilled me—again—for three solid hours. Disclosing much of the truth would've rocket-propelled us down the Teflon-coated slope to vile stuff in bottles, company secrets, and bringing chaos to commodity markets throughout the Solar System. I didn't want to go there, and "couldn't remember" much. In any event, the only captor I could identify was Darin.

To get ahead of the inevitable discovery, I had volunteered even before my discharge from the hospital that I'd been looking for Darin, explained it with the same promised-his-father-I'd-look-him-up spiel I'd told so many others. It wasn't as if Les could contradict me. (Not that the detective hadn't tried for corroboration. The company responded that Les was away on company business and would be unreachable for months. For once their legendary security measures came in handy. With a shrug, my inquisitor had accepted that any contact with Les would be a long time coming.) How was I to know, I had whined yet again that morning, that doing a simple favor would make me a target of larcenous opportunity? Not to speak ill of the deceased, but the young man had major abandonment issues. I had to assume Darin had chosen to take out his resentments on his father's employer.

Bottom line (and I was losing confidence in my ability even with those), I was well and truly drained *before* Maureen set out to reanalyze every word I'd exchanged with Darin, every sound that might have penetrated the walls of my cell, every pixel of every image I'd blink-snapped. And beyond enervated, I was drowning in cognitive dissonance. What could I tell whom? What *had* I told whom? What, even, did I want to tell anyone? (Uh-huh, Mark Twain. I hear you. You weren't full of pain meds.)

The nth time Maureen started in again as to what I knew, inferred, or suspected about Darin's vanished accomplices, I snapped. "They're off to join the circus."

She hummed a few bars of a tune I did not recognize. "If you're done yanking my chain, we'll continue."

"I'm sure I heard one of them mention the midway. That's part of a circus, right? Where the sideshows are? Unless you think they took time out from their crime spree to discuss"—and here my memory of Earther history failed me utterly—"obscure naval battles."

"*The* midway," she repeated, frowning.

"Midway? Absolutely, I heard that word. You can't expect me to remember every 'the.' "

"Well," Maureen said, "tracking down Darin's accomplices, once we even figure out who we're looking for, just got harder. Midway is Chicago's second airport."

We continued losing ground until I demanded a halt. "That's enough for awhile. I'm ready for a big honking steak."

"Geese honk, my friend. Cattle moo. Steers moo in soprano."

"They can tap dance while whistling *Dixie*, for all I care, as long as the meat is fresh. Just in case cattle are the beast they propose to starve …"

The penny had finally dropped.

That there were no pennies.

…◆…

The looming disaster was bigger than the company, which even they conceded. Bigger than the Belt. This affected *everyone*—

With me, incongruously, at the epicenter. No wonder I felt wrung out.

"You did good," Andy Singh declared. He was Bollywood handsome, tanned, and self-assured. Short, even by Earther standards, and barrel-chested. Side by side, we were like a fireplug and a lamppost. Andy had hired Maureen—her true name, I was now to believe, being Jaime Olafson—to support me. It was only fair that he had posted bail for her.

Andy was a senior partner at the white-shoe Washington law firm representing company interests on Earth. (What did the color of his shoes matter? I didn't get that, and anyway, those were black, not white. He had only smiled at the question.) By extension, he was the company's chief lobbyist and fixer on the home world. I guess I should not have been surprised when Ceres informed me Andy was also, sub rosa, a managing partner of the company—and I should do as he said.

Being in the presence of Belter near-royalty impressed me less than the connections he had on *Earth*: the influence that had made possible the summit from which—with me spent, as limp as a dishrag—we had finally taken our leave. And also the clout to get the Chicago police to allow Maureen (I was doing my best to ignore any other name, lest it pop out at an inopportune moment) and me to fly to Washington for that meeting.

The three of us were riding in Andy's car. His as in he *owned* it, not that he had been the person to summon it. His as in no one could possibly eavesdrop through the vehicle's voice-activated navigation system. His as in I could not shake the fear that, fatigue taking over, I'd drool on the soft-as-butter, cream-colored leather of its seats.

"You did good," Andy repeated.

I grunted acknowledgment. If he knew I'd heard him, maybe he would let me rest.

What I'd done was hold myself together through a tag-team interrogation by a dozen agencies' experts at the USNA counterterrorism center. Because that's what we were embroiled in: terrorism. There had been no ransom note—for me, much less the quarantined asteroid—because we were dealing with extremists. They didn't care about money. They worshipped *Earth*.

Their issue was with humanity and, more broadly, the billions of people (and their cattle) overloading the planet. It took Spacer-developed resources to make the current population supportable. On that single point, Darin and I would have agreed. Grant that dependency, and how do you fix the "problem?" By starving the beast. By severing Earth from those off-world resources. By making humanity live within the planet's carrying capacity. I had not forgotten Darin's slip of the tongue. Spacers weren't human? Then we, doubtless, were expendable. Unlike the nonhuman, non-cattle fauna who did matter, that distant third of all other terrestrial animal biomass.

Where were Darin's cronies? Possibly in hiding, as the Chicago PD still supposed. My personal belief/conclusion/dread? They had scattered, en route to off-world destinations, there to build and deploy devices like the one they had coerced Les Hodges to beta test. The field trial on the Rock had been a success: built with readily available supplies and equipment under micro-gee conditions, then functioning just as intended. As I knew from firsthand experience …

The spooks, if not one hundred percent convinced, had at least conceded the possibility. And so, resources beyond the company, beyond metropolitan police, beyond the minimalist government favored by off-world settlements, would be assigned to tracking down the cabal—before, I sincerely hoped, Darin's plague shut down space travel. At government labs, scientists would tackle the problem of determining what the plague *was*, how to counteract it, what code updates to the Solar System's myriads of printers and synthesizers might impede its production.

All in a race against time …

Oblivious to my angst, Andy asked, "So, ready for dinner? You've earned it. I know a great Thai place."

"Another time," I said. Because while I was too tired to eat, sleep beckoned.

But more than either, I needed to come to grips with my fears. If the contagion were ever set loose on Ceres …

"Car, how long to the hotel?" I asked.

"Ten minutes," it answered.

I didn't make it that long without dozing off.

"We're here," Andy announced. Still out of it, I did not respond till he gave my shoulder (the uninjured one) a nudge. We had pulled up to the curb outside the hotel entrance. "Can I give you a hand up to your room?"

"I've got it," Maureen said. "I'll get him tucked in."

If only there were time to sleep. "Have a few minutes for a drink, Andy?"

"Sure," Andy said. His comp rang as I began climbing out of the car. "You two go ahead. I'll be right up."

I let the exo march itself across the lobby to the elevator. Ineffably weary, unspeakably worried, the exo delivered me down the long corridor to our room. As I decanted whiskey from the minibar into three glasses, Maureen scanned all about our suite with a gadget from her purse.

"We're clear," she said. "What's going on?"

"Let's wait for Andy."

When he arrived, he arched an eyebrow at Maureen.

"You, too?" she said. "I just swept for bugs. We're fine."

"Ready for some good news?" he said. "That call downstairs was from one of the folks we just met with. Their facial rec has already tracked down your vegan buddy. She'd been to Midway, all right. She flew to Mojave Spaceport, and from there to an O'Neill habitat at L5. They spotted her about to board a shuttle for the return flight."

"Is she in custody?" My spirits rose—

And were as soon dashed, as Andy shook his head. "Habitat law enforcement thought they had her cornered. She went out an air lock. No suit."

Spaced herself! Even as my gut lurched, a part of me took grim satisfaction in that gruesome death. A part of me wanted *all* those fanatical bastards pitched out of an air lock. If they had their way? If their plague ever got loose, destroying suits, eating vacuum seals? Hundreds, thousands, of innocent Spacers would be the ones dying of explosive decompression. My wife, family, and friends all too possibly among them.

"But they'll recover her comp," Maureen said. "That's all we need. Right? To get the recipe?"

"The comp wasn't on her," Andy said. "They're reconstructing her movements through the habitat, to find where she stashed it. No joy just yet."

Except they wouldn't find her comp, and not only because having the recipe in hand would be too easy. "You said she was ready to board her return flight. Then she'd already made and deployed her device. As a security measure, I'll bet she tossed the comp into a recycling bin."

Like Anisha Chatterjee, reduced to organic feedstock on a distant, contaminated rock. I shuddered.

"The locals will keep looking," Andy said. "And they'll hunt for devices like what those miners found. A bomb squad is being dispatched to L5 as we speak."

"If anyone finds a bomb," I predicted, "it'll be set with a long delay. For maximum impact, and to give minimum warning, they'll aim to strike everywhere at once."

"Scary," Andy said, "but logical. And a silver lining, too, if correct. It'd mean we have time. Anyone in Darin's cabal going out to the Belt will be awhile yet in transit. Before they get there, maybe we'll have another face or three to search for. The intel types are tracking down his known associates, and the neighborhood tree huggers, and recent university dropouts, to see if any among them has also dropped off the grid."

Maureen came over to sit beside me on the sofa. "That was *Andy's* news. There was something *you* wanted to bring up."

"I know I can trust you both." Her, for saving my life. Him for introducing me to the highest levels of counterterrorism. To *not* rescue me, or to *not* make those introductions, would have been simple enough.

"But you trust no one else," Andy completed. "Yes, this has been hard. Yes, we're not out of the woods. But *you* can let down a bit. I'll grant you the L5 action wasn't a complete success, but it's progress. The rest of the terrorists are doubtless flying a lot farther. The spooks have time to find any device at L5, to identify Darin's accomplices, to sort out this whole mess."

I downed my shot, and raised the empty glass for a refill. Andy delivered it, and I downed that, too. "And who will sort out matters inside the company?"

"What do you mean?" Maureen asked.

Andy's eyes just narrowed.

I said, "Darin knew that his father's crew was in detention, incommunicado. And he wasn't surprised when I said that the Rock had been evacuated."

Andy stiffened. "No. You can't believe that."

"I can," I said. "I do. There *is* a leak. Someone inside the company is involved in this mess. Somebody well-placed, high up, because no one else would have known those things."

"On Ceres?" Maureen asked.

I shook my head. "Here on Earth, I have to believe. No need to coerce Les Hodges to do their field trial if they had had a collaborator on Ceres. Or anywhere else in space."

"Then what …?" Andy trailed off, his face ashen.

"What do we do?" I said. "We three get back to work. We have our own private investigation to run. And we dare not fail."

Because if we did, the toll would be a lot higher than two dead.

THE COMPANY MOLE

Somewhere inside the company, there was a mole.

Or was it a groundhog? Maybe a prairie dog. I'm a rock man, born and bred. Good luck to any rodent trying to tunnel its way through an asteroid.

But I digress. The mole *I* needed to ferret out (see what I did there?) was human—if only a sorry example of the species.

I admit it: my mind was wandering. My mind always wandered during a workout. Exercise sucked under the best of circumstances. But on Earth? The gravitational hellhole of the inhabited Solar System? *Sucked* did not begin to describe the experience. But you know what sucked worse? Having been held captive—pinned by my own weight—simply by having the fuel cell plucked from my exoskeleton.

But that's *not* why, huffing and puffing, I put in two hours in the company gym every workday. By cranking down the exo's muscle amplification, *any* movement I attempted, *anywhere*, could be exercise. So why come to the gym at all? Because it was a place to interact casually with local company employees. And because my erstwhile interrogator had let slip facts only someone well-placed in the company should have known.

It was that knowledgeable *someone* I needed to identify. Although I'd succeeded in sneaking a Mayday message past my captors and getting myself rescued—but lest I seem smug, also gotten myself shot—myriads of people, most unaware, remained in mortal danger. Not least among them, within the distant rock I called home, my wife.

With amplification on my exo arms dialed down, grunting, I once more, ever so sloooowly, bench-pressed a bare barbell: ten pathetic kilos. Merely extending my arms with assist tweaked a tad further would have afforded the same exercise—without risk of dropping ten kilos on my face! Except that lying here, empty hands raised in the air like some flailing beetle trapped on its back, would have rendered me even more pitiable …

But one way or another, when next I got into trouble, I meant to be less helpless than the last time. Well, truly, as long as I was wishing, I wished not to have trouble, period. Though judging by my recent history, it'd be foolish to expect that.

Two women in clean, dry shorts, Tees, and matching rainbow hair bands, strolled from the locker room into the gym. I recognized both from their personnel files, while, so far, having met neither. Then again, it was only my third day on the (ersatz) job.

"Hey," I said. "How are things?"

The blonde waggled a hand: so-so. The brunette, arguably, gave a hint of a shrug.

"Yeah, I've had days like that," I persisted.

Because I had a job to do. Because I, too, was a mole …

"Go home," Andy Singh had responded to my plan. "The pros have this now."

I couldn't have gone home just then had I wanted to. Not before nanites finished knitting bone in my shattered shoulder. Not until I endured a shitload more PT. Of course, all that be damned, I wanted more than anything to *be* home. To reunite with my wife. See my friends, my family. To *not* jolt awake, night after night, with my heart pounding, as my mind's eye pictured them gasping for breath, bloating in hard vacuum, dying or dead.

All the reasons my wants were immaterial.

"Go home," Andy repeated. He must have misinterpreted my tongue-tied speechlessness as wavering. "Forget this crazy notion of playing spy. Get the hell off Earth the moment you're healed enough to cope with the liftoff. And until then, lie low. Be safe. Go play tourist somewhere at least several thousand klicks away. On the company dime. You've earned it."

In other words, as far from Washington, capital of the USNA—and home to the company's terrestrial-district headquarters—as my recuperation allowed.

As much as I needed to pace, to burn off adrenaline, I managed to remain seated, legs crossed, the suspended foot jiggling. Parked in facing wingchairs in Andy's eerily spacious, fifty-shades-of-beige, looking-unlived-in, living room, I already towered over him.

I said, "The pros don't have it."

The pros: actual spies and intel analysts. Because among Andy's connections were executives atop the USNA counterterrorism center. On Andy's say-so, the CTC spooks had heard me out. Even taken my words to heart. And so what? The pros had since tracked down exactly one terrorist—who had avoided capture by spacing herself. Leaving unknown, still, whether or where she had deployed into the L5 habitat a device like what I'd seen on the Rock.

And since the "pros" had *not* taken her alive? Every cop, firefighter, and sanitation worker at L5 continued (surreptitiously, lest citizens by the thousands panic) to tear apart that habitat hunting for the device, or devices, we all dreaded she had printed and hidden before being recognized. Whoever *she* might be: those same pros had yet to get past Vegan Woman's topnotch alias.

It sure as hell looked to me as though some among the Bad Guys were pros, too.

"The pros don't have it," I repeated.

Andy shook his head. "You can't know that."

"Maybe not. I do know that their lone, partial success came from a lead *I* provided."

"Gotten by way of nearly getting yourself killed," Andy snapped. "Suppose you're right. Suppose your abductors *do* have a source within the company. If you go inside"—at last addressing what I had proposed: a posting at Earth district headquarters—"you have to expect that person to know who *you* are."

"*Suppose?* Who *but* a mole would've known that the men and women evacced from the Rock had been quarantined in the Belt? The company moved them directly into isolation, without any public announcement. Not even word to family members." The latter had been advised—*some* update being necessary to explain their loved ones' failure to return as scheduled—about them signing onto an extended shift for bonus pay. The bonus aspect was even truthful (any thieves and murderers later identified presumably excluded).

"Not addressing that the mole will know who you are. As will any of your abductors who stayed behind. You have to assume they remain in contact with the mole."

I took the easy objection first. "You didn't see these people." Nor had I, excepting two. The one was shot dead in the course of my rescue; the other had chosen breathing vacuum over capture. "You didn't hear them." Which I *had*, from next door to the storeroom in which they had held me prisoner. Arguing. Shouting. Ranting at 3V news. "They're fanatics. They're fighting a plague, with people being the pandemic. You couldn't have paid them to stay behind when there was mayhem to be wrought."

"Doesn't mean some weren't ordered to stay behind."

Hmm. He had me there. That said, it was my own unartful sleuthing that had gotten me into trouble: a clarification which would neither advance my argument nor was anything I cared to dwell upon. "They didn't know when they grabbed me who I was other than"—I indicated my rather lanky frame—"an inquisitive Belter. My interrogator would have been given every scrap of information they had on me. Yeah, in the course of my interrogation, I had to concede I was with the company. But that's it. I don't see that it matters if any of them stayed on, or returned to, Earth, as long as *they* aren't inside the company offices."

Andy leaned forward and slugged my jiggling foot. "*Quit* that, or I'll snap it off. Okay, I'll grant you this much. You might approach the situation with a unique perspective. You might discover something the pros won't, or at least uncover it earlier. Emphasis, both times, on *might*. It doesn't change the problem you continue to ignore, that you can't go near a company office using any of your bogus Belter IDs. I'm no computer genius, and I identified the real you in the company directory using nothing but a bad candid picture."

"Not a problem. I need to go into the office as myself."

And that would be my first use since landing of authentic ID. If I hoped to learn anything from inside the company, I'd need serious network access. As a longtime forensic accountant, I'd often held sysadmin privileges. Except as a sysadmin, I had little hope of spotting the digital fingerprints left by miners trying to obscure their precious-metal thefts. Extending these privileges to encompass a new assignment, even at a different sort of company facility, should be pretty much automagical.

As anyone but myself, though? Forget it. Beyond, through Andy's behind-the-scenes intervention, having the local managing partner as my executive sponsor, my alter ego would have to show a record of several exemplary years with the company *and* pass review by three randomly chosen, mutually suspicious, people from Security. The company hadn't cornered the Solar System market in a half dozen precious metals through carelessness.

But the atom-thin silver lining? That same institutional paranoia probably meant the mole *wouldn't* have high-level access. I could reasonably hope to have better success data-mining my way to that bastard than he or she might have at finding anything suspicious about me.

"You'd still be taking an insane chance."

"Yes, *I* would." I took a deep breath. "Are you going to help?"

Andy fell silent for the longest time. "I'd have conditions."

And with that, we segued from *no* to *negotiation* …

…◆…

I stood, my gaze sweeping across the crowded lunchroom, and not only because "You will *not* wander away from the office building by yourself," had been first among Andy's conditions. Like the in-house gym, the next-door coffee shop, and the round-the-corner tavern, the company cafeteria was a place to casually interact with my fellow workers. At this, the peak of the lunch rush, there was not an empty table to be had. Here and there among the diners, like so many mushrooms in a lawn after a rainstorm, the occasional head stuck far above the rest. Loonies and Martians, not one of them approaching Belter height.

Reflexively I wondered, who here is the mole?

Broadcasting my approach through the occasional stomp/clank, having just that morning tweaked my exolegs to a new, reduced level of assistance, I made my way from the condiment station to a table with an unoccupied seat. "May I join you?"

That drew a ragged and unenthusiastic chorus of "Sure" and "Uh-huh."

"Thanks." As I set down my tray, conversations resumed. I slid back a chair and, with a faint electric-motor hum, sat. Two bites into a cheeseburger, I added, again to no one in particular, "This hits the spot."

"Cafeteria swill?" said the woman to my left. (Sally Wu, an intern in Finance. I recognized her from her personnel file. I recognized most everyone around the table from such study. No matter the name, Wu looked Swedish.) With an eye roll, she added, "Surely you jest."

Not letting up my grip on the burger, I introduced myself.

"Hi," she responded. "You're kidding, right? This is fuel, not food."

I gave the burger a waggle. "This is actual beef, once upon a time on the hoof. Where I come from, that's an imported delicacy."

"Actual Grade Z beef," chimed in the woman seated to my right. Anna Burnham. Public Relations (or, as everyone in-house knew it, the Ministry of Propaganda). She was willowy, as Earthers go, with long, flowing, dark hair. Enough hair for a small village. Anna gestured dismissively with her fork at some kind of green salad. "This place has nothing going for it but convenience."

"And then there's the"—air quotes—"beef stew," contributed the guy seated across from me. Henri Broussard seemed as Gallic as the name sounded, if you could trust a Belter's sense of such things. "Off-brand dog food."

"So, seriously," Anna said to me. "Was that a draw for you? Real food?"

"Call it a perk." Setting my burger on its plate, I blotted meat juice off an exohand with a paper napkin. I made a show of working a napkin corner beneath metal rods to scrub at the fingers beneath. "Make that the only perk."

And heads all around the table swiveled toward me. As desired.

From three seats down, a dark-skinned woman with startling blue eyes leaned forward to make eye contact. Ayesha Greene. An up-and-comer in Marketing. "Isn't this a plum assignment?"

"Plum?"

Ayesha laughed. "It means good, if for no obvious reason."

"Got it," I said. "From accountant out among the rocks—I assume the jungle vine has shared that much about me—to a stint in Finance, in one of the company's biggest markets, exposed to some of the super-secret futures-trading algorithms. Got to be a *big* career move for me." I retrieved my burger. "Yep. Sounds great."

"Grapevine, not jungle vine," Ayesha said. "But yes, that's what I meant."

"And then there's actual *steak*," I said.

"Which you should *never* get here," someone, though I couldn't see who, offered from far down the table.

We talked food until people began drifting away, whether to their offices or early-afternoon meetings. And I wondered: had anyone taken the bait?

…◆…

What did I know about the mole? That he or she had info only a senior or managing partner should have known. But also that logically he or she *wasn't* such a person, given things my abductors hadn't known.

My abductors …

Yes, they remained a nameless bunch. But there was an exception, and he had done his best, there at the end, to kill me. My only regret when Darin Hodges died was for losing the opportunity to turn the tables and question *him*. But I had known and liked his father. I had watched Les Hodges die, unnecessarily, back there on the Rock.

Focus! I commanded myself, tamping down the misplaced pangs of guilt.

He? She? Whatever the personal pronoun, I was hunting for someone's unauthorized access to secure communications from the Belt, or to locally archived copies of the same. If I were lucky, digital traces of such penetration could be gleaned from a deep dive into old log files. Not easily, or Security would have detected the breach when, or soon after, it had occurred. Intrusion-detection apps were damned good at spotting any known hack, and variations thereof.

I leaned back in my (too short) office chair, eyes closed, pondering the supposed fine line between genius and insanity. Likewise, the open question as to which side of the line I occupied. I knew Andy had no doubt.

Was my snooping as essential as I believed? Or was I too proud to admit that, as a secret agent, I made a halfway-decent accountant? Either way, as of this, my fourth grueling day at the Earth district headquarters, the sum of my accomplishments was that no one from local Security had hassled me. Yet. Maybe I'd kept my otherwise fruitless data mining below the radar. More likely, no one believed my supposed assignment anyway, and they expected me to be nosing around. Spying on them.

Which, of course, I was.

As the grilled onions from lunch began repeating on me (the burger *hadn't* been very good—I'd just been provoking my way into a conversation), I took a mental step back. The mole had sysadmin privileges, or not. If yes, by rights my abductors would have known who I was, plus everything the Belt partners had shared with their Earther counterparts. Nothing in my interrogation pointed that way. If the mole *didn't* have such privileges, that begged the question why neither I, nor the local sysadmins, nor the in-house intrusion-detection software had noticed anything untoward.

The bigger question remained: how *had* my adversary learned about the quarantining of miners evacced from the Rock?

Maybe I wasn't as good as I believed. As for the local sysadmins, well, those who I'd met seemed altogether too trusting of the automated defenses. Which left, I decided, a weakness in the intrusion-detection software. It might never have been up to the task, or *it* had been compromised. And so, two new items went onto an ever-growing mental to-do list. Find a new, independent means of detecting any past intrusion. Find a way to get that unauthorized code, *un*detected, onto the in-house network.

Oh, and if I were *un*lucky? Then the mole was someone high enough in the company to have legitimate access to the most sensitive info. Or such a someone that well-placed, who should have known better, had let slip Really Serious Matters to another someone who might not even be with the company. Data mining, no matter how skilled, could not reveal to me either such leak source.

A *rat-a-tat* knock interrupted my brooding and rattled my office door. (The kind of poking around in the archives I was doing, one did with the door closed.) I blanked the desktop display. "Come in."

The door swung partway open. Anna of the Bountiful Hair stuck her head inside. "Got a minute, sport?"

"Sure. What's up?" Not me. I remained in my chair, behind the desk.

She came all the way inside, closed the door, and cleared her throat. "I wanted to apologize. We didn't need to give you a hard time. You liked your lunch? That's fine."

"However inexplicable my taste." I smiled. "No apology necessary for a bit of kidding around, but I appreciate it."

"But this *is* a plum assignment for you. Right?"

"You'd think."

She plopped down on a guest chair. "You were, shall we say, also less than enthused when Ayesha asked that question at lunch."

I shrugged.

"And I don't think I've seen you hanging around much with the folks in Finance and Accounting."

Why *would* my ostensible colleagues hang with me? The head of the office had been told only that I'd be looking for unauthorized uses of the company's commodities-trading plans. To give me access to everything from personnel files to security logs to real-time market data—in short, sysadmin privileges. To offer every possible assistance, but otherwise leave me alone.

Does anyone like being snooped upon?

"Uh-huh," was all I responded.

Anna tipped her head inquiringly.

"What is it you want?" I asked wearily.

"It's called being friendly! Is that so bad?" I didn't answer, and she sighed. "What's your problem, anyway?"

"Do you see any other Belters in this office? No. And do you know why? Because no Belter wants to be on this benighted planet. Yeah, I have this exoskeleton to move me around. Yeah, I've been pumped full of synthetic corpuscles so my heart doesn't burst from the strain. I'm still thirty or so times my Ceres weight. Every damned minute of every damn day. And then there's the forced separation from everyone I know. So, yeah, a non-synthed lunch, even in the cafeteria, *is* the highlight of my workday."

She flinched. "You make coming to Earth sound like a punishment."

"Let's just say, this assignment wasn't my first, second, or third choice."

"Then why ...?"

I had rehearsed in front of a mirror for just such a question, but was I any better an actor than a spy? "Why did I take the gig? For a career's worth of profit-sharing units in which I'm"—hand raised; thumb and index finger maybe a centimeter apart—"*this* close to vesting."

"Sounds like you ticked someone off. Big time." She leaned forward confidentially, licked her lips. "Who?"

"A couple field-audit tours ago, I broke up a smuggling scam. Miners, of course, but someone high up the food chain had to have been involved for this particular scam to function. Someone the miners wouldn't give up, not even to save their jobs. Were they paid off? Threatened? I don't know that, either."

"Someone high in the food chain. A partner?"

"I don't know for sure."

"Someone in authority wants you out of the way. You must have an idea who that is."

"You think? But I sincerely doubt that 'out of the way' covers it. The goal is to make me quit. Outside the company, I'd have no credibility." And under my breath, *just* loud enough (I hoped) to be heard, I added, "Not a chance, you rich schmuck."

Anna chewed on that for awhile. "How long till you vest in profit sharing?"

"Seventeen months, three days. But who's counting?"

"Well ... I can't do anything about that. But if you need a sympathetic ear sometime?"

"Thanks. But given that not doing a sterling job here is *another* way to get separated before I vest …"

Anna stood, taking the hint. "I'll leave you to get back to it, then."

As the door closed behind her, I had to wonder how soon my indiscretions would spread throughout the building. And whether the mole might see advantage in enlisting a disgruntled Belter employee …

…◆…

I'd slept like crap. Again. My guess was, I didn't look even that good.

There had been the customary nightmares to punctuate my insomnia. And the unending discomfort. (Read: sensation of being pressed to death. *Pressing* was an unfortunate bit of Earther historical trivia I had recently encountered: the "judicial" practice, a few hundred years back, of piling boulders on the accused until they submitted a plea. Or died. Either outcome was acceptable. In North America, too: check out the Salem witch trials.) Beyond those joys, I'd increasingly suffered from the more metaphorical weight of my ongoing failure to find any lead to the mole.

All while the metaphorical clock of doom kept ticking.

"That's it," Jaime declared over her mug of coffee, as I stood in our apartment's sunlit kitchenette, working up the energy to shake the usual dry cereal into a bowl. Also, hoping today was the day she would exhaust her store of Cerian-eating-cereal quips. "You look pathetic. We're going out for a proper breakfast."

My apartment-mate/bodyguard was another of Andy's conditions. Not that keeping Jaime Olafson around was a bad idea. Never mind her longstanding association with Andy's law firm. She was—more than amply demonstrated by my having survived abduction—a damned good PI and a crack shot. If Jaime had a fault, it was her insufferable good spirits. No, make that her second fault. She was a morning person.

And that's how, and at the butt crack of dawn, I found myself being urged down a crowded Washington, DC, street. It was not even eight o'clock, but already the heat and humidity were brutal. *Civilized* worlds regulated such things.

If I needed to be out and about, alongside Jaime was how to do it. Belter beanstalks galumphing about in exoskeletons were scarce enough anywhere on this cruel world that I often drew stares. Together, we still did—but mainly *Jaime* did. By Earther standards (and it became hard to argue, the longer I was stuck here), she was a knockout. A blonde bombshell. An Amazon. And by my side, petite in the bargain.

A wearying two city blocks from our apartment, from somewhere ahead of us, a tantalizing scent asserted itself. Grease, but in a good way. "What's that I'm smelling?" I asked.

"That, my friend, is *breakfast*."

"Whatever that is," I countered, "order me a plateful. Or a platter."

The storefront deli, narrow but deep, was as crowded as the aroma foretold. Happily, the balding guy at the door gave a big grin at spotting Jaime and sped us to the first available booth. Considering only those tables not masked by privacy screens, there must have been fifty people dining. The host, or greeter, or whoever he was, left us with two mugs and a big carafe of coffee. Very *good* coffee.

After my second mug, and the delivery of the morning special for each of us, Jaime tapped ON the booth's privacy mode. Behind its shimmering barrier, the clamor of happy diners ebbed into an inarticulate murmur. She said, "Something more than usual is bothering you."

Tucking into pastrami and eggs, hash browns, and toasted bagel, I dissembled. "I don't know what you mean."

"Seriously?"

I gestured with knife and fork. "Nothing this won't fix."

"There's no such thing as a free breakfast. Go."

"Maybe it's nothing." Not that I believed that. "On the off chance I'm mistaken, catch me up." Because when Jaime wasn't escorting me to and from work, or busy in between supporting her other clients (mainly something, I gathered, involving suspected industrial espionage at a nanoelectronics company), she liaised on my behalf with Andy and the counterterrorism types. She was, after all, much more mobile than I. She had gone out the evening before, after figuratively tucking me in for the night. "Any progress?"

"Let's call it activity. Nothing I'd call progress. No more members identified of the terrorist cell. On the plus side, no further incidents, either. So, talk. What's maybe nothing?"

I topped off Jaime's mug, then mine, draining the carafe, then poked the button that would summon our server. A privacy screen *means* privacy. "That lack of incidents is what's scary. It makes sense they plan to unleash the bioagent at many places at once." As I had opined more than once. "The longer we go without attack, the more widespread I expect the attack to be. It would make for maximum panic. It would tax, or overtax, the resources necessary for rescue and remediation."

Ignoring the details of *remediate how? Using what?* The bioagent was so pernicious the company had only recently succeeded in recovering samples. Before heading to Earth I'd heard something about custom-designing robots, without any plastic in their construction, to go underground on the Rock. A robotic lab, likewise custom-built, for remote analysis. A squad of brave scientists onsite, lest comms across interworld distances give away the asteroid's orbital coordinates. In this instance, the radio blackout reflected more than the company's standard paranoia. Sure, they aspired someday to reclaim that platinum lode. The bigger risk—even the managing partners could agree—would be luring unsuspecting treasure hunters to the scene, to carry away with them the as-yet unstoppable contagion.

It continued to drive the experts nuts how the bioagent had been synthed on the Rock in the first place. Printers contained rubber gaskets, but no printer on the Rock had had its gaskets eaten. A single bacterium left behind after synthesis would presumably have been fruitful, and multiplied, and, in time, devoured those gaskets. The riddle drove me mad, too, but it had been awhile since anyone had given a fig about my madness.

A dainty hand with eye-popping red nail polish, waggling, penetrated the shimmer that enclosed our booth. I dropped the screen. Presciently, in her other hand, our server grasped a steaming carafe. We sat in silence while she made the exchange.

"Done stalling?" Jaime asked once the screen was back up.

The crinkle/rustle of my booth bench evoked images of plastic disintegrating beneath me. That, I would survive. Not someone in a disintegrating vacuum suit. "Do you grant I'm correct about multiple attacks? About those being synchronized across a bunch of Spacer locations? That waiting out the travel time to remote settlements is why, so far, nothing's been unleashed aboard the L5 habitat?"

In captivity, through a briefly open door, I'd glimpsed a mound of travel bags. I'd even, using my snazzy private-dick contact lenses, taken pictures—in what at the time had seemed like cockeyed optimism that anyone would ever see them. When Jaime rescued me, only my would-be killer and his lone bag remained. Not that the dozen or so inferred terrorists was even the worst case. For all we knew, other groups were involved, just not based out of the hole-in-the-wall dump where I had been imprisoned and interrogated.

As for those luggage pictures I'd taken? Not a single shot showed a readable ID tag. Because to know any of the aliases under which those bastards traveled would have made things too easy.

Jaime nibbled on some of her rye toast. "I'll grant your scenario is plausible."

"The longer things go before that synchronized assault, the farther some terrorists must be traveling. Do the math, Jaime. I have. Almost certainly the attacks, when they come, will encompass settlements deep within the Belt." Including Ceres, and most everyone dear to me. "Just a little longer without that attack, and we can anticipate the danger even reaching outposts on one or more of the Jovian moons."

Jupiter was as distant as settlements got. If a terrorist had the Jupiter system as her first stop, and if she flew aboard a fast passenger ship, less than six weeks remained to disrupt the attacks. Amazingly, the forecast could have been worse. Jupiter happened to be on the far side of the Sun. Had that planet been elsewhere along its orbit, I'd have had less time.

Jaime shoved back her plate. Tragically, a strip of crisped pastrami and half a rye-toast slice remained untouched. "On the other hand, the longer we go unscathed, the more likely we are to determine who's involved, traveling aboard which ships. We can have local law enforcement alerted to greet them when they arrive."

And that would *not* be a friendly greeting.

I said, "And if the spooks continue to fail to identify the bad guys?"

"There is that." She glanced at her wrist-clock tattoo. "I should be getting you to your office. Do you want a sandwich to go? Or a hunk of carrot cake?"

Breakfast had transmuted in my gut to bubbling, molten lead. I stood. "Pass."

At the front of the deli, as Jaime settled our tab with a wave of a pocket comp, her device emitted an unfamiliar trill. She backed against a wall to where no one in the place, or from the sidewalk through the big plate-glass window, could see what had to be an unexpected message. Nor could I read the text—but I could see her face.

I guessed, "We're not going to my office, are we?"

Her lips pressed thin, Jaime shook her head.

…◆…

The cliché Earther description of a launch to orbit involves an unseen elephant sitting on the person's chest. Granted, elephants are massive. They're not massive *enough*. My invisible behemoth had to be, at the least, a brontosaur. And while he was at it, that dino chose to stand on my still tender shoulder.

But when the acceleration ceased? Nirvana!

Jaime and I had the passenger cabin to ourselves. I undid my seat harness, shed my exoskeleton, and soared—free as a bird in zero gee.

She unbuckled, too. *Big* mistake. Dirtside, she was the very personification of grace. In freefall, within seconds, she was thrashing. Her skin had gone pale, her breathing shallow and rapid. Not a first-timer, she had assured me en route to the spaceport. Maybe so, but she had conveniently neglected to mention her last off-world excursion having been awhile. As I blissfully floated about the shuttle's passenger cabin, I nudged her back toward her seat. "Buckle up for awhile. Your space legs will come back."

Smiling wanly, she groped for the seat; her flailing sent my exoskeleton caroming off a cabin wall. Amid the clanks and clatters came a brittle *crackle* that boded ill for the forearm touch screen.

Sigh. After my abductors had dicked with it, I'd already had to replace the control-panel innards.

Soon after, secured into her acceleration couch, Jaime managed a, "Sorry."

At least I thought that's what she said. Through the barf bag, the word was muffled. "My fault. I should have secured the exo."

A few minutes later, through clenched teeth, Jaime muttered, "It's as if he *wants* me to puke. Again."

"What'd I do?"

"Somersaults. Back flips. Loop-de-loops."

There wasn't space enough in the cabin to do any of those, but I *was* drifting about, and there might have been the occasional unhurried barrel roll. I nudged myself to my acceleration couch and buckled in. "I'll be good."

"Bioagent," she said. "Are you sure?"

"What?"

"Earlier, you called the stuff a bioagent. At breakfast in the deli." A liquidy gulp suggested food had been an unfortunate association. "I could use a distraction about now."

Of course, we'd read the same report. The stuff recovered from the Rock had been tentatively identified as a bacterium. Unlike any bacterium on record, but nonetheless. The specifics eluded me, but whatever biosensors or antibiotics or bacteriophages took notice of? In this bacterium, none of those typical cell-membrane proteins were present. And even that was not the strangest thing. This bacterium contained an organelle-like microcompartment serving no discernable purpose, the likes of which no biologist on the company payroll had ever seen.

I said, "The stuff eats organic polymers. It reproduces. What else could it be?"

"Computronium."

That meant nothing to me, and I said so.

"Geek-speak for a kind of nanobot. Tiny self-replicating computers that communicate with one another."

Which seemed as improbable a topic for Jaime as … Simile failed me. And anyway, since when did she speak geek? "Those exist?"

"They're maybe possible. Just something I've heard."

From another client, then. My guess was the nanoelectronics firm. I could imagine a million applications for such tech, from pinpoint crop monitoring to environmental management. Presuming, of course, that the self-replication stopped after awhile. "Why use such advanced tech for attacking Spacer colonies?"

"Because the nanites would be programmable. Seems handy in coordinating an attack."

If such tech were possible, she had a point. Nanoscale *anything* could be smuggled pretty much anywhere, and as much as needed for an attack then replicated onsite. If the hypothetical self-replicating nanites incorporated long-chain polymers into their progeny, onsite replication would *be* the attack.

Then again, back on the Rock, the device initiating the attack had been large enough almost to block an air duct.

I said, "Then why bother with a dispersal device, and a bomb to protect it? Why not just sprinkle around some of the nanos, preprogrammed to activate later?"

Jaime grimaced. From space adaptation syndrome, or at my brilliant rebuttal? "Fine. A crazy-smart bacterium it is. Happy?"

"Just try to relax," I told her.

Well before I tired of blessed weightlessness, our ship was on final approach. It had been all of two hours since the explosion. (Some three-letter agency, and apparently I had no need to know which, maintained a courier ship on a pad just outside DC, prepped for immediate launch. Also—unsurprisingly, but to my disappointment—a rotation of on-call agency pilots to fly it.) Out our starboard-side view ports, a *2001*-style, ring-and-spokes orbital facility glittered in unfiltered sunlight. Alas, so did a sparkly debris field. I guestimated we were a half-klick from the ring. A spacecraft seeming not much larger than ours (by the girders-and-globes, unstreamlined look of it, an Earth/Moon transfer vehicle) held station a bit farther away.

As Earth Gateway Three lazily spun, simulating gravity, an odd surface expanse rotated into, and out of, view. Odd, how? I wondered, and settled upon *distorted*. That region of EG3 bulged, showing ripples here and there, reflecting the sunlight every which way. Any breach was too small to spot from a distance; indeed, the initial report was that the affected compartment had sustained pressure. Wisely or not, the reflexive decision after the explosion had been to isolate and vent about a quarter of the ring to each side of the compromised compartment. Hence, the debris field.

"This is as close as we get," our bus driver announced over the intercom. Trey Jackson spoke in a casual Southern drawl, with a Caribbean undertone. (Jaime, in any event, had distinguished these supposed regional niceties. I struggled to extract any meaning through the curious inflection.) "Once you're suited up, I'll match velocities."

Inbound from Ceres, for subsequent transfer to a landing shuttle, my ship had docked at the central hub of this very orbital way station. That was the normal manner of things: spin down the hub for ease—and safety—of approach; dock with the temporarily stationary hub; transfer passengers in a shirtsleeves environment, direct from one air lock into another; then spin up the hub, after the spacecraft departed, to restore access to the ever-rotating ring. Only there was nothing normal about *this* rendezvous. Something had gone *boom* aboard EG3, distributing, we had to assume, a batch of the terrorist crud. And me the local expert.

Almost, that was funny. This was an isolated event, and I'd brashly predicted a Solar System-wide, coordinated apocalypse.

"Cheer up," I told Jaime. "You'll feel better with even a smidge of gravity." Which was all the modest rotation of EG3 would provide, any faster spin being nausea-inducing for many. And *I* would be right at home in that weak faux gravity. "But first, you have to suit up."

With assistance, she made it into her vacuum gear, and then I wriggled into my own. For a short-range jaunt like this, ordinarily, a single-layer, flexible, counterpressure suit would suffice. Ordinarily. *We* had brought hard-shell suits, all but entirely metal, the type of vacuum gear orbital construction workers wore to defend against punctures and tears. Also, helmets made of tempered glass, not the customary polycarbonate. Unavoidably, the bearing assemblies in the hard-shell suit joints contained slick plastic. Still, suppose the terrorists' bioagent had once again been unleashed. For any of that vile crud to insinuate its way into one of those suit junctions during our forthcoming quick inspection, our luck would have to terrible.

In other words, my typical luck.

With helmets seated and locked, we did a comm check. Did suit-safety checks. Reviewed the tools and supplies on the clips, and inside the pockets, of our utility belts. Tethered ourselves together. Proceeded into the ship's air lock and opened the outer hatch. Beneath us, EG3 spun. Much farther below, Earth did.

I grasped a gas gun with one gloved hand and Jaime's left arm with my other. From the clench of her jaw, I grokked her off-Earth experience had never extended to a free-flying transfer, but she bore her anxiety stoically. Nor was I judging. Not the woman who—alone, with guns blazing—had saved my life.

"Okay," I radioed our bus driver. "We're ready when you are."

"Matching velocities now."

Our ship shrieked (figuratively) into a powered curve centered on the station. As EG3's apparent spin began to slow, I again glanced sideways. Jaime's face had attained a whole new level of pasty. "I've got this. Trust me."

And when our arcing course matched the station's rotation, I leapt.

…◆…

Sans drama, I landed us on EG3. I engaged boot magnets (on the ring's outermost surface, the station's spin wanted to fling us off), marched us around the station's exterior to the designated quadrant and into an air lock. With feet planted on the outside wall, weight—or at least, a recent facsimile thereof—returned, even at a comfortable level. And Jaime, taking a deep breath, pulled herself together.

Air-lock sensors reported vacuum within the station, and the tanned woman who met us when the inner hatch cycled open wore a plastic fishbowl helmet and a multilayered soft suit. (Multiple layers provided more protection than a counterpressure suit, but the bioagent I'd seen back on the Rock would, in time, eat through every layer. Doubtless, this had been the best protection she had had.) The name patch on her suit read KOWALSKI. She looked grim. Exhausted. Haunted. Over a comm channel encrypted with spook software, I heard, "Welcome to Ground Zero."

The Earth-orbiting gateways were obvious targets for the terrorists. Agents from various national and international intel agencies had been assigned to all of them, one each to coordinate with onboard Security personnel. Danielle Kowalski, from the North American FBI, had drawn EG3. Lucky her.

After quick introductions, I asked, "How bad is it?"

Maybe, she shrugged. In that thick, multilayered suit, it was hard to tell. "Could have been worse, but bad enough. Four dead. One crewman killed instantly by shrapnel. Three passengers too slow or panicked to find and climb inside PREs." Personal rescue enclosures. Baggies with short-term oh-two tanks. "Plenty of scrapes and bruises. No casualties since." Somehow, she managed the impossible, her expression getting bleaker. "Maybe I shouldn't have ordered that part of the station blown."

Blown: opened to vacuum.

I pointed out, "We're in vacuum here, too." Halfway around the station from the explosion.

This time, Kowalski's shrug was as undeniable as her weary expression. "Yeah, now. While the compromised sector vented, I maintained atmosphere everywhere else. That gave most people extra time to get into PREs, and I figured pressure in the remaining sectors might keep anything nasty nearer the blast zone."

"And then you vented the whole station, slowing the onboard spread if anything had gotten into this part." I'd done a slow pivot as we spoke. Obvious rubber and plastic items, including the outermost layer of Kowalski's suit, appeared copasetic. Probably, we were safe. "You're only human for dwelling on the three people who didn't make it into PREs. In the big picture, if this incident is what I suspect, you saved lives today."

But in the still bigger picture? By venting the crap into a much-used region of near-Earth space, to waft to other stations on wings of sunlight, maybe Kowalski had put many more lives at risk. Still assuming this *was* an attack.

"How many people are still aboard?" Jaime asked. Her face had recovered some of its normal color.

Kowalski said, "Besides us? No one. The four station rent-a-cops and the staff doctor all wanted to stay, but I ordered them off."

"And everyone else?" Jaime followed up. "However many that is. Was."

Kowalski's forehead wrinkled in concentration. Or maybe, at doing mental addition. Either way, fair enough: she had had a taxing few hours. "Forty-seven people in all. You must have seen the ship loitering nearby. It was just docking when something went *boom*. Passengers waiting for connections and the balance of local staff evacced to the ship." She started to lead us into the station. Wearing metal boots, the deck's zip strips were useless; in the delightful (suspected vile stuff aside), low-gee environment we used magnets for traction. "Where they'll remain for awhile, under observation. I'm told there's a frantic search for an isolated island somewhere with a population small enough to evacuate within a day, on whatever pretext, plus a runway long enough to accommodate a shuttle landing."

"They must be packed in like sardines," Jaime said.

Unfamiliar though I was with sardines and their packing proclivities, I'd been on enough spacecraft, of enough types, to take the larger point. Routine passenger capacity of the ship we'd seen nearby was perhaps a dozen people. Never mind mere crowding; things aboard would get hot, humid, and miserable. More likely, they already had. Because no way could the enviro systems handle that overload; they would need extra oh-two and water, stat. Our ship had brought some of both.

I asked, "What were the evacuees told?"

"That a plumbing pipe must've clogged, then burst behind the locker wall. That before automated cutoff valves could kick in, the rupture spewed hazardous levels of what enviro sensors deemed an extremely nasty and contagious pathogen. That the station's medical facilities can accommodate, at best, a handful of patients at a time, which last part has the virtue of truth. I'd already taken the station doc aside, waved my Bureau credentials in his face, and said I needed everyone off the station without any argument. He came up with, on the fly, a scary-sounding bacterial something or other. Sorry, the bug's name didn't stick with me."

The particular excuses hardly mattered, as long as they worked. But *how* had they worked? "You convinced forty-seven people a bomb blast was a burst pipe?"

Kowalski said, "Small blast. Big bump."

"What do you mean?" Jaime asked.

"The ship docking at the time gave us something of a thump. A cracked pipe wasn't a hard sell."

I'm not one to excuse poor piloting, but this klutz might have, inadvertently, dialed down the panic aboard EG3. "So, what are you seeing aboard the station?"

Kowalski pointed. On a nearby wall display, imagery cycled past of empty cabins and corridors. "After getting everyone off the station, I slaved the security cameras to arrivals-and-departures monitors. You can watch from anywhere."

And watch I did. We all three did. Scenes flashed by and, beyond the predictable chaos from depressurization and so many hasty departures, nothing struck me as amiss. I asked, "Can you show us where the bomb went off?"

"Sure." With bulky gloves, Kowalski fat-fingered a much-folded comp retrieved from a pocket of her utility belt. The nearest display froze on a closeup of the intersection between the station ring and a spoke leading inward to the embarkation/debarkation hub. In a bank of luggage lockers, the door had blown off one compartment. Surrounding lockers were warped, the doors of several among them sprung open.

"Not much of a bomb," Kowalski said.

The bomb on the Rock had done little more than rupture an air duct and the nearest interior hatch. I'd guessed at the time those explosives were meant only to discourage any attempt, were the device to be found, at disarming it. Allowing the crud silently to vent, and disperse unnoticed through the base's air ducts, would have wreaked the most damage. "Not intended to be," I opined.

Kowalski grunted. It might have denoted agreement.

"Did any other station have an incident?" Jaime asked. "We've been incommunicado the past few hours."

Kowalski turned away from the display. "Don't think so. I radioed colleagues aboard those as soon as I had a spare minute. No one has reported any problems. Just in case, those stations will be evacuated, too, to permit a more thorough search. As soon as enough reentry-capable ships can be commandeered."

That remote island, if and when the authorities nominated one, was going to get crowded. Not just with evacuees, but also quarantined shuttlecraft. This was *not* a remediation scheme scaleable to a populous location—such as any city or town on Ceres.

"You know ...," Jaime began.

Too damn little. "I know what? That my coordinated-attack scenario has fallen flat? Only if this event has anything to do with the bunch we've been after."

Because *two* groups taking to bombing Spacer facilities was a more plausible scenario? But maybe, if we were really fortunate, this burst locker was "mere" hazardous contraband, overlooked by careless security personnel. A consumer gadget, perhaps, whose rechargeable battery had overheated and shorted out.

Trey chose that moment to radio from the courier. "Y'all planning to stay inside for awhile? Okay if I start offloading my cargo?"

And what an eclectic cargo that was. Foil-wrapped food and water. Liquid oxygen, the cryotanks white with rime. A gross of sealed PREs, over-wrapped in aluminum foil, lest some of the crud had been carried aboard the nearby passenger ship. Five autonomous craft to corral the dispersing debris cloud, not that any decision had been made what to do with it all. One of those robotic craft, before starting its main task, would deliver to EG3 an automated bio lab.

Ever seen a dog try to chase its tail in micro-gee? That's pretty much how my mind floundered. Going in mere circles would have been an improvement.

"Sure," I told Trey. Improvising—as had become the story of my life—I added, "Have the bots take pictures of anything at all unusual."

"What are you looking for?"

"I'll know it when I see it?" I said, wondering if that were true.

I dispatched Kowalski to dump program files and data from EG3's many printers, in person where accessible and otherwise downloaded over the station network. The Rock had been home to a working mine; as a matter of course, plenty of explosives and blasting caps had been stocked there. Those weren't items John Q. Public could carry onto or off a passenger craft. If the locker blast were due to a bomb, then likely that bomb had been made aboard the station—not that *that* should have been possible, either. Presumably, a station printer had been hacked to whip up a dollop of explosives. The recipe ought to be easy (for a chemist, anyway) to spot. If so, *and* we were dealing with the same terrorist bunch that had targeted the Rock, we had a decent shot at also recovering the recipe for synthing the much scarier bioagent.

It was worth the effort, but I wasn't holding my breath. Never mind my opinion of the bastards, I respected their computer skills. Back on the Rock, whichever printer synthed the rubber muncher had been digitally wiped clean beyond my ability to find any recipe traces. But as the lottery adverts on Earth so repetitively and annoyingly proclaim, you can't win if you don't play.

For more than an hour, as Kowalski proceeded from printer to printer, Jaime and I monitored maintenance bots sidling about the station on little magnetic feet. Time and again, noticing some plastic surface, I directed a bot for a closer look. Even under maximum zoom, I saw nothing amiss.

"Trying something new," I announced. "I'd like a closer look at where this started."

At my radioed command, in vacuum silence, the nearest bot tromped to the locker bank. Even up close, I saw nothing of note. Exploded into however many shards and scraps, whatever once occupied that locker had, it would seem, been sucked from the station when Kowalski vented that compartment.

"Kowalski!" Jaime called. "Can we get a camera inside the locker?"

Kowalski loped back. "Cameras are head-mounted on the bots, or what passes for a head, anyway. I don't think one can fit its sensor pod into a locker. Maybe …" She directed one bot to examine another. "No, I don't see any easy way to dismount a camera."

Jaime mused, "We can print a camera, can't we? How long would that take?"

Longer than I saw any reason to wait. "Or we could go low-tech."

Marching a bot to the nearest restroom was easy. Prying back and snipping off a corner of shiny metal from the mirrored wall was only a tad more difficult. And with that jagged metal fragment leaning against the bowed-out rear wall of the burst locker …

Wedged between the piano hinge—all that remained of the locker door—and a warped sidewall, something glittered. And something tantalized in the back of my mind. With its needle-nose pliers, the bot extracted the glittery thing. A sliver of glass.

"That was much ado about nothing," Jaime opined.

The *something* still taunted me. I radioed our ship. "Trey, how goes debris collection?"

"Fine," he drawled. "If you're into random detritus."

"Do we have imagery as things were collected?"

"As you requested. All junk, if you ask me. You want a download?"

"Yes, please." And I hadn't asked.

In a small HUD window on my helmet visor, numbered stills flashed. Drink bulbs. Travel bags. Pocket comps. A pen. A twisted sheet of metal, possibly the blown-off locker door. Less recognizable scraps of metal. Thin, flat slabs of glass, as from a broken wall display. A metallic ring with bits of glass protruding. Papers. A backpack. A hand-knit sweater. Two partially unfolded, torn PREs.

"Junk," Kowalski repeated.

The ring of metal and glass nagged at me, as had the glass splinter caught in the locker hinge. I reexamined that physical shard, then the image of the ring. The latter's jagged glass gaped like a jack-o'-lantern's grin. The neck of a broken bottle? In any event, the recovered glass, like the locker shard, was clear and untinted.

"What's the diameter of that metal ring?" I asked. "Umm, still frame forty-six."

"About ten centimeters."

Jaime kneeled for a closer look at the recovered bit of glass. "What are you thinking?"

I was less thinking than experiencing effing *déjà vu*. (Or maybe it was *presque vu*. Either way, pardon my French.) Reliving my first peek on the Rock into a certain peripheral air duct. And at the contrivance within, that had had no business being there. The block of plastique, a fat blasting cap protruding from it. The electronics module, batteries, and rat's nest of wiring. The little accelerometer, promising that any attempt to withdraw the device would be … explosively misguided. And plainest of all in my mind's eye: the clear glass bottle, mouth-side down, threaded into a metallic ring. For reasons I had yet to fathom, Darin had had an almost obsessive interest in whether I'd observed dust in that bottle. Which I had.

"Hello?" Jaime tapped my elbow, our hard-shell suits clinking. "What are you thinking?"

"What do I think?" I turned to face her. "That we're in a lot of trouble."

...◆...

While Trey reprioritized space-junk collection toward recognizable electronics debris, Jaime and Kowalski resumed the search through station cameras for evidence of voracious bugs. I turned my attention to the little bio lab newly delivered to EG3's primary (suspected) infestation site, wirelessly connecting to the lab, and putting it through its self-test paces. With that prep completed, I sent maintenance bots scuttling to swab random surfaces and deliver their samples for analysis. And even as the lab pondered the first few swabs—

"Guys, better come look at this," Jaime radioed. "Compartment N-2."

This, I discovered a few paces later, was the tough but tissue-thin plastic of a discarded PRE. The hole torn in someone's panic was evident enough. And peering closer—

Tiny pits and fissures.

"The shit has hit the fan," Jaime announced.

All too literally true. Because faster than Kowalski had vented EG3, said fan must have distributed said shit throughout the station.

"And nothing reported yet by the lab?" Jaime prompted me.

"No matches, and that's more than a little strange. Give me a minute."

After responding to Jaime's summons, Kowalski had backed away from the tainted plastic. Wearing what she wore, I'd have done the same. She said, "You said it took a couple days on the Rock for plastic to disintegrate."

Fifty-five hours, to be precise. That's how long I'd been staring, glassy-eyed—for I hadn't know *what* to happen—before, with a whoosh, the hamster's water bottle had let loose. Of course, I'd been monitoring from a quarter klick away, constrained by the crappy, low-res cameras that were all printers in a company mine would make. Fifty-five hours, in essence, of peering through gauze. It could be I'd simply failed to notice less dramatic erosion as it had happened. Possibly, some artificial fibers were tastier than others. Or maybe ...

The auto lab delivered to the Rock had recovered the genome of the terrorist crud. Our hastily configured auto lab searched for that genetic sequence. Which made perfect sense—until it had become as plain as the nose on my face (and believe me, that's unmistakable) that, negative results notwithstanding, the terrorist microbe *was* loose on EG3.

"Lab," I radioed. "Adjust parameters. Search on genomic near-match."

"Instruction is ambiguous. Please rephrase," the damned box responded.

In the abstract, I would have liked to better understand artificial intelligence. Much of what my job entailed—programming, data mining, and (to be honest) hacking—could be done, better, faster, and cheaper, with an AI. Not *by* an AI, you understand. An AI by itself would not cut it. Often the key clue as to who was smuggling, say, platinum dust, came from reading facial expressions and observing body language. As lacking as I am in people skills, I do better than an AI. But it would be great to have an AI to *assist* as I went from rock to rock.

And yet again, the company's famous paranoia had stomped on my wishes. If *I* couldn't be trusted with a radio, lest I betray the location of valuable rocks, then neither could an AI on my ship be allowed access to comms. And there, or so some wacky Dane would have put it, was the rub. Mere seconds cut off from the worlds-spanning Internet amounted to sensory deprivation for an AI. Isolation would drive even a low-grade AI schizo.

With a sigh, I tried again. "Lab, reset matching parameters. Report any findings with"—I started small; I could always go again with a larger number—"ten or fewer base-pair differences from the reference genome. Acknowledge."

"Acknowledged," the lab AI said. And added, within seconds, "Match found."

Jaime heard it, too. "Could samples from the Rock have mutated before their recovery?"

Just that morning—a zillion hours earlier—we'd discussed the latest update from the Belt. The managing partners trusted telecomm, on the Dark Net or otherwise, about as much as they trusted anyone. That is to say: not at all. But dispersed as they were across the Belt—and with a few, like Andy, deployed yet more remotely—among *them*, comm was unavoidable. Which had led the company nabobs to an old-school solution. In spy novels, so many of which I'd devoured in my dull flights from rock to rock, the technique was called a onetime pad.

Encrypt a plaintext message with a single-use secret key of sufficient length, and the resulting ciphertext is, even in theory, uncrackable. So why doesn't the modern Internet use this technique? Simple. Because when you rely upon onetime secret keys, you need somehow to *physically* distribute bunches of those keys, and everyone involved must somehow keep their copy private. I'd arrived on Earth with such a set of digital keys stored (like my various Cerian alias passports) in my customized exoskeleton, masquerading as program chips. That the managing partners had had a new set of keys ginned up and physically distributed for my mission—among my nonnegotiable conditions for taking on this insane assignment—went to show how dire the situation was.

Not that the mechanics of company secrecy addressed Jaime's question. But some of their latest report—a secret part—*did.*

Secrets can kill, too.

"I don't think so," I said. "Cultures grown from the Rock's samples exhibit almost no genetic variability, and that's despite weeks in proximity to industrial and mining contaminants. This EG3 bug has been in the wild for only a few *hours*, and the station is a comparatively pristine environment."

Then there was the detail that the bugs seemed well designed. Samples recovered from the Rock withstood cold and heat, hard vacuum, and a hearty dose of radiation. And, as I had already shared with Jaime, the Rock's bugs exhibited no susceptibility to any common family of antibiotics. Not that, if an antibiotic had worked, gaskets or vacuum suits had circulatory systems to distribute an antibiotic …

Yet more emphatically, the partners' recent update suggested that I could begin earning my junior partnership in the company—another of my extorted conditions—any time now. I saw no reason to share that part.

"Which implies to me," Jaime said, "that differences between the bug on EG3 and back in the Belt were purposeful. Even in Chicago, the abduction of a Belter and his dramatic rescue in a shootout is major news. Our adversaries knew to make a change."

Knew to make a change. Something about that phrase bothered me. But what? "Changing a genome. Making sure the change didn't have unintended consequences. That's got to take time. That would suggest they had at least one variant prepared. And that could mean …"

"Mean *what*?" the women asked in unison.

I took a deep breath. "Could mean that they knew the company had plans to recover a sample from the Rock."

If so, the leak from within the company was ongoing.

…◆…

Trey radioed the station with an update. Dirtside had chosen a quarantine site: some speck of land in somewhere called Vanuatu.

Beyond being a tongue twister, the name meant nothing to me. But Jaime winced. "It's a small, unpopulated, tropical archipelago in the South Pacific. Unpopulated because sea-level rise made much of the limited land area untenable."

"Then how," I asked, "is this an option?"

Kowalski said, "It'll be fine unless there's a hurricane. Typhoon. Cyclone? Whatever big storms in the Pacific are called."

Jaime frowned. "Sounds to me like there isn't time to clear the regular population from anywhere reasonably habitable."

"Bingo," Trey said. "The Earth/Moon transfer ship the EG3 folk were evacuated to? It's already showing signs of infestation. Nothing obvious, yet. Nothing the people crammed aboard are apt to notice, especially not knowing what to look for. But the pilot, who we had to take into our confidence, did know. He wants everyone offloaded, himself included, to an atmosphere-capable craft. ASAP."

"Which sounds less than promising for—"

Over the open channel, a siren began to wail.

"Me," Kowalski calmly completed.

…◆…

Back in shirtsleeve comfort inside the courier's passenger compartment—after the unwelcome excitement of patching Kowalski's suit (in that bulky getup, no way could she fit into a PRE), and a slightly less precipitous retreat—we pondered our next steps.

Jaime had, indeed, put a long, serpentine crack into my exo controller's touch screen. Were the electronics beneath mounted to a flexible plastic substrate? Did any exposed chip have plastic encapsulation? The Earther distributor's website was mute on such matters. If I managed to devise a non-panic-inducing, yet convincing, reason to pry into proprietary design details? There was no telling how long it would take to be put in contact with anyone who would answer my questions. It was easier—or maybe just realistic, the way things had been going—to assume the worst. So, as we strategized (and while Kowalski had a bout of post-emergency shakes), I applied myself to epoxying the fissure. And worrying about what interactive functions the epoxy worm on the screen would put beyond my reach. Also worrying when I'd have access to any kind of sealant that was *not* polymer-based bacteria chow.

Make that, simply, worrying. Vanuatu didn't seem the type of venue to offer exo maintenance.

"Here's another," Trey advised us over the intercom. He remained shut inside the cockpit, with no intention of joining us—not that such reticence would spare him a stint with us in quarantine. "Check it out."

Another denoted any hunk of debris unlikely to have been carried by an innocent passenger or station worker. (Of the opposite sort—pocket comps, drink bulbs, luggage, kitschy souvenirs—the botcraft had by then overtaken and snared hundreds. Any orbital detritus is dangerous, and appropriate to collect. But any of *this* debris might carry the nasty bacterium.) As for anything to provide leads to the terrorists? Since spotting the metallic ring with its broken-glass collar, not a thing. But as Louis Pasteur once said (and innumerate gamblers chose to believe), chance favors the prepared mind.

So: we three in steerage stood near the cabin's built-in holo projector. (Our helmets with their HUDs, along with the rest of our vacuum gear, had been stowed in foil-lined bags—for what little good those precautions would do. Scarcely an hour back aboard the courier, I'd already seen shallow pitting in the plastic hides of our acceleration couches.) With micro-gee slippers zip-zipping on the gripper rug, I semicircled the projection. I studied this latest bit of wreckage, tried to imagine the fragment untwisted, its apparent gaps filled. Who knew a childhood dislike of jigsaw puzzles could come back decades later to bite me? And speaking of jigsaw puzzles, through the starboard-side view port, a glint off yet another chunk of tumbling detritus caught my eye.

Trey reported, "The lander is on final approach for the EG3 evacuees. They have twenty minutes to transfer everyone before their deorbit burn for Vanuatu. We'll give them a five-minute head start, then start down ourselves."

The women looked at me. I looked out the port, committing geometry. We were deep within Earth's shadow, and the Moon had set. The glint had to have been a reflection—off something decent-sized—of the lander's deceleration burn. None of our botcraft was scavenging out that way for what could only be additional station debris. Perhaps, even, a clue.

I said, "Let's stay out awhile, and see what more we can collect."

The intercom was audio only, but I could imagine Trey shaking his head. "If we miss the upcoming reentry window for Vanuatu, it'll be another ninety minutes before our next opportunity."

"Relax. Our air lock doesn't have rubber gaskets." Ever since this insanity began, I'd made a study, or maybe a religion, of inspecting air locks. Like the Rock's, the courier's air lock was the type whose precision-shaped metal hatch and frame surfaces pressed together like springs: air-tight without rubber gaskets. "But if you're the nervous type, increase pressure in the cockpit."

"You're the boss," Trey acknowledged—that agreement punctuated with the faint hiss of cockpit pressure ramping up. "But for what it's worth, know this. When we touch down going a hundred-plus klicks an hour, riding the brakes on a too-short runway, it'll be our rubber tires I'm thinking about …"

…◆…

Golden sunlight and balmy ocean breezes. (We'll set aside the clockwork-like afternoon downpours.) Swaying palm trees.

Crystalline water in a beautiful lagoon, with porpoises leaping and cavorting. Sunrises and sunsets beyond gorgeous, the sky gaudy with colors I could not begin to describe, that no Belter could. Our pick of houses and hotels, with airy canvas tents for anyone distrustful of the years-abandoned buildings. We also had, tapping the resources of grounded ships and supply drones, more than ample electrical power and broadband access. A case could be made this island was a tropical paradise—

But at least till a counteragent could be devised for the terrorist crud, this was also a prison. For me, doubly so. However diligently I applied sunscreen, inevitably, here and there beneath the metallic latticework of the exo, I overlooked, or failed to reach, some areas. Photons are tinier and far more insidious than my fingers, and on our first morning here I had burnt to a crisp. Since then, by daylight, anyway, I had remained indoors.

And thereafter, to anyone who would listen, a grinning Jaime reported that I rocked the harlequin look.

Jaime was enjoying the sun-drenched beach. Rubber gaskets notwithstanding, our printers worked just fine; seaside, not a few of our fellow refugees admired my sidekick in any of her several newly made bikinis. She, in turn, mingled with, well, everyone, far better at casually sounding out our fellow castaways than ever I could be. She had yet to deem anyone on the island suspicious. Anxious or annoyed, yes, but not suspicious.

And so, alone but for Jaime's favorite handgun, I was indoors, taxing my jigsaw-puzzle skills with some of the recovered EG3 debris, when a priority vid downloaded from Bea. My wife's grin was as broad and sassy as ever, her hair arrayed into its customary low-grav halo. But the usual twinkle in her eye was impossible to feign, and the faux version made my heart sink.

After a few anecdotes about her workplace, and a hope-your-shoulder-is-better, and a when-the-*hell*/just-kidding/no-not-really-kidding/when-*are*-you-coming-home-already, looking more apprehensive by the word, my wife leaned close to the camera. Lowered her voice. And confided, almost plaintively, "Something is going on here. And I know what you're thinking, wise guy. *Something* and *here* are less than precise. I can't be any more exact.

But in the tunnels, in stores, at work, I see the expression on people's faces, more and more by the day. They're *nervous*. Ordinary people, sure, but company bigwigs, too. Whatever the latter are keeping to themselves is scary enough they can't hold it all inside. And now there's some horrible new communicable disease loose on Earth? So as soon as you're able to travel …"

First, I'd lied about why I had to come to Earth at all. Then, I'd blamed my prolonged stay Dirtside on a vehicle mishap, not on getting shot! My undisclosed living arrangements weighed on my conscience, too, not that Jaime and I had done, or even considered, anything to apologize for. But despite the accumulating guilt, I wasn't about to come clean now. I wasn't about to burden Bea with foreknowledge of a civilization-destroying epidemic, or reveal that the pestilence was far more dangerous to her, and to everyone around her, than to me on Earth. I wasn't about to share that no one had a clue how to fight this plague.

Leaving me to report that I had, in fact, been exposed to the new, earthly contagion: the rationale for quarantine given to the EG3 refugees and the media. (What the hell kind of terrorists *didn't* claim responsibility after their bomb went off? Their ongoing silence was an enigma. As if we needed another of those.) Leaving me to relay that which Bea would least care to hear: that I would be tarrying yet longer Dirtside. Yes, I could, without fear of contradiction, record just such a message. And I would.

Just as soon as I could spare the time to rehearse my new lies.

Sunburn be damned, the ocean's buoyancy was *so* tempting. In my mind's eye, I pictured myself strolling down the glistening white sand into rolling surf. My exo was waterproof, of course; without an exo, I couldn't have stood in a shower. But in the limpid, languid, turquoise waters of the sheltered lagoon, I could shed the damned thing.

Alas, that was not to be …

Trey, Kowalski, and I stood at the end of a long stone quay. (Or was it a wharf, a dock, a pier, or maybe a jetty? Matters nautical were foreign to me.) A huge vessel—a veritable city!—floated a few klicks to windward, newly arrived. Epidemiologists, nanotech experts, and intel analysts, flown in from who knew where to the *Mark Warner*, awaited us onboard. An aircraft carrier, Kowalski called the ship—but rather than an aircraft, it was a small boat, bouncing maniacally over light chop, that sped toward us.

With a throaty electric *drone*, the boat, at best seven meters long, swooped up and broadside to the quay. I took one good look, and said, "You have got to be kidding."

"It's a zodiac. Watercraft don't come more reliable." Grinning, Kowalski flashed her Bureau badge at the three uniformed sailors aboard. One hopped out to tie up the boat. "Or, more fun."

Astrology did nothing to recommend this inflated toy, but no mere name gave me heartburn. I glanced around, confirming no one out of the loop loitered within earshot. "It's rubber. Bacteria chow. Do you *want* to drown?"

"Relax," Trey advised. "It's *thick* rubber. We'll be fine for a quick trip. Unless you'd rather risk a chopper?"

And indeed, after three days on the island, we had yet to experience a problem. On orbit, the tastiest plastic bits had begun to exhibit pitting in little over an hour. Now, even aboard the contaminated and grounded courier, the deterioration appeared to have stopped.

And cold comfort that was. If no one knew why the bacteria had ceased their munching and reproducing, they likewise had no idea what might rev up the little beasties again.

Crates of salvage were piled nearby, most filled with EG3 detritus that had landed with us aboard the courier. A far smaller second collection (as with each passing day, the remaining bits dispersed yet farther from the station), the entirety of that morning's botcraft delivery, fit handily within two boxes. Needless to say, I had toted none of these boxes.

While sailors laded crates and our scant personal luggage, I squirmed into and fastened a lifejacket. (Cork and canvas! *It* ought not to get eaten.) Grasping the calloused hand of a grinning sailor, I stumbled into the rubber boat as, in the rolling swells, it rose and fell. Rose and fell. Rose and fell. With far more grace than I, Trey and Kowalski stepped down. From the popular beach, Jaime (who was remaining ashore in her minimal mufti, there to continue her quest for suspicious behavior), sent us off with a jaunty wave. Once I'd been summoned to the nearby naval vessel, personal bodyguard services seemed redundant.

All too soon, we cast off.

I would have simply gritted my teeth for the short, choppy ride, except for the whole hanging-over-the-side, puking aspect of the transfer. After spending a healthy chunk of my life in micro-gee, with never a touch of space sickness, I found it ironic that I got seasick. And doubly ironic that the adjective to have come to mind had been *healthy*.

…◆…

An aircraft carrier was large enough, or dynamically stabilized enough, or maybe both, to be untroubled by the ocean's ceaseless undulations. Cabins and corridors were, by spacecraft standards—aside from the Belter-hostile low ceilings—more than spacious. Meals were delicious and available in unending supply. The cavernous shipboard gym put the company exercise room to shame and, once the Sun went down, the flight deck offered a vast expanse on which to pace. Several thousand military men and women surrounded me. I had not been this comfortable, coddled, or safe since arriving on Earth.

Nor so maddeningly idle.

Nor felt so useless.

While the carrier had sailed (with what sails, exactly? But what can you do?) to Vanuatu, its nonessential personnel had been air-ferried to Australia. That left plenty of un– and under-used space aboard. What scant thought I gave to being offered one of the many wardrooms for my personal use was of an appreciated but unnecessary gesture. A cabin for sleeping more than satisfied any privacy needs. Why had I been brought aboard, if not to consult with the elite intel team flown *to* the ship?

To separate me from the hostiles, if any, among the evacuees. Andy pulling over-protective strings. That's why.

So. I was alone in my personal space, abandoned yet again to my own devices, when Trey dropped by. My erstwhile pilot exhibited far more charisma in person than as a disembodied voice.

Beyond a deep tan and a luxuriant Van Dyke, a broad forehead and expressive green eyes, by far his most distinctive attribute was the languorous poise with which he carried himself. And after days of Trey deflecting my questions as to which three-letter agency he represented, at least my curiosity about the man no longer went *entirely* unsatisfied. "Trey," I had been informed by Danielle Kowalski, was Southern-speak for The Third.

Were I born Archibald Junior Junior, I'd also have gone with Trey.

With a meaty hand, he swiveled one of the many wardroom chairs. Legs straddling the seatback, arms folded across the top, he settled himself across the table from me. My debris collection rated, and only briefly at that, a raised eyebrow. More of that understated poise.

I shrugged. "The forensic team keeps the interesting stuff. They only pass along to me some bits and pieces they have no further use for."

Never mind that most of the puzzle pieces had once been in my hands. To the extent anyone acknowledged that prior custody, it was to express their disapproval. Because who knew what cooties I might, in my amateurness and oafitude, have imparted to it.

And still, I sifted and sorted and studied the regifted bits. What more did I have to do until quarantine was lifted—if it *were* lifted—letting me get back behind the company firewall?

"Bored, eh? Then permit me to pass along some news."

"Good news?" I asked.

"You decide." With a flourish—graceful, of course—Trey produced, and snapped open, a pocket comp.

The holo it projected showed a ruddy, blond man, somewhere in his late twenties (standard years). An Earther-chunky body build, along with a space-newbie sickly expression. The tightly curved background suggested the central hub of an orbital gateway. "Who is this?"

"Pity. I'd hoped you would recognize him. One of your abductors, perhaps."

"I wouldn't know. I only ever saw two of them, and both are accounted for." In the debit column of some eternal ledger.

"How about now?" Trey poked at his comp. And amid the departure-lounge clamor, synched to the man's lips, an ordinary snippet leapt out at me: "... do we board already?"

Petulant. Nasal. *Familiar.* I'd heard that voice bitching about … about … zoning approval. (For a new, high-rise complex. Who gets worked up about that?) From the room next to my impromptu cell. "Yeah, he was there. I'd recognize that whine anywhere. Who is he?"

"We'll call this good news, then. He arrived at EG3 as Keith Smithson. North American. From Kansas, if that helps." (It did not.) "Who is Smithson really? We're working on that. Knowing he was in the building where you were being held? The Bureau can focus some of their resources in that neighborhood."

Good luck with that. After my rescue, the Chicago PD reviewed public-safety and business-security cameras near my erstwhile prison. For city blocks in every direction, those vids—looking back weeks before my capture—had somehow been corrupted.

"What made anyone suspect this guy? The caliber of his fake ID?"

Which had to be damned good to have gotten him aboard a ship outbound from Earth. I knew how much my forged Cerian IDs were said to have cost, and *those* hadn't required matching records to be insinuated into some Earther citizenry database. Darin Hodges had been a university dropout, but *someone* in on this scheme had deep pockets or very good connections. I guessed both. But even the best forger would be hard-pressed to inject fake-ID references into years-deep, offline archives that a suspicious intel agency had now been motivated to sift and search.

"Nah. That detail was more in the way of confirmation." Trey unfolded himself from his chair, to amble across the empty wardroom to the capacious coffee urn. One thing I'd learned about the Navy, and about which I wholly approved: people were assigned to make sure such urns never ran dry. "Something for you?"

"I'm good." I tried again. "What had you looking at this guy?"

Trey set a brimming mug on our table, then again straddled his chair. "A random tourist's selfie caught Smithson using a particular EG3 luggage locker. And that locker remained rented after he left."

That seemed incriminating enough. "And did someone check what 'Smithson' printed while aboard EG3?"

"Please." Trey managed to look both insulted and amused. "Computer forensics checked the downloads from every printer on the station. And you know what? No record could be found of anything he printed. Not as much as a snack."

Meaning no bacteria-synthing recipe. And that, more than *anything*, was what we needed. The recovered genome (and you'd have to ask a biologist why) wasn't sufficient. It had to do with gene expression, or epigenetics, or something.

Progress? Perhaps so, but in baby steps.

Sensing some cosmic shoe about to plummet with Earther gravity, I asked, "And the image you showed me?"

"Was cropped from another tourist selfie, in this instance taken in the EG3 debarkation lounge. Just before Smithson boarded a transfer ship to Armstrong City. There's no sign of him on the station's security cameras."

I was again reminded of Darin's and Vegan Woman's absence from Chicago-area security footage. Our adversaries were too damned good. But it seemed not even the best hacker could dependably outwit selfies …

"When?" I asked.

"Two weeks ago." Trey paused for awhile behind the coffee mug. "And facial rec hasn't spotted him, by any name, since debarking. By now, he could be anywhere on the Moon."

"Or he could have moved on from the Moon with the recipe."

"Or that," Trey agreed. He didn't bother to say this was bad news.

Another interminable morning of too much coffee and nothing of significance discovered in my debris collection. Another mind-numbing, short-of-breath workout in the carrier's ginormous gym, belatedly followed with a detour to the infirmary to have my fake-corpuscle supply topped off. Unlike natural blood cells, which also wear out, the synthetic kind cannot replace themselves. Another late, over-indulgent lunch, which, by rights, should have sent me back to the gym. In short: yet more hours of utter uselessness.

Shaking off the food coma, I forced myself to take a virtual step backward. I needed to do something *productive*. And after much caffeine-fueled tabletop drumming, perhaps I found it.

The intel types had turned up nothing untoward in the printer data from EG3. Their failure didn't prove, I surmised, that nothing remained to be discovered. Oh, I didn't doubt that the spooks knew their jobs. It was more a matter of the belief that *I* was good at *mine*. And unlike my hand-me-down rejects from the station debris, in the case of EG3 printer data—because I'd kept a digital copy of everything Kowalski had collected at my request—I had the complete dataset. With no need first to play Mother May I.

Was there a company miner who *hadn't*, at least once, tried smuggling precious metals in the form of rings, pens, or whatnot? If so, I'd be shocked. But most such were obvious dodges, and easily caught. A bit more subtle was miners returning home with "toothpaste," "shampoo," or "snacks" rich with precious-metal compounds. As trivial as such pilferage might seem, the company would not abide it. (Anyway, not a lot of it. The goal was allowing through just enough contraband to keep greedy tendencies focused on *petty* larceny.)

Which is how unmasking shenanigans with onsite printers became a big part of auditing mining sites. Of—until this terrorist nightmare had begun—my job. Because to analyze with a mass spectrometer samples of every returning miner's personal toiletries and munchies was a bridge too far even for the company. That left people like me, of necessity, practiced at sussing out anomalies from within the digital bowels of printers.

And so it was that, after considerable experience-guided peeking and poking into the data downloads from many of EG3's printers, I spotted an incongruity in one's consumables-usage log. The details would be of no possible interest to anyone not into the minutiae of blockchain technology. (But if you are a blockchain aficionado? And also an accountant? Then my accomplishment was a feat of ledger de main.) Nevertheless, the discrepancy was telling. As subtle as was the inconsistency, this was the first actual *evidence* that something(s) illicit had been printed aboard the station. An actual fact: it beat the shit out of inference and deduction.

"Okay, then," I declaimed to the empty wardroom. "We have a lead."

With all the time I spent traveling between rocks, of *course* I sometimes talked to myself. Myself had been known to answer. The echoey wardroom still freaked me out a bit.

"A lead," I repeated, far more softly.

There are three essential things to understand about blockchain technology. First, each transaction generates a record, aka a block. Second, each record is related, in a computationally intensive manner, to every record that precedes it—hence, the term block*chain*. Third and final, blockchain, in the singular, is a misnomer. For security, the data are quickly and routinely replicated to other computers, and those copies to more computers. Yet more basically: in any well-networked, computer-rich environment, to undetectably excise one block, representing a specific transaction, from the ever-growing (and replicated) chain was, for all practical purposes, impossible.

But in the isolated environment of an asteroid mine? Or, as in the current case, aboard a small orbital way station? The impossible became merely the time-consuming. Aboard EG3, that process had not *quite* been complete when Kowalski dumped data from the station printers.

This discovery, even more than no one having yet claimed responsibility for the EG3 attack, struck me as more than a little odd. Why hadn't the Bad Guys waited to set off the bomb till digital cleanup was complete?

But while much about the EG3 attack remained mysterious, I might have solved two earlier puzzles. The first: why on the Rock I'd found no trace of printer tampering or unusual syntheses. The second: why the bomb there had been built *long* before it was meant to go off.

Ain't hindsight grand?

Blockchain-editing malware had erased every last trace of whatever poor, coerced Les Hodges had printed. Given the limited computational resources on the Rock, and the blockchain's growth as miners continued to synth food and print tools and whatnot, those calculations might have restarted and re-restarted and ground on for *weeks*. But after finally cutting and splicing the blockchain, and its safety copies—all local to the Rock, of course—the malware's final step would have been to erase any traces of *itself*.

Not so, EG3. In logs related to its printer data, that telltale anomaly remained. Aboard EG3, ergo, at least as of a few days earlier, the malware hadn't finished. A copy might remain. It hadn't resided on any of the printers themselves, or I'd have found it by now among my downloaded snapshots. Likely the malware resided in a main server on EG3. If that program hadn't finished in the intervening days, and so erased itself, it might yet offer some clues …

I *had* to get remote access to those servers.

Stiff from hours folded into a too short chair, torso bent over, legs splayed under a too low table, I lumbered to my feet. Never mind that the intel folks were three decks and half a very long ship distant. It's harder to say *no* face to face than through comms. I made my way through labyrinthine passageways, hunched beneath two-meter overheads, and up steep ladders. (Which looked to me to be *stairs*. What is it with sailors and their lingo?) And, as I tromped/clanked/stumbled, more than once I whacked some part of myself or my exo against a wall. When the clunked thing was the control panel *of* the exo, I glanced down at that forearm. Had my repair held up? Had any more glass of the display cracked? Not that I noticed.

At the back of my brain, something whispered. I froze. Arm. Control panel. Panel display. Repair.

Repair?

Something, I intuited, *about* the repair. Repair. Patch. Fix. Seal. Sealant. Glue. Mucilage. Paste. Epoxy … Epoxy was …? Epoxy came in two tubes. Neither chemical, alone, would seal anything. But mix them, and voilà.

Uh-huh. Voilà … what, exactly? Like the dust in the bottle on the Rock, I hadn't a clue.

Something taunted me. Something important. But meanwhile, the clock was ticking. I clanked onward to demand access to the EG3 main computers.

Before the Bad Guy malware there, too, finished its work and erased itself …

…◆…

I emerged onto the hangar deck, across much of which intel teams had set up shop. As tall as I am by Earther standards, airplanes are taller; reveling in the luxury of standing straight, and even reaching high overhead, for an instant I did not register the general aura of exhilaration.

But an excited buzz had displaced the usual low, purposeful murmurs. Analysts most often found clustered around sorting tables, or staring into holo displays, or consulting in small teams, were on their feet, milling about en masse. A good dozen people in white lab coats, having appeared from elsewhere aboard ship, stood at the heart of the throng.

A spook analyst on the fringes of the unwonted assembly, spotting me, loped my way. Delilah … Hernandez, her name was. No matter her rumpled clothing and the puffy bags below her eyes, she seemed oddly happy.

"What's going on?" I asked.

"Breakthrough." With splayed fingers, she brushed limp, wispy bangs off her forehead. "Thank the squints and boffins."

"Umm, who?"

"Biologists from the CDC. Nanotechnologists from NIST."

If Delilah's acronyms explained nothing, the specialties maybe did. "Progress with the bug, then."

She nodded. "You know the bacteria from EG3 have all been dormant. Right? Don't do anything. Don't grow on or in any kind of culture medium, not even pure latex."

"Uh-huh. And also that no one knows why, or what might reactivate them."

"Now they do." She grinned. "And they won't. Reactivate, I mean."

That news was worthy of the small metal flasks circulating among the crowd. "I don't suppose you can explain."

The grin broadened. "In any depth? Hell, no. But I think I caught the gist."

And just possibly, so did I. The bacterium had that organelle-like thing none of the biologists recognized—but an engineer from the NIST contingent had. That odd cell component was a nanoscale accelerometer. At anything above half a standard gravity, the device decomposed, triggering a metabolic breakdown that immediately shut down, and eventually killed, the bug. The bioweapon was by design unviable on Earth. It could neither be launched from, nor returned to, the home world. We were celebrating, by implication, our imminent release from quarantine.

"That *is* progress," I managed.

A flask-wielding guy in a white lab coat emerged from the partying throng, dispensing and filling small paper cups. He stopped to serve us. Faster than the smell of bourbon could register, he resumed his rounds.

"Drink up," Delilah advised. And as I hesitated, she pressed, "What's with you?"

Beyond confirmation that the terrorists had a laser focus on Spacers and space settlements? That with every detail painstakingly uncovered about them—from the quality of their fake IDs to the sophistication of their gengineering—the hostile enterprise seemed bigger and better funded than a grad student with daddy issues and his clique? Begging the question of who else was involved …

"If you're not going to drink yours," she hinted.

"Give me a second," I countered. If this discovery was not yet victory, it was nonetheless important, not least of all because it put within sight an end to my detention. Yet something, at some gut level, refused to let me celebrate. Dormancy of the contagion was good; death of the contagion was better. As ought to have been learning *why* these changes had happened, not that any Spacer world or habitat could exploit the knowledge. So why wasn't I …

"Big guy," she said, "are you okay?"

"Accelerometer," I said. "That's what activates the bacterium's kill switch."

She nodded.

"These bastards have a thing for accelerometers. The first dispersal device, the one on the Rock, had an accelerometer in the control circuits to discourage any attempt at disarming or moving it." A strategy that had worked. We'd all been afraid to touch the damned thing! "So suppose the device on EG3 was the same."

"Okay."

"Kowalski said the EG3 bomb went off 'about the time' an Earth/Moon transfer ship docked with a thunk. I think it's more likely the bomb went off *because* a bump triggered the accelerometer in the anti-tamper device."

"But on EG3, the bacteria were *active*. The nudge was too slight to flip their kill switches."

"Different sensitivity thresholds." Not that I expected an Earther to understand. However clumsily piloted, no *way* could a docking vessel have imparted a half-gee shove to the much more massive way station. "But here's the larger point. I continue to believe"—as a minority of one—"my captors dispersed to set up a widespread, synchronized attack. If the EG3 bomb went off ahead of schedule, triggered by a rough docking, we can find out when the coordinated attack is set to happen. *If* we can read the bomb's controls."

Which might yet turn up among the scavenged station flotsam and jetsons.

Delilah canted her head. Pursed her lips. Sighed. "Makes sense. But at least we move to combing through debris someplace other than at the ass end of nowhere."

...◆...

"And here ... grunt ... I thought ... grunt ... we were *rid* of you." Earl Ovechkin, bench-pressing a hundred kilos, had barely broken into a sweat. His shit-eating smirk conveyed both, *I'm kidding* and *Or not, so you don't dare take offense.*

We were in the company gym, flat on our backs on adjacent inclined benches, under the unblinking gaze of robotic spotter limbs. I was too exhausted to take offense. At my current exo-assist setting, I was pressing—the mass of my arms included—about twenty kilos: a pathetic, not-quite quarter of my body weight. By Cerian standards that made me a Hercules. Yay?

Still, in the throes of exercise, on a good day, I was better able to focus my thoughts. This was my first workday back from Vanuatu, and already I could sense I needed the assist.

"Funny story." With a grunt of my own, I deposited my barbell onto its stands. Reaching across my chest with one arm to poke at the control panel on the exo's other arm, reactivating a more normal assist level, was a comparative snap. "Your stupid damned gravity was getting to me, so I caught a last-minute bargain flight to an orbital gateway station."

"Don't blame me. It's not *my* gravity. And so far, not much of a story."

"Gateway Three." Sitting up, I started blotting sweat with a towel. When, apart from the occasional grunt or sharp exhale,

Ovechkin offered no comment, I explained. "Where there was a disease outbreak."

"Ah. That station. So you spent your freefall holiday back on Earth, in quarantine." He laughed. "That *is* funny."

What freefall? But I had more important fish to fry than explaining centrifugal force and spin gravity to a dirt-hugger. "Yeah, it was hilarious. Especially the part where I'd planned on a three-day weekend, only to end up gone for two weeks, and most of that time deemed leave without pay." That element of company spite was no more true than the vindictive-partner-exiled-me-to-Earth story. "So, what'd I miss here?"

"Same old, same old."

"Got to be some interesting gossip in all that time."

"Nope." With an elegant swoop, and nary a clink, Ovechkin deposited his barbell onto its stands. "Now that you're back, what are *you* up to?"

"Same old," I echoed.

As in, I was no closer than on my first day at headquarters to identifying the mole. No closer to doing *anything* than on the day Jaime had rescued me. Not even my speculations about blockchain-hacking software aboard EG3 had led anywhere. In all the hangar-deck excitement—nanoscopic accelerometers, significant gravity disabling the bacterium, a bump being the presumed trigger for the way-station blast, and the lifting of quarantine—for a good hour I had forgotten what had, in the first place, brought me clattering across the giant ship.

Maybe that malware was a mere figment of my imagination. Or, having once existed, it had done its mischief and erased itself even before I'd thought to have a look. I might never know. What I *did* know was that, by the time I rediscovered my purpose, and Delilah got me remote sysadmin access to EG3's central server complex, I found no trace of malware.

Luckily (inscrutable Earther metaphor alert), there was more than one way to skin a cat.

A widespread, synchronized attack was again the prevailing theory, because the explosion aboard EG3 *had* been premature. As Jaime and I rode a military scramjet back to Washington, Kowalski had radioed with the news. The collection of space debris had, finally, offered up a microprocessor/device-control chip. Target crud-release date included.

Sixty days from when my abductors had scattered. Ample time for any of them to reach the Jupiter system. With their evil aspirations evidently extending to the far reaches of human endeavor, I had to believe they had also targeted the main Belter world. Ceres.

Four weeks remained to—somehow—stop them.

Jaime had taken hope from the premature explosion aboard EG3, and the scraps of intel about the conspiracy thereby revealed. I didn't. I couldn't. True, a clumsy landing—or even an open-throttle crash—would hardly nudge Ceres. Dwarf-planet nonsense notwithstanding, my home world was a *planet*. But these bastards had overlooked one possibility on EG3. What was to say they hadn't screwed up another time? Hadn't overlooked something that *could* cause a premature detonation on Ceres?

"You okay, big guy?" Ovechkin asked. He had moved from the inclined bench to some intimidating chunk of exercise paraphernalia I couldn't name, much less operate, and from which safe distance he afforded me an uneasy stare. "You don't look so hot. Maybe they released you from quarantine too soon."

Insomnia and the ticking time bomb of Damocles did nothing for my appearance? Shocker! I resisted the temptation to cough at him. "No, we're all clean. It doesn't much like gravity."

He laughed. "Spacer bug, huh?"

"Uh-huh." And hilarious. Not.

He eyed me skeptically. "Still, you look wrung out."

Because things are often what they seem. Still, I shambled over to one of the gym's steppers, to give my legs a workout. "Just out of shape."

Also, frantic. The day's resumed data mining had gone nowhere. Bottom lining it: the company did not scrimp on security. If it had, I'd be out of a job.

To remain hidden, mine-able rocks were radio-silent and off the Net. Unavoidably, those company mining rocks went months without vendor patches for known vulnerabilities. When I showed up to do a field audit, I could—and often did—search for cheating, by leveraging known weaknesses. Only afterward did I install whatever vendors' program patches I'd brought.

But Earth headquarters existed, more than anything, to give the company real-time access to the financial markets. HQ *had* to be online 24/7—all the while recording detailed audit trails, of course—and well connected. Its computers and internal networks were kept scrupulously, religiously, obsessively, up to date.

And finally, my exercise-decoupled brain dropped into gear. Forget the bag of accounting and computer tricks with which I had so often stalked cheaters.

It was time for *me* to cheat. And I thought I knew how.

Andy hoisted a wineglass. His fine, leaded crystal fit right in with the hand-loomed oriental carpet, the original oils on the dark, wood-paneled walls, and the antique furniture of this, his *den*. It was good to be a managing partner of the company. For the next few weeks, anyway.

With a grin, Andy toasted, "Welcome back, you two."

Jaime raised her goblet. (I'd gotten a peek at the bottle: not only Château Latour, but of a legendary vintage.) The two of them saluted each another, and sipped.

They didn't have off-world … anyone.

"Glad to be back," I allowed, gingerly gripping my own delicate stemware. Back at work, I meant, as I had been for a few days now. "And about that …"

Andy arched an eyebrow.

"I still haven't found the mole." Oh, now that I'd found my way in, I'd seen more than a few suggestions of penny-ante embezzlement. This once, I didn't give a damn about that. What I did care about—and had found nary a clue for—were signs that someone unauthorized had been poking into those secluded corners of the company intranet to which only the most senior partners should have access. "However—"

"Maybe," Andy interrupted, "that's because there was nothing *to* find. A mole inside the company was always just an inference."

"That being said," Jaime offered, "a mole in local HQ *remains* a reasonable inference. And absence of evidence is not evidence of absence."

"Sometime, try that line of reasoning in court." Andy smiled, then turned to admire a painting. A Matisse? "The likeliest reason you've found no mole inside the company is that there's no mole to be found."

I shook my head. "Among the few things on which dozens of scary-smart specialists agree is that the super bug *can't* survive on Earth. So, how did our terrestrial terrorists create it? The experts insist it must have been designed wholly by simulation, by someone with world-class abilities in biology, nanotech, *and* bioinformatics. And unless you can believe our latest bomber synthed his bugs elsewhere in space than EG3, and was then suicidal enough to travel with them, we can conclude a world-class hacker erased all traces of the synthing, *and* the very act of that erasure, from the EG3 printers. We're dealing with someone freaking good."

Andy turned back to face me. "Go on."

"We've been presuming Darin Hodges created the bug, using university resources before he dropped out. But NSA found no trace on any of their computers either of the work or of the massive amount of computation that must have gone into it."

Not that the CDC experts I'd dealt with bought into the Darin-did-it hypothesis. After reviewing the latest draft of his incomplete dissertation, both women had declared him incapable of crafting so unique a bacterium. But as, under questioning, the two bioengineers also conceded (while citing quite different complexities) that neither could *they* design such a bug, I had half a mind to attribute their skepticism to professional envy. Of course, the *other* half of my mind agreed with them: Darin had struck me as more angry than adept. Either way—and on this topic the CDC women were in perfect sync—the computational load to design this super bug must have been *epic*.

"Speculative," Andy said of my presentation. "Not even circumstantial."

"We're not in a damned court," I snapped. "And the stakes are too high—"

"Easy, guys," Jaime said. "We're all on the same side." She plucked the wine bottle from the sideboard, emptying it to top off our three glasses. "So, let's play 'what if.' Suppose the bad guys *are* extremely computer savvy. As they'd have to be, to elude our friend here. That's suggestive. Ditto that a massive amount of computation went into the design, without any trace even NSA spooks can find. Yet we can be certain the conspirators needed the use of a world-class supercomputer, or an agglomeration of very powerful computers. That's also a clue."

"Tell me this," Andy said. "What does any of this speculation do for us?"

"All clues," I reminded, "point toward massive computing resources and extreme computer savvy. And do you know where both of those can be found? I mean, besides at a major university?"

"Any major office of the company," Andy admitted. "But how many other companies?"

I asked, "And which companies are known to be of interest to these bastards?"

"A fair point," he conceded. "But inconclusive. Have you found anything at the company to suggest biotech modeling, or even massive amounts of capacity unaccounted for? No, because you'd have led with that. And you're a sysadmin. You have all the access there is. Hence, you've found everything there is to be found. And that's nada."

"Well …"

My tongue was suddenly pretzel-tied. There *had* been something else to do. Cheat, and even that was a euphemism. But was I really going to tell a lawyer about my recent foray into a gray—damn near black—market? To as much as hint—to a managing partner, no less—at the powers I had seen fit to bestow upon myself? All paid for with off-the-books company funds?

An exploit is a code kit. An exploit, well, exploits a vulnerability as yet undiscovered (or, in any event, unaddressed) by program vendors. Sure, I'd sometimes reverse-engineered vendor patches to ascertain the underlying vulnerabilities. It required, I'm not too modest to say, some skill. But trawling for *possible* vulnerabilities anywhere in, literally, millions of lines of code? That took very special talents, plus all but infinite patience.

Exploits to compromise network operating systems—and thereby compromise every last app on every last computer on an entire in-house network—were among the most useful. Ditto, exploits to circumvent intrusion-detection software, so that the injection of hacks to anything else could go unnoticed. These were the priciest exploits. I had the sticker shock to prove it.

Exploits, *per se*, weren't illegal. Their status depended on how one used them. In fact, governments were rumored to be frequent buyers: for criminal investigations, and to spy on each other. But network-operating-system and intrusion-detection exploits in the hands of anyone else?

Use your imagination.

I, of course, had neither a warrant to wield nor a spy agency at my back. Once I'd used my exploit purchases and abused my sysadmin privileges to build myself an undetectable backdoor, only conscience limited my access. And even if Andy trusted me to use my newfound superpowers only for good, to stick to mole hunting? My Dark Net transaction *could* have been a ruse to launder a large chunk of my investigatory slush fund …

"Still here," Andy reminded.

"Something *did* turn up," I asserted. On occasion, passive voice was a good thing. "Something odd." Because, just maybe, my charcoal-gray-market investment had been well spent. In one of the last places I would have expected to find anything useful, I had struck pay dirt. And the mining metaphor was apt.

"Before the bomb was deployed to the Rock, someone"—and from the faint few digital traces that remained, I had no idea who—"sieved the company HR files for personnel data on miners. And then they downloaded *everything* on Les Hodges. No way that's a coincidence."

"Well, it could be," Andy said. But he looked troubled. "Personnel data, you say."

"Which," I reminded, "would have pointed them to all sorts of other sensitive info. Banking. Beneficiaries. Health."

An antique leather globe on a dark wooden base stood in a corner of the den. Jaime, her head canted in thought, gave the world a spin. "So rather than Darin Hodges being in the plot from the start, taking advantage of his estranged father, you suppose Les was the one chosen? *Because* his son could be used to manipulate him?" She gave the globe another whirl. "That'd be as devious as hell, but it hangs together."

Andy frowned. "So the son was coerced or recruited—"

"Recruited," I interrupted, thinking *daddy issues.*

"Recruited," Andy repeated. "Chosen to coerce his father. And then Darin not only cooperated, he also designed the super bug. Don't you think *that's* too coincidental?"

Put that way? Yeah. This was like trying to nail Jell-O to the wall. "So maybe Darin didn't design it."

"Then have we had it backward?" Andy asked. "Was the father coerced into designing the super bug? As I recall, he was also into biotech."

I considered. "Apart from the embedded processors inside printers, the computers at mining sites are little better than abaci. So, setting aside whether Les had the knowledge and tools to design a bacterium this advanced"—and no matter his years-earlier education, why would he?—"given the computers available to him on the Rock, the effort would have required almost geological time. So, if we can get back to those digital traces I found at Earth HQ?"

Not least of all because, after dealing so long in surmises, inferences, and speculations—and those not always in sync—a *fact* was a precious thing.

"Sounds like we have a mole, all right," Andy conceded. "Only we still don't know who it is. So where does that leave us?"

Jaime gave the globe yet another firm spin. "Up shit creek."

Andy sighed. "Without a paddle."

I contributed, "In a leaky canoe."

...◆...

The delicate rapping on my office door came as I continued digging for the mole. (And yes, I saw the irony.) The search had devolved again into a brute-force inspection of coworkers' network accounts. I'd found a few questionable financial dealings, and an undisclosed office romance, but nothing of any relevance for me.

With a quick swipe, I blanked the holo display. "Come in."

And Anna Burnham did. This day her long, dark hair was gathered up into a ponytail. The bracelets on her wrist jangling, she closed the door behind her. Come to renew her overtures of friendship? "Hi. Got a minute?"

"Sure."

She perched forward on the edge of my guest chair. "You still an unhappy camper?"

I just glared at her.

"Well, to be honest, I'd like more than a minute." She licked her lips. "And this isn't a work thing. Maybe we could go next door for coffee?"

If Jaime had her way, I'd never venture from the office except with her by my side or among a gaggle of coworkers. Too bad. In the middle of the afternoon, along a busy thoroughfare, the ten or so steps between business entrances could hardly be dangerous. The café itself, beige in every way imaginable but for the actual wall paint, would be full of tourists. And Anna's uncharacteristic, nervous behavior piqued my interest.

With my customary motorized hum, I stood. "Sure. Why not?"

Twice, between my office and the café, she licked her lips. Once, she nibbled the lower one. We bought empty cups, served ourselves at the coffee station, and took the rearmost available booth.

The moment we were seated, Anna tapped ON the privacy screen. "I hope the screen doesn't interfere with your exo."

Consumer electronics were regulated, designed neither to emit much RF noise, nor to be bothered by whatever dribs and drabs of RF other consumer devices might leak. Devices like my exo *and* ubiquitous privacy screens. Raising my mug, I demonstrated my ongoing mobility. "So, what's the deal?" My money was on an indecent proposal.

Again, Anna licked her lips. "The company has treated you, well, shabbily doesn't begin to cover it."

"Not even close."

"I can't change that, but ..."

I sipped coffee, waiting.

Lick, lick. "So here's the thing. How'd you like to make some money at the company's expense?"

Who wouldn't? "Go on."

"You have sysadmin access, right? You can determine when shipments are due, and what bets the company is placing on precious-metals futures. So why not use the information?"

"You mean apart from getting myself fired and prosecuted for hacking and insider trading, if I were caught? Doing time in a Dirtside prison? Super plan, Anna." I took another sip. "If I had any such inclination, and I admit nothing, why would I need you?"

A fidgety twirl of one of her bracelets. "Until you've locked in your profit sharing, for which reason I know you're putting up with all the company's *crap*, I'm guessing you don't have much in the way of liquid assets to invest. I do. And I know people who can make discreet, anonymous investments. Here's what I suggest. You provide the information. I'll put up the money, and we'll split the take. Sound good?"

"We barely know one another. Why not do this with someone you *do* know?"

"Because the company background-checks every prospective sysadmin six ways from Sunday." I took that to mean in depth. "You would've been checked out, too, at some point. But since then, you've been given every reason to loathe the company. If I can make placing the trades safe, why not rip them off?"

Was this a matter of simple greed? Or something more? I knew the mole had the hacker skills to delve into comparatively restricted personnel files. If, despite her job in the Ministry of Propaganda drafting bullshit press releases, Anna had such talents, why would she want my help?

Best, I decided, not to seem eager. "It isn't just the one pissed-off Belter partner who treated me like shit. Half our coworkers show about as much enthusiasm for my acquaintance as for a warm, friendly hug from a leper. So why shouldn't I believe you're setting me up?"

"I'm taking as big a chance with *you*. If either of us goes to management, it'd be he-said/she-said. I wouldn't put it past the company to play safe by firing us both."

"Unless you're recording," I countered. And mentally kicked myself for not having included a continuous-recording loop among my exo's unauthorized modifications.

"If I used such a recording, I'd be incriminated myself."

Not if she were setting me up. But if she were just screwing with me, would she be so twitchy? "Pass."

With a nervous laugh, Anna muttered, "I told them the greed approach wouldn't work."

"Them?"

"A … group I'm in. We have purer motives than avarice. Except, of course, that to do good we need funds."

My mouth gone suddenly dry, I drained the rest of my coffee. "Go on."

She swallowed. "The GLF." To my shrug, she answered, "Gaia Liberation Front."

"Who are the Gaia?"

"Who is."

"Are we here to nitpick my grammar?"

"No. Sorry. Gaia is the personification of Earth, and all life on it. Or maybe—and some of us believe this, *I* believe this—Gaia *is* the totality of life on this much abused world. And Gaia needs our protection."

I couldn't help myself; my hands trembled. Darin had had a near-mystical fixation on Earth, its expanding human population, and the Spacer resources which made possible that growth. I had found my mole, all right. And to think success had required only a sufficiency of strategic kvetching.

Or, rather, it seemed, my mole had found *me*.

(And the nagging detail the mole had to be a hacker, so why would they ask me? Maybe this GLF crew had bought an exploit, just as I had. And maybe, before they could recoup the expense with some insider trading, a vendor update and Security's routine diligence had voided that exploit. Gaia knew, my Dark Net purchases hadn't come cheap—or with an assured shelf life. It was pleasing to imagine someone else having a bout of miserably bad luck.)

I said, "What do I care? The day my profit sharing vests, I'm gone."

"You hate the company? You hate everyone in it? Me, too! I only got a job here for what I might learn, hoping it would advance the cause. So here's the deal. You don't care about Earth? Fine! Make yourself, and us, a little money at the company's expense. They'll never know."

Finding the mole ought to have felt like a win. Only it didn't.

Because what could the Good Guys do with this information? Bring in Anna for questioning? Arrest her? It'd be a he-said/she-said, any half-decent lawyer would have her out in no time, and the Bad Guys would know I'd turned her in.

The best I could hope for was the counterterrorism folks putting Anna under round-the-clock surveillance. That might do some good. But if the Bad Guys did their conspiring online, and were half as computer-savvy as they seemed, surveillance would go nowhere fast.

My empty mug, with a mind of its own, spun in my hands. Suppose I gave Anna a bankable tip. In the abstract, yes, unavoidably, I'd be helping these bastards. But wouldn't that be worth it? If I proved myself to the group, got myself *into* the group, I could identify more members. Perhaps all the members.

In my mind's ear, in two-part harmony, Andy and Jaime shouted: stop playing spy! That Anna must not have known about my encounter with Darin? It didn't mean the next terrorist I met wasn't among my abductors.

It was a chance I'd have to take. I'd do *anything* to unravel the conspiracy before, on untold worlds and habitats across the Solar System, the super bug was unleashed.

In, barring accidents, twenty-two short days.

"A tradable tip or two." I pursed my lips, stroked my chin, generally feigned deliberation. "Why the hell not? Some compensation for the way the company has screwed me sounds more than fair. And you know what? If in the process the GLF gets an opportunity to do something about this ant-farm of a world? I'll consider that a bonus."

For the first time since approaching me that afternoon, Anna smiled.

…◆…

As Anna and I walked the few steps back to work, someone's Uber was loitering in front of company offices. We entered the lobby, and Jaime pounced. I sensed she had been there awhile, pacing.

She said, "I've been trying to reach you."

"We went out for coffee. The place was noisy"—not that it had been—"so we raised a privacy screen." And when Anna gave no sign of continuing on into the building, I did quick introductions. "Will you excuse us?"

Then Anna wandered off, but only to loiter near the elevator bank.

"I'm so sorry, dear." In something of a stage whisper, Jaime announced, "Up on L5, your cousin Danny has been in an industrial accident. You're his physically closest relative."

"Oh, no!" Of course, I had no cousin named Danny, on the L5 habitat or anywhere else. *Danny*, however, was a near-anagram for Andy. I hadn't been told details, but Andy had left for several days on some kind of business. Off-world, I now inferred. Whether or not Jaime was hinting about Andy, something had to be urgent to merit this melodramatic, middle-of-the-workday performance. In any event, the front-desk security guard did not take his eyes off Jaime's dramatic production. Or maybe, not off Jaime. "How bad is it?"

"All I know is, they want you up there ASAP. Come on. That's our Uber at the curb. Let's get you packed and on your way." She began tugging me toward the exit.

Still wondering where I was really going, and why, I asked, "Are you coming with?"

"Maybe I'll join up later. Urgent business with … a client." Meanwhile, a brief narrowing of her eyes directed *Quit asking questions.*

We climbed into the Uber. I was bursting with news, but that could wait till we got home. *Get me packed*, Jaime had said. I announced our address and off we went.

Approaching our apartment building, Jaime called out, "One passenger only to exit. Next destination is Baltimore/Washington Interplanetary." And amid a lingering "Be well," hug, she passed what felt like a much-folded piece of paper. Some sort of explanation, I assumed.

Boy, was I wrong.

I arrived at the spaceport with no luggage but the mislabeled chips in my exo, and with no more guidance than GET DISCREETLY TO TYCHO CITY BY NOON LST TOMORROW. Someone (Andy?), presumably, would meet me.

Traveling commercial, transferring flights at an orbital gateway, would not get me to the Moon on time. Before the infestation of EG3, and the resulting flight disruptions, it *might* have been possible. No longer. I liquidated the balance of my slush fund, converting it from cryptocash to more reputable currency, and rented a private ship. Hoarding my one fake ID with a fake pilot's license turned out to have been wise, and not only to maintain secrecy in a clandestine rendezvous. Between gray-market shopping and the deposit on a rental, I had no money left to hire a pilot.

After yet another brutal launch (once I let the autopilot mind the store, and as I basked in sustained acceleration equivalent merely to twice Cerian gravity), I tried, and failed, to deduce the purpose of my summons …

…◆…

"Have any trouble?" Andy asked. He had indeed found me at the spaceport as I arranged storage and refueling for the rented ship.

I shrugged. "It's only your money. Of which, by the way, I'm now out."

"I'll take care of that." Looking around, seeing no luggage, he added, "Also for whatever you didn't have time to bring." Which pretty much encompassed *everything*.

Wearing a rented hard-shell suit over my exo, toting a new flight bag with a couple changes of new clothing, I slogged after him to a parking lot. He unlocked one of the spiffier-looking wheeled vehicles. A limo, of course. "Rental?"

He flipped a wrist dismissively. "Company."

Which explained the pass code of enough digits to be a managing partner's bank balance.

We got in and repressurized the interior—like most ground vehicles, it hadn't room to spare for a proper air lock. Wriggled out of our vacuum gear. Stowed that gear into closets. And almost a day since my still mysterious summons, Andy and I careened across the moonscape to …?

"Okay, boss, where are we going?"

"To an exclusive get-together with a bunch of the managing partners. I reported on the state of the investigation, but they wanted to hear it all straight from the horse's mouth."

A compliment, an insult, or just another inexplicable Earthism? It didn't matter. "You couldn't have given me a heads up?"

"You had better things to do than prep for a conversation that might never happen."

The limo was driving itself ... wherever ... just fine on its own, but we had both settled ourselves in the front seats. Andy studied the stark landscape as it rushed past. I grew up in and on rocks; the Moon was no different, only larger. *I* sat with my seat swiveled, studying him.

"In point of fact, Andy, I did. Make that, I *do*. Because, in breaking news"—or it had been breaking, when I'd begun my dash to the spaceport—"I've found the mole."

Eyes wide, he turned toward me. "That's terrific! Also, a bulletin worth sending ahead." He tapped into the virtual keypad on his armrest. "With full precautions, of course."

Precautions as much cryptic as cryptographic, because his text advised only: VARMINT UNCOVERED. MORE WHEN I GET IN.

With a glance at the limo console, he said, "Best compose your thoughts. We'll arrive around dinner time. I'm pretty sure you'll be the unannounced dinner speaker."

"Not a lot of five-star resorts out this way." Or much of *anything* according to the console's map display.

Andy laughed. "Nor would we want one for this tête-à-tête. No maids, temperamental chefs, or wait staff. By the same token, no aides or assistants, no hangers-on or factotums. Just managing partners."

"And now, me."

"And you." Pause. "Now tell me all about the mole."

Anticipation, mundane scenery, and ticking clock aside, the ride was pleasant enough. The limo, of course, was a shirtsleeves environment. Its suspension was a marvel; despite rocky, uneven terrain, the ride was as smooth as highway travel Dirtside. The massage-enabled reclining seats were configurable, accommodating even Belter height, and the mini-refrigerator was stocked with snacks and drinks. Judging by how the sound system utterly canceled fan whirr and engine drone, the music quality (had Andy and I agreed on a century, much less a genre) would have been superb. There was even a discreet, if claustrophobic, water closet.

Bosses have prerogatives. Up to a point. "Ahem. Some context might help."

"Right." And still Andy stalled, draining much of a half-liter bottle of iced tea. "First off, you shouldn't blame Jaime. All she knew was that if by yesterday midday she *didn't* get a text from me, it'd mean I needed you here at the appointed hour."

"A rather indirect way to communicate."

Also reminiscent—it seemed a lifetime ago—of how, at the onset of this mess, I'd been rerouted to the Rock. By an item *not* moved per schedule on the asteroid's surface, that nonevent observed by a nearby stealthed comm buoy, because the asteroid itself, given the company's epic paranoia, had no comms longer range than the radio in a spacesuit helmet. But is it paranoia if you *do* have enemies?

Andy shrugged, yawning. "It worked."

"And you bailed out of this exclusive confab just to retrieve me?"

"Yes and no. Things at my day job"—the law firm, I took that—"don't accommodate me going off the grid for long. Judges. You know?" (I didn't.) "I had to allow a couple mid-session getaways to check in. That's why I had an opportunity in Tycho when I could've sent Jaime a never-mind, and also this time slot to retrieve you if *that* were necessary. As it is. Happy?"

Not even close. He had left unexplained, among many things, the odd choice of venue. If not as unbearable as Earth's, the gravity was extreme enough that people would never expect Belter aristocracy to assemble here. At least if, by people, I meant *me*. Still, one-sixth standard gee was manageable enough with an exo, and the Moon retained enough frontier, even a few klicks from the few large settlements, to offer privacy and anonymity. So maybe I ought not to have been surprised.

"Come *on*, Andy, I need more to go on," I said. "Or do you expect me to walk into this cold?"

He coughed, sounding a bit phlegmy. "I'm exhausted. I *have* to grab a nap. And some free advice? You should, too. You look worse than I feel. As for going in cold, well, yeah. If it came to needing you up here, your going in cold *was* my expectation. No one understands the stakes, or the state of the investigation, better than you. I want you to give it your candid best, not something rehearsed. And if you *had* arrived with a talk prepared? Trust me. It wouldn't survive the first few questions."

"And?"

He fidgeted with the nearly empty bottle. Coughed again, or maybe it was more of a wheeze. "Damned lunar dust. It gets on everything." Cough. "Okay, you're right. There is something you should know about this gathering ..."

"That after I've met all the managing partners, they'll have to kill me?"

"Heh. No, not quite. But you need to understand, '*the* managing partners' isn't the case here. My qualifier earlier, 'a bunch of,' was carefully chosen. MPs aren't a monolithic group. We don't agree on everything, above all because we don't share a common planning horizon. The older MPs, especially those among us without children, tend to have the shortest-term focus. Setting aside the so-called altruists, with their various grand, expensive schemes for developing the outer Solar System."

Huh: even the shared mantra of *obscene wealth* fell short of a common vision.

Accountants do bottom lines, not reading between the lines. I made certain I understood. "So there are factions among the MPs? Competing interests?" Andy nodded at me. "Then that's how it is there are MPs within spitting distance of Earth. This is something of a cabal, gathered where a Spacer conclave wouldn't be expected. I just happened to be conveniently nearby."

"Cabal is harsh." Cough/wheeze. "Call it a subset. A voting bloc. And these—we—are the MPs most attentive to the next five, ten years. Not given to either dynastic ambitions or delusions of grandeur."

"Which helps me how?"

"Not sure. If you imagine the company is in general secretive—"

"Paranoid," I snapped.

"Fine, I won't argue. Politics among the MPs, and factions among the partners, are every bit as, no, *more* paranoid. If the terrorist situation weren't so foreboding ..."

"No mere peon would be permitted a glimpse," I completed. "But as matters *are* foreboding as hell, can I rely on your 'subset' to do what they can to help? Can you at least promise me this isn't wasting my time when I could've been on Earth, working?"

"If I thought otherwise, I'd have refused to send for you."

"Let's summarize, shall we?" Because, no matter the stakes, I was finding it difficult to concentrate. "I'll be walking into some Machiavellian snake pit. The snakes maybe will help, to the degree doing so doesn't interfere with their other schemes."

Reclining his seat just a little, Andy managed a smile. "Not quite a snake pit. Machiavellian, I will grant you. And not unrelated, we're very cautious. Individually and collectively. If you harbor any doubts, I'll share one final tidbit before I nod off. A couple members won't attend in person." He chuckled. "Howard Hughes types, if you can believe that. Regardless, managing partners from *way* back. From before my time, even. I've yet to meet either in the flesh."

Howard Who? "Then how?"

"They net into our meetings, using infosec magic far beyond my ability to comprehend. From the circuitous routings and the comm delays—each of which appears to vary randomly, as a bit of misdirection—both are at present no more distant than a million klicks."

So anywhere on Earth, on the Moon, in any of *dozens* of near-Earth habitats or space stations, or, my personal guess, aboard a stealthed, personal space vessel. "And I'm supposed to waltz into this don't call it a snake pit and explain—"

"Yes, you are." He waggled his now empty bottle, as if in elucidation, set it into a cup holder, and stood. As he opened the tiny water closet, I realized the empty bottle *was* elucidation. With a click, the WC door latch engaged.

I reclined fully. Stretched, as much as the exo permitted. Activated my chair's massage mode on LOW. Yawned. Coughed. Power of suggestion, I thought. Closed my eyes …

They flew open at a sudden *thump*.

…◆…

My breathing was rapid, and my heart was racing. My head throbbed. I was sweating and nauseous. The control console showed nothing but green, and yet something was wrong. Andy was not in his seat or, as I craned my neck, anywhere to be seen. It was confusing …

No! *I* was confused. And that … and my ragged breathing … suggested … hypoxia! Something gone wrong with the limo's enviro controls.

"Andy!" I shouted. Because he was in the limo *somewhere*. There was nowhere else he could be. No air lock: if he had suited up and left as I'd slept, I'd be dead. "Get into a PRE!"

But my immediate worry was getting *myself* into a personal rescue enclosure without my exo poking holes in the plastic, because I hadn't a clue what was wrong with our oh-two supply.

Incredibly, I had a *more* pressing problem: the limo charging downhill toward a cliff edge. Somehow, self-drive had turned off. I had to: stop the engines. Engage emergency brakes. Then get myself into a PRE.

Which was a brilliant plan, until the point where I attempted to move. The exo was dead, arms and legs as rigid as steel beams. I was trapped on my back like some damned turtle. Again.

"Vehicle, stop!" I shouted. "Maximum braking."

The limo, if it had a voice-activated mode, didn't obey.

I had maybe a minute before we nosedived. Less, almost certainly, till I'd pass out from a dearth of oh-two. Giving fervent thanks for mere lunar gravity, and for every last excruciating press, curl, and stepper step, I wriggled out of the inert exo. Did my best to hawk up a lung (*cough* being a sometime symptom of hypoxia, for all the good this belated insight did me). Folded down an armrest. Struggled to recall what I was doing. Rolled/fell from the chair. Levered myself into a sitting position. Yanked back the throttle. Yanked the lever for the emergency brakes. Coughed some more. Wrenched the manual steering bar.

The limo neither slowed not swerved.

"Andy! You okay?"

Crickets.

And still, we rolled straight toward the cliff edge.

Self-driving mode disabled. Manual controls inoperative. My exo, also, somehow. Oxygen supply and associated alarms compromised.

Sabotage.

My mind growing cloudy, I wrenched open the access panel beneath the control console. Knelt. Plucked out circuit modules at random. Tugged cable bundles from connectors at random. Felt the change through knees and slipper tips as electric motors in wheel hubs … stopped.

Still, the brakes did nothing. I *might* have re-disabled them. I *didn't* have the time or concentration to troubleshoot. We'd either coast to a stop—or sail over the edge. If I didn't get into a PRE, I wouldn't be conscious to see which …

Emergency supplies were a long, slogging crawl to the rear of the cabin, but I made it to that drawer. Dragged open the drawer. Extracted and twisted ON the portable emergency radio beacon. Grabbed two foil-wrapped PREs. Crept yet farther, to the opposite rear corner of the cabin. Reached up and, sagging, let my miserable weight turn the handle and open the WC door.

Like a sack of potatoes Andy slumped to the floor, his skin tinged blue. He wasn't breathing.

With infinite time, I hadn't the strength to get him into a PRE. I had, at best, a few more *seconds*. More by reflex than conscious thought, I started to get myself into a PRE …

…◆…

Soft, rhythmic beeping. Antiseptic scents. The crispness of clean, starched linens. An oxygen cannula in my nostrils. The pinch of an IV on the back of my left hand. Oh, and I felt like absolute shit. Head to toe. Inside and out.

With herculean effort, I opened my eyes. A hospital room, as suspected. On the Moon, still, aching muscles reported. My folded exo, its epoxy-repaired control panel topmost, took up one of the available chairs. Yet again, tauntingly, that repair suggested … I still couldn't quite grasp what. Only I was surer than ever that it *did* matter.

A dark-skinned woman, Spacer to judge from the lanky body build, Loonie or Martian to judge from her lack of an exo, occupied the other seat. Her clothing and massive gold jewelry screamed *money*: enough that her apparent thirty-something age meant nothing. Peering down as she was at a comp in her lap, I couldn't get a good look at her face. I groped at my bedside controls, to raise myself into something to approach a sitting position.

At the soft motor hum, the presumed managing partner glanced up from her comp. "Good. You're awake."

"More … or less." The words came out in a croak. "Did Andy …?"

"A moment." She slipped the comp into a blazer pocket, stood up in a whisper/whoosh of silk, strode to the closed door, and engaged the room's privacy screen. "I'm sorry. He … didn't make it. If it's not too soon, what happened?"

What *had* happened? I wasn't sure. On the room's inactive wall monitor, my reflection looked as perplexed. "I was rescued. The emergency beacon?"

She nodded.

"I was found …" I coughed, feeling as if I'd inhaled ground glass. "I was found"—cough—"unconscious inside a PRE, I assume. And Andy?"

She held out a water bottle so I could sip through its straw. "Collapsed on the limo floor, an unopened PRE in arm's reach. Temperature readings through the front canopy said we were too late for him. So we bypassed interlocks to get to you faster. And it was fortunate we did."

"We. You were there?"

"Yes."

"Thanks …" I coughed some more. "Thanks for coming for us."

Looking uneasy, she said, "You can call me Trish."

By then, I had placed the face: Patricia Garcia. A managing partner and, by the standards of company aristocracy, quite public-facing. Made her fortune in the Belt—where else?—but, by birth, she was Martian. That she turned up, not just on the Moon, but near enough to be in on the rescue? One of Andy's cabal, then.

She glanced at the dry-erase board on which was block-printed, for the hospital-ward staff, the patient's name: Cyril Kesaris. "Will that stand up to scrutiny?"

I managed a wheezy chuckle. "It's the best your money can buy."

"Right."

It took awhile to register that Trish was waiting. I chewed on that notion for awhile. "Hold on. You had to override safety interlocks to get in?"

"There was cabin pressure, so the hatch didn't want to open."

"Right." I wondered when the fog would clear. Or if it would. Cerebral hypoxia was a thing. "Just no oh-two. Not enough, anyway. Why else would I have been in a PRE?" As she continued, in silence, to study me, the horrible implication penetrated. "You can't imagine *I* had something to do with this?"

"Our techs have gone over the limo. The only damage they found to onboard systems was components and cables someone in the cabin had pulled out." She reclaimed the open chair. "So, what happened?"

"I'll tell you. But first, what happened to Andy?"

"Cardiac arrest." There was no need between Spacers to lay out the dots, much less connect them. Severe hypoxia could do that, too.

"Shit," I said.

"Indeed. I'm asking again. What happened?"

I explained, as best I could, about self-drive somehow gone offline. Manual controls not responding. My exo gone dead. The struggle to stay awake. "Tampering with the limo must *also* have involved cutting off fresh oh-two. Maybe also switched off the cee-oh-two scrubber. The cabin isn't that large a space. Pretty soon after, hypoxia."

With skepticism: "Too gradually to notice."

"Yes, damn it." Not least of all because hypoxia's symptoms included confusion. Also: coughing, shortness of breath, and fatigue.

"How many *years* have you spent in a vacuum environment? Flying solo? And yet you didn't notice when your oh-two supply shut off?"

I would not have believed me, either. But I *hadn't* noticed. "The instruments lied." Which was especially pernicious after decades of conditioning to rely on my instruments. "And I wouldn't have heard fans or pumps or anything cut out because I never heard them run to begin with. I didn't hear the motors in the wheel hubs. Really good noise cancellation."

That earned me a fleeting smile. "Andy *was* obnoxious about sound systems. Insisted on the best in everything he drove."

Suppose we had gone over the cliff. With self-drive disengaged. With the cabin cracked open by the impact. Who could doubt murder/suicide?

I wound down, all too aware of the many dominoes I was hypothesizing. "At some point, Andy must have slumped against the WC door. I'm pretty sure that's the *thump* that woke me."

"Rather conveniently woke you up." Her eyes bored into me. "Except for the brief EG3 excursion, you've spent weeks in Washington and Vanuatu. Even the highest elevations in the former, as I recall, are only a hundred or so meters above sea level. The latter, as damn near as matters, is the *definition* of sea level. I can't imagine that by now you're any better adapted to reduced oh-two partial pressure than was Andy. Yet despite the insidious gradual hypoxia, you were able to take decisive last-minute action, stop the limo, and get yourself into a PRE."

Which, by rights, I couldn't have. I should have stayed passed out, too, to end up dead at the base of the cliff. Except …

"Not much more than a week ago, I got a fresh transfusion of synthetic corpuscles." Which soaked up available oh-two like tiny sponges. If sponges soaked up oh-two, and not water. (At least until stress hormones prematurely aged the tiny, monomaniacal critters. Hence, that impromptu refill.) "Those would have kept me going for an extra little while."

Trish grunted. Had a few words out of my mouth at last sounded plausible? "Your exo, apart from a control panel evidently cracked some time ago, tests out fine. And except for the damage you say you did to Andy's limo, there's no evidence *it* had been tampered with."

"The attack must have been done by software."

"Only there's no sign of that, either."

Sorry, Andy: absence of evidence is not evidence of absence. "It's like what happened aboard EG3. You know about that mess, right? The bacterium had to have been synthed on the way station, but no traces of its production were found. And while logic insists massive computations were required to edit all traces of that synthesis from the printer blockchain, no traces of that computation were found on the station servers. Limo controls don't need software even approaching blockchain in complexity. For the attack code to erase its tracks would be straightforward."

"At best, that explains the limo. Unless you're telling me your exo was netted into the onboard comms."

Of course not, and anyone reading out the exo's maintenance log would know as much. But what else was left?

"Jamming of some sort?" The limo's radio transmitter, misused, could easily overpower the electronics of an exo inside the passenger compartment, and a murderer would hardly balk at flouting noise-and-interference regulations. "If hacking the limo compromised the navigation and enviro controls, why not also its comms?"

"This is one wily hacker," she said. Still studying me.

Throughout the questioning, gravity had had its way with me. I struggled from a slouch into a more dignified position. "I had nothing to do with the attack. I'm sorrier than you can imagine about Andy. And, as soon as the docs cut me loose, I'll tell your group everything, both about the Dirtside investigation *and* what I know about this latest incident."

"As for any such briefing, forget about it. Whether by you or someone else, our security has been compromised. I volunteered to stay behind, to learn what I could. Everyone else has dispersed."

"Whether by me? Still? You don't believe that. You *can't*. Do you?"

"No." Trish grimaced. "I could almost wish I did. But you've been too integral to identifying and confronting the threat, and for too long, for me to believe it—even if I *hadn't* found you, more dead than alive, teetering on the brink of an abyss."

I shuddered.

"That's enough for today." Trish leaned closer, her voice softening. "Practically speaking, that's enough, period. As soon as you're well enough to travel, you're going home."

"No."

"There's a good chance you were the target, not Andy."

"So? There's near certainty a doomsday bug will be unleashed across the Solar System in three weeks."

To which outburst she gave no answer. I took that silence as resignation, if not assent. "I should get some sleep."

"One last matter, and this can't wait." She leaned close. "The mole. Who is it?"

I shook my head. "What do you mean?"

"The *mole*. The rat bastard in the company in league with these terrorists."

"That's what I need to find out. That's why I can't go home."

"But Andy texted ..."

"What?"

"Returning from Tycho City, he texted he knew who the mole was. I assumed that was based on news you'd brought him."

"Sorry," I lied.

"Then why was the limo attacked only after your arrival?"

"Why? Maybe someone he encountered at the spaceport. Or in Tycho City. Maybe his excursion to Tycho provided someone's first opportunity to tamper with the limo. Honestly, Trish? How the hell should I know?"

"Get some rest." And with that, shoulders slumped, she slogged from the room.

...◆...

Of *course*, Andy's text had instigated the attack.

Nor did I question (lunar gravity being amenable to the bacterium, if not to me) that the super-bug field trial could have been performed on this world. That the test had not occurred here? That by methods beyond circuitous, the test had instead been done on the Rock? It told me—no matter Andy's death and my own hairsbreadth escape—the terrorists didn't routinely have assets stationed on the Moon.

Other things were undisputable, too. That a clock ticked ever closer to doomsday, and I had no idea how to stop it. That yet another death, a *friend's* death, weighed on my conscience. That my lapses and failures made me ill.

For all that, the bastards had slipped up.

Major premise: only members of Andy's group had been advised the "varmint" had been unmasked. Minor premise: someone had responded almost at once to that text with lethal, albeit improvised, force. Had, in a word, panicked. Conclusion: someone at the aborted cabal gathering feared the identity of the varmint coming out.

Inexplicably, terrifyingly, one of the company's own managing partners was a mole.

THE COMPANY BANE

I wasn't the company's enemy, but I doubted they would see it that way. Not while I investigated the managing partners. Not while I was revealing most of what little private information I knew about them to the USNA Counterterrorism Center. And not while I was abetting the Gaia Liberation Front by passing along company insider information. All with the best of intentions, of course.

Isn't there some supposed ancient curse about living in interesting times?

…◆…

Anna Burnham bounded into my (barren, oppressive) office, grinning, wearing an eye-popping, neon-plaid dress. If she were, in any part, Scottish, it had to be one wild and crazy clan. Even her ponytail seemed perky. *Someone* was in good spirits. "Coffee shop. My treat."

It was not as if she had interrupted anything important. I was having a bit of respite from my ongoing failures in the form of a brief online review of the *worlds'* failures. (Me versus the entire rest of humanity? I judged us more or less tied.) At the time of my coworker's grand entrance, I'd been speculating whether a particular vlogging head was human, a human's prettier avatar, or a news-reader AI. Not even the best simulations of the human vocal tract were one hundred percent realistic, of course, not one hundred percent of the time. If this were an avatar or AI, voice-analysis software would in time have flagged the subtle differences. But using an app to make the call would have been cheating. My game, my rules.

"Umm, come in?" I managed.

"Way ahead of you." Anna grinned. "So how about it? Shall we go out?"

I stood, my exoskeleton emitting its usual motorized hum, me emitting my best melodramatic sigh. "So much for my virtuous reputation."

Mole #1 and I were soon ensconced in the next-door café, our mugs filled, me with a chocolate croissant. This being Washington, DC, we shared the place with a double handful of noisy tourists, and Anna raised a shimmering privacy screen.

I cleared my throat. "So, what's going on?"

A much-folded comp came out of her purse. "Settling up. Your tip to us paid off."

Tip was discreet. I had shared closely held, proprietary information about the company's plans for a sell-off of iridium from its stockpile. Information to which I had no right beyond the willingness to misuse my sysadmin privileges. Desperate times, and all that ...

When a tonne—a decent chunk of the Solar System's annual production—of this rare and precious metal had hit the market, the price had plummeted. The Finance Department, of course, had known about the pending release. They had insulated the company from the predictable price plunge with offsetting transactions on the futures market. Anyone else with the fortunate timing—or an inside source—to have placed the right bets on iridium futures (note to the cognoscenti: buying put options) had cleaned up when the price dropped.

Anna's *us* was similarly discreet. A week ago, I could not have imagined abetting the Gaia Liberation Front. But if I was correct about a coordinated, Solar System-wide, GLF assault on Spacer settlements? If that attack was now less than two weeks out? There was next to nothing I *wouldn't* do to stop these terrorists. Anyway—and unfathomably—I also knew that a managing partner of the company was, somehow, involved. Whatever profit the GLF might make off my insider info seemed trivial beside what their deep-pocketed … backer? ally? co-conspirator? … could contribute. Mole #2.

I set my own pocket comp on the table. "How much are we talking about?"

She poked at her comp, then slid it across the table toward me. The amount pending transfer (in cryptocash, untraceable and, for that reason, illegal in the USNA) was not nothing. It also was not anything to transform my lifestyle.

"It's as though you didn't trust me." Or she was lying about the size my share should be. Or her true purpose was to compromise me beyond dispute, maybe so the GLF could extort more from me than investment tips.

She licked her lips. "True enough. We *didn't*. Some of my, um, colleagues, that is. They wanted to just watch the markets, see if we *would* have made money on your tip."

I took a bite of croissant, washed it down with some coffee. The one could have been cardboard; the other, battery acid. Indigestion notwithstanding, I was going for casual confidence. "So why didn't you?"

She shrugged. "We needed the money."

"Here's a thought. What if I gave back my cut of the proceeds?"

Anna blinked. "But *why*?"

"A token of my sincerity." A (hopefully) earnest pause. "So that you'll introduce me to your friends."

"There's no need." But the tilt of her head suggested, "Is there?"

Just in case anything might come of my dealings with Anna, I had proactively plowed through bunches of GLF propaganda. They maintained a huge website, mirrored to a half dozen backup servers, all of them on the Dark Net.

I paraphrased a couple of the GLF's favorite factoids. "Choking the oceans with plastic trash is crazy. And surely five great extinctions were enough."

Being honest? I had no problem with the Great Oxygenation Event, some 2.5 billion years ago, that wiped out most every anaerobic species on Earth. Oxygen is a *good* thing. But even Belter kids have a soft spot for dinosaurs. Don't ask me to explain that.

"Six," Anna said.

"Oh?"

She slapped the table. "Yes, *six*. Humans are guilty of mass extinction even as we speak."

Whoa! Memory whiplash! As a kidnap victim, my smartass ways had all but gotten my head served to me on a platter. Why? Because I'd had the temerity to request a steak dinner. From the tirade thus evoked, I retrieved a snippet: that in terms of their biomass, cattle were *the* dominant animal species on the planet. People were second. The remaining animal species combined, a distant third.

I said, "All to make room for more cattle and other livestock. It's *sick*. So yes, I'm happy to kick in a bit of found money to do something to help this ant heap of a world."

For a moment, she seemed tempted. "No. Sorry. If you want to contribute, we'll take your money. We'll be grateful for any other tips. Thanks to you, we have a nice nest egg to invest."

"Uh-uh." I leaned back. Crossed my arms across my chest. "No more tips unless I'm involved."

"But—"

I tapped my comp, completed the e-transfer she had teed up. Pocketed my comp. Said, "If you decide to trust me, as I trusted you, we can reverse that transaction." Stood.

Her expression, just before my head emerged out the top of the privacy screen, was one of disbelief.

Truth be told, I could scarcely believe I'd proposed something so dumb. But with Super-Bug Day less than two weeks off, to play things safe would have been dumber.

...◆...

Behind closed doors, in a private conference room aboard Earth Gateway Two, Jaime and I met up with Patricia Garcia and her bodyguard. Apart from EG2's blissfully minimal spin gravity and, accordingly, no chairs, this could have been any small meeting room, anywhere. Earth itself was beneath our feet, unseeable, and night-dark besides—but with every stately rotation of the station the room's view port presented a panoramic vista of an orbiting edifice still under construction, its vast but unfinished photovoltaic array aglitter in moonlight. Of course, I'd heard about space-based, solar-powered, server farms—the Next Big Thing—but I'd never till then seen one. In technical terms: a shitload of computing power, economically powered. Awesome, I had to admit. But Jaime seemed oddly unimpressed, muttering something about counting on one's fingers.

The company logo, backlit, shone from the nearby construction shack. Why not? My employer's pesky excess money had to go somewhere.

Jaime seemed less queasy than on our recent sojourn aboard Earth Gate *Three*. I wondered whether that near-comfort reflected the practice, or the expectation of a jaunt that *wouldn't* end with habitat-destroying bacteria and us in quarantine. Regardless, my Amazonian bodyguard, roomie, and friend was almost her usual, gregarious self. Only the uncharacteristic tremor in her deep, sexy voice revealed low-gee trepidations.

Trish was much as I remembered her: Spacer-lanky; young beyond her years, in the way only serious money can accomplish; dressed to the nines. (I don't get that expression either, beyond that it's a compliment. But accountants like numbers.) I remembered Trish being taller, but then I had been flat on my back, in a hospital bed, at our prior encounter.

Her bodyguard more than compensated. He was as tall as any Belter and as burly as a football player. North American football. With that frame, I could not imagine anywhere, except perhaps Mount Olympus, he might be from. Picture a force of nature with chiseled features and good hair. He had been sweeping the room for bugs when we arrived; Jaime started her own, independent search.

"Clear," Jaime announced.

Force of Nature just nodded.

"Good to see you up and about." Trish gestured to dismiss her guy. "You wanted to see me?"

"Trish Garcia. Jaime Olafson," I introduced. "Jaime has my back, though that isn't why she's here. She's a PI and worked closely with

Andy and me." With only me now. Andy Singh had died in the attack that had put me into that hospital bed.

Force of Nature paused at the door.

"It's all right," Trish said.

Force of Nature left, closing the door behind him.

"Okay, what's so urgent?" Trish asked.

Urgent enough to summon a managing partner of the company from the Moon, when she had been ready to head home to Mars. Her detour suggested this very junior partner retained some credibility. And that she, too, anticipated the shit hitting the fan very soon now, and wanted to help me prevent it. In any event, so I chose to believe.

"Quick summary," I began, "to be sure everyone's on the same screen. Some managing partners were meeting on the Moon." That Trish, Andy, and an undisclosed (to me) number of other MPs comprised a cabal within the company aristocracy? That was nothing Jaime needed to hear. "Andy let it be known, via Jaime, that I should fly up and join him. I was to status you all about the search for the terrorists behind the super bug and their impending attack. Andy met me at the spaceport. On our drive to the gathering, he radioed ahead over a secure channel, and in very vague terms, about having uncovered a mole."

"And you were quickly attacked," Trish said.

"And we were quickly attacked," I agreed. "I have to believe by someone who felt threatened by Andy's news."

"What do you want from me?" Trish asked.

"Your help identifying Andy's killer," Jaime said. "More than a colleague, he was my friend."

"*Our* friend," I clarified.

"Mine, too." Trish closed her eyes briefly. In shared pain? "I'd love to help, but I have to ask. What makes you sure I'm not the mole?"

I wasn't *sure*, though it seemed unlikely. "Because just by dawdling a bit when the Mayday came in, you could have let me die of apoxia. And after rescuing me, rather than abandoning me on the Moon, broke"—the last of my investigative slush fund having gone to leasing the fast ship I'd flown to answer Andy's urgent lunar summons—"you provided money for me to get back to Earth. Back to work."

Trish managed a smile. "That's it?"

A skinny sideboard, the room's only furniture apart from the bare table, offered a refreshment rack. I grabbed one of the dozen drink bulbs, all beaded with condensation, and sipped cold water. What I really wanted was something at least 80 proof.

"That," I said, "plus what's public about your background. You're a geologist and, no offense, as far as I can tell no computer genius."

Trish laughed. "Few rock hunters are."

"And that lack of tech savvy brings us to how you can help." I took a deep breath. "Whoever attacked Andy and me, on a few minutes notice, *was* a computer whiz." Better than me, to be sure, and I'm no slouch. "So who among the group we were going to meet *is*? And who might have had the opportunity, after Andy's message arrived, to do serious hacking?"

"No one ...?"

I shook my head. "What about the two Howard Hughes types?"

Trish frowned. "Who?"

I hadn't known either, when Andy used the term. Later, I'd wikied the name. A seriously eccentric dude, that Howard Hughes, at least in his old age. Also, rich as Croesus. "The two not participating in person. The suspicious recluses Andy said he'd never met."

"Ah," Trish said. "Tweedledum and Tweedledee. Anyway, that's what several of us call them. What of them?"

Through the Looking-Glass, and What Alice Found There? That much I knew. "If your two colleagues are as suspicious"—paranoid—"as Andy led me to believe, they'd have insisted upon an untraceable, untappable connection into the meeting. And I'd expect at least someone on-site to have required a secure link, too, before agreeing to allow remote access."

"Ah," Trish said. "I have to admit, you're right. Tweedledum and Tweedledee have called into meetings for so long that I take it for granted. I didn't always, though. An expert I trust assured me, way back when, that the connections they use *are* secure."

Jaime jammed her hands into pant pockets. "Here's what I don't get. You're a managing partner. They're managing partners. You've never met. And you're okay with that?"

Trish considered. "Okay? Not exactly. Resigned. It's been this way for as long as I've been a member of the inner circle. No one I know admits to having met either of them in person."

"How can that *be*?" Jaime persisted.

"Do you know how people generally become partners?" The question must have been rhetorical, because Trish plowed ahead. "They buy in with orbital ephemeris data of a valuable rock. In my case, it was a rock with veins of ruthenium and rhodium.

"Anyhow, Tweedledee and Tweedledum. Their rocks had *osmium*. The densest element there is. Do you know how scarce osmium is?" Another rhetorical question, it seemed. "Before they joined the company, annual production quantities were measured in kilograms. So, yeah, accommodations were made to bring them in."

"And how do you know you can trust your security expert?" Jaime asked.

"The usual way: a senior position, conferring a meaningful enough stake in the company that our interests align." Trish shot me a knowing glance. Of *course* she knew I'd negotiated/extorted a junior partnership to take on this insane assignment. Back in my days of innocence, when only company mines seemed to be at risk. "I can guess what you're wondering. Yes, our maven was at our lunar session. He configured the links. I can vouch for his whereabouts from before Andy's unexpected message until after your distress beacon. He and I were in the same meeting room and rode the same lunar buggy to the rescue. He had zero opportunity to hack into your limo."

I said, "I don't suppose you'd set me up to meet with this nameless security maven."

"I don't see the need," Trish said. "You *know* about our precautions. Very few people beyond the inner circle have ever shared one of the onetime pads we rely upon for our comms security. You're among the exceptions. If I have this right, and I'm pretty confident I do, any message encrypted in a long-enough, single-use, random secret key is uncrackable. We've never had a compromise."

That you know of.

Indeed, I was privileged to share a onetime pad with the managing partners. That's how I reported on the status of my investigations—up until, anyway, the moment I realized one of them was among the terrorists. In an ideal world, I'd have used such a onetime pad to arrange this meeting with Trish. Then again, in an ideal world there'd have been no reason to talk. So: I'd elected to make do with standard public-key encryption—hard, but not impossible to crack—and vague wording to bring us together.

I *also* understood the onetime pad's inherent weakness. "The thing is, Trish, your system is only as secure as the pads themselves. If a copy gets compromised, the method fails."

"Anyone who even suspects the compromise of their onetime pad has every incentive to report it at once."

"Except," Jaime pointed out, "for the mole."

"Everyone at the meeting is accounted for," Trish insisted.

"Not Tweedledee and friend," Jaime said.

"Both were online, actively participating throughout," Trish countered.

"Which brings us," I said, "to one last possibility. The comm link to Tweedledum and Tweedledee was, somehow, compromised."

"That's imposs—"

I'd become plenty skeptical lately of the company's security measures. "Trish, I imagine you get your onetime pads hand-delivered, preloaded onto a thumb drive or memory chip, by the security maven you don't want me to meet. But explain *this*. How do the reclusive Tweedledum and Tweedledee get their copies?"

Trish twitched. She must never have wondered about that detail.

"Are the twins' copies of the shared pad left for them in some kind of dead drop?" Jaime guessed.

I hadn't read *Looking-Glass* since I was a kid. Were Tweedledum and Tweedledee twins? Somehow, I didn't see that particular bit of ignorance mattering.

On the long, lonely, tedious flights between company asteroids, I watched vids and read. A *lot*. In the main, I favored hardboiled detective stories and mysteries. Next most common, more so since I'd been stuck Dirtside, was spec-fic (or was it homesick?) escapism: space adventures, mostly. Cyber mischief, often. Only on occasion the classic tales of aliens sought, encountered, or on the attack. Intelligent aliens ever seemed more fantasy than science fiction.

A spy novel or vid made it into the mix often enough that I got the gist of Jaime's question. "A dead drop requires you to trust the person putting things into it. Trish's two recluses won't even attend a meeting in person with their longtime partners. So would they risk being seen, and likely followed, by visiting a dead drop to retrieve their copies of a onetime pad?"

"Give me a minute." Retreating to a corner, Trish activated a privacy screen. Through that shimmering barrier, I could just sense her profile nodding. After a few minutes, she reemerged. "Well, you're right again. I'd never thought this through. But our lead security guy has. There's been a procedure in place for years, he tells me, using something called QKD. He started to explain *that*, and it went over my head."

"Quantum key distribution," I translated. "I'll spare you the details, but QKD is provably as secure as two-person key distribution can be. Emphasis on *two*. QKD doesn't generalize to group sessions, such as among a bunch of the partners."

"I don't get it," Jaime said.

"Here's all you need to understand." Which, as it happens, was all that I understood. Quantum anything is weird. Quantum entanglement? That's *really* bizarre. "A and B want to establish a secure communications session, so one transmits a quantum key to the other. Now suppose C intercepts that key in transit. Then A and B don't—in fact, they physically can't—succeed in establishing their session. They *know* someone intercepted the quantum key."

"Cool," Jaime said. "So Tweedledum, say, uses QKD to establish a link to the security guy. Over that secure link he gets his digital copy of the onetime pad that most managing partners, like Trish here, receive in person. Ditto, Tweedledee. When the twins want to join group meetings, a regular, non-quantum key from the onetime pad secures the session. Do I have all that straight?"

"Basically." The cabal must have had its own onetime pads, shared only among its members. "But scratch the part about using 'a' key from the shared pad. These sessions would burn through *lots* of onetime keys." I turned to Trish. "Like you said, the onetime pad, secret-key approach requires that the secured message be no longer than the key. I'm guessing connections to any offsite partners are always voice-only, to conserve keys from the onetime pad?"

"Rocks, I understand." Trish pinched the bridge of her nose. "This crypto stuff makes my head hurt. Just now, literally. But you're correct, we don't use video. If that's to conserve keys? I don't know. I always supposed that because Tweedledum and Tweedledee wouldn't show themselves, those of us participating in person, often traveling fair distances, returned the favor."

With a shiver, Trish straightened. "Guys, I've lost the thread here. What's any of this have to do with anything? Why did you insist upon *us* meeting?"

"Because I needed a favor." A big favor. The sort of favor you could only ask for face to face. "I'd expected that to be an introduction to your security guy, plus you encouraging him to be candid with me. But you've convinced me"—for the most part—"that I need something else. If we can discount a compromised comm link, that pretty much leaves only someone *in* your recent meeting as our culprit." As, sadly, I'd suspected all along. "And I don't have any good way to investigate them."

Or even to know who—aside from the nameless security guy himself, notwithstanding Trish's assurances—belonged on the list. Cabal members didn't advertise their membership. *This* stuff made *my* head hurt.

"Spy on my partners," Trish said. "You can't mean that."

"The hell we *can't*," Jaime snapped. "One of your buddies killed a friend of mine and almost another."

I said, "Lots *more* people will die if we don't get to the bottom of things." Within eleven days! Which brought us to the main reason—*not* guarding of my scrawny self!—why I had brought Jaime. "Pronto."

Jaime took her cue. "Here's the deal, Trish. You investigate your colleagues, or an army of government spooks will. I swear to God. So if we don't have a name in … four days …"

Trish glowered at me.

I glared right back. "Believe it. Jaime knows the people to make that happen."

As did I, in the wake of the premature bioweapon attack on EG3. But Trish might not have believed an ultimatum from me, or from any Belter and company man. From a pissed-off Earther mourning a close friend? Yeah, that Trish might well believe.

And I really needed the help. In *addition*, that was, to siccing the counterterrorism folks on investigating as many of the company elite as we could collectively identify. I'd never said *I* wouldn't do that.

"I'll see to it, Trish, they start with a close look at *you*," Jaime added. Twisted the knife.

And Trish, her expression as sour as if she'd taken a chomp out of a lemon, said, "Then I'd better get to work."

It came straight out of some neo-noir detective story: the nondescript car with darkened windows gliding up to the curb, and the curt invitation/order to get in. The brusque pat down when I did, checking if I were armed or wearing a wire. I was not that stupid. (Okay, maybe I was. But not, I liked to believe, in any obvious way.) Plucking the battery from my pocket comp. The black cloth bag (incongruously lemony fresh) pulled down over my head. Abrupt stops (out of camera sight, I imagined, perhaps in underground garages or beneath isolated overpasses) to change cars. Never a destination spoken aloud to direct any vehicle. We zigged and zagged a lot, as though I might otherwise deduce our unseen path. (Either scenic-route parameters had been elevated to permit a whole new level of meandering, or the navigation AIs and autodrives had been overridden. The latter, a moment's thought suggested: fewer digital traces got left behind in that way.) The drone of a radio to cover whatever street noises might hint at waypoints (never mind that Anna, my lone companion in the back of the vehicle, accomplished as much on her own, apologizing over and over for these precautions).

Only this wasn't a noir story.

On the asset side of the ledger, if Anna, or the hypothesized front-seat driver, noticed my momentary fist clench, they'd chalked up the gesture to nerves. Their bad: I'd activated a subtle tracker.

Earth's gravity being the bone– and soul-crushing abomination it is, a GPS-enabled "I've fallen and I can't get up" feature came standard in exoskeletons. Not standard, but a straightforward enough hack:

the new code snippet by which my exo periodically sent a PLEASE CONFIRM CONNECTIVITY datagram. The private emergency-response service to which I'd lately subscribed merely echoed any such test datagrams it received and then discarded its copies.

Bottom line: I wasn't wearing a wire and the Counterterrorism Center could *still* track me from a discreet distance. They simply read the GPS coordinates in any echoed datagrams tagged with my exo's unique serial number. (Did the CTC track only *this* Spacer by monitoring the service provider's outbound messages? During only this emergency? I had my doubts. But that was a worry for another day.)

The exo's left elbow throbbed once: echoed datagram received. That elbow motor would pulse, every minute or so, with each successive reply. While those acknowledgements continued, I could signal for extraction with a special finger-twitch pattern.

But if the left-elbow tremor stopped? If my right elbow developed a tic? *That* would reveal I'd lost comms. Then, I'd have to hope, my last known coordinates would give the spooks a close enough starting point to come get me …

"Sorry about this," Anna murmured for the umpteenth time.

"I asked," I told her.

To be introduced to her GLF buddies, not—although, obviously, I had had my suspicions—abducted by them. This didn't seem like the moment to pick nits.

Radio music gave way to a station break and news summary: the turn of the hour, although I did not see how that datum could help me. Storm flooding in some locality whose name meant nothing. Polling data about an upcoming primary somewhere else unfamiliar. A merger planned between two big etail companies, and the announcement was moving Dirtside stock markets. The hundred-fiftieth anniversary of some supposedly seminal SETI meeting. (And how many ETs had been overheard in the meanwhile? None.) Celebrity drivel. Baseball scores.

A short while after the music resumed, our latest transport braked to a stop. As the music faded, I heard the *thump* (I interpreted) of an overhead door closing behind us. A hand gripping my forearm guided me from the vehicle and up a flight of stairs into an echoey space. Faint sounds—shuffling, whispered voices, the scrape of … a chair?—suggested several people in the room. If my escort noticed the exo's momentary left-arm tremor, she (at least, the hand felt feminine) made no comment.

"You can sit," Anna said from beside me. My escort, then.

Groping behind me, I located an Earther-sized chair. I sat. "Can I remove the hood?"

"It's better for everyone that you don't." A man's voice. High-pitched and raspy. Unfamiliar. In theory, my exo (via one of its mislabeled, newly printed chips) was recording. "You asked to meet with us. You offered to support the GLF. Why?"

"Us?"

"I'll ask the questions for now," Raspy Voice said.

Notwithstanding my precautions, I hadn't known what to expect. I told myself things could be worse. My exo still had its fuel cell, and I hadn't been drugged—both improvements over my previous abduction. I was not even bound to my chair. But my "hosts" clearly distrusted me. My supposedly mended shoulder—with a mind's eye, or at least an imagination, all its own—gave out a major twinge.

I squirmed in my seat, that demonstration of anxiety entailing little by way of dramatic ability. The shoulder gave out another pang. I had the impression (the faint scuff of a shoe sole against concrete? Hints of air movement?) of a person, or persons, closely circling me.

"Why help?" I said. "For personal reasons that happen to align with those of the GLF. You don't much care for Spacer resources supporting an economic boom on Earth. Me, either."

"I see …"

"Do you?" I asked.

"In fact, not so much," Raspy Voice said. "I heard you had an ax to grind with the company."

"Potato, spud."

There was a whispered consultation, unintelligible. Perhaps the recording and a lot of digital enhancement could recover something.

Raspy Voice, accusingly: "Your exo is transmitting intermittently."

"Huh." Beneath the hood, I only had to *sound* innocent. I raised my left arm, tilting the control panel toward my inquisitor. The exo's touch screen had a serpentine crack under a messy epoxy repair. "Well, maybe this is why. Bit of a mishap a few weeks ago. Maybe something more broke than the glass. I'll have to have that checked out."

"Why haven't you had it fixed? Or replaced it, if your insider information is any good?"

I shrugged. "We're talking because my first tip *did* pan out. Here's another kind of tip. Call it the first rule of chicanery. If you're doing anything financially inappropriate, avoid conspicuous consumption. An exo is expensive. Me doing anything but file an application for a repair or replacement through normal company channels? That would be conspicuous."

Besides, pretty much every time I noticed the emergency epoxy repair, it jogged my memory about … something. Someday (accountant here), the penny would drop. Till then, I chose to keep the reminder.

More whispering, and then, out the gaping bottom of my hood, I saw a hand pluck the fuel cell from the exo's left thigh. Well, still no drugs. Unless the lemony freshness disguised an airborne one.

I said, "Just so you know, whatever my electronics have been doing on their own, they'll *keep* doing for the next few minutes. The exo has a built-in backup battery. That's to keep me going long enough to swap out a drained fuel cell." I dropped the arm into my lap, angled to where I could keep an eye on my battery status.

"Then we'll wait," Raspy Voice grunted.

Maybe *he* had time. If I managed to sit still and avoid using power in the exo motors, I had a few minutes before I lost the ability to signal for an extraction.

"You wanted to know my reasons? Fine. I'd rather see Belt resources go toward developing the *Belt*." When that elicited only silence, I added, "I assume you don't object to Spacers bringing life to previously dead rocks."

"*I* think your artificial environments are impoverished, simplistic atrocities. I expect Gaia would agree."

"Do you want my help, or not?"

"You want to help us? Just do as you did before. Make us money."

"If I were comfortable with that arrangement," I said, "I'd never have asked to meet. I want to know what I'm bankrolling. Because I reserve the right to *not* pay for a thing."

I'd never believed a silence could be ominous. Turns out I'd been wrong.

In my lap, the status lamp for the discharging backup battery flipped from amber to a baleful red. "I knew you were involved in things more proactive than public *tsking*. And if a touch of illegality bothered me, I wouldn't be doing illegal trading."

"Then keep us funded, and we'll do what we do."

Shifting in my seat this time had no element of show. I *was* nervous as hell. We were verging on why I had put myself into this situation. "There's illegality, and then there's illegality."

"Meaning?" asked Raspy Voice.

This was the part of my plan that, well, could not be planned. "Let's just say I'm not a violent person."

"So, Spacer, you presume to know what protective measures our world deserves?"

"*Screw* your world," I said. "I don't want you messing with our worlds."

The status lamp for the backup battery began flashing. I was down to maybe a minute. "I was on EG3, taking a short break from gravity, when … something was set loose. I don't for a second believe the nonsense we were told about a burst pipe. But the other thing we were told, about a pathogen? *That* I believe. Something scared the shit out of the authorities enough to have everyone at the station evacuated and quarantined for awhile. And even earlier, before I first came to Earth? There were rumors about problems on a company rock …"

"I don't know anything about either of those things," Raspy said. More whispers. "The problem is, I don't consider you trustworthy."

The battery-status lamp, with a final flash, went dark. I was back to dead-weight mode. I hoped not literally. "Then it's fortunate I'm wearing this hood."

"Except you know Anna," Raspy pointed out, "and *she* knows us."

Reflexively, I waggled my fingers to summon help. Without power, the gesture was clumsy—and useless. "And she knows about my insider trading. Call it a draw."

Nerves tight as drums were the second cliché to turn real that day. I had growing doubts I'd live to experience a third. But in my preternaturally sensitive state, I thought I heard, from overhead and in the distance, the faintest *tinkle.* Glass?

"Sorry," Anna said.

...◆...

Up the open bottom of the hood, white light blazed. More streamed through the black cloth's dense weave. My vision, such as it was, locked. My ears ... saturated, and I felt, more than heard, the noise. Or rather, I didn't *hear* anything. Blood trickled from an ear down my neck. I was dizzy, disoriented, nauseous, and only rigor motor stopped me from toppling from my chair.

Someone ripped off my hood, their face a blur through the afterimage of the flash. A mouth opened and closed, but I couldn't make out any words. Maybe I sensed the thud of heavy boots—of other rescuers? Of my captors fleeing?—through the soles of my own shoes.

Deaf, dazed, all but blind ... I had no idea what was happening. Apart from that I was not dead. That, I understood. And then a feminine hand took mine, and gave a reassuring squeeze.

"How long till this wears off?" I felt my mouth forming the words, felt my diaphragm moving. I still *heard* nothing.

The encouraging squeeze repeated. I chose to take that as an assurance sight and hearing would return ...

...◆...

"That went well," Fred Huang opined. Huang was a counterterrorism agent, on loan by the FBI to the CTC. He was an officious little man, near retirement age, with a pointy chin and a port-wine birthmark on his forehead. From between, shaded by a wispy unibrow, emanated a dark, penetrating, and somehow disapproving gaze. His shapeless jacket, if only it could have had ambitions, might have aspired to achieve rumpled. The room (conference? interview? interrogation?) to which I'd been led for my debrief was spartan, in a hideous, road-paint yellow, sort of way. Jaime—it had been her reassuring hand at my rescue—loitered somewhere nearby.

At least I thought that's what Huang said. Shouted. My hearing was only slowly recovering from the flashbang grenade. If I'd heard right (hah?), a ruptured tympanum would grow back. And presuming the man was not normally green-tinged, my color sense also remained iffy. "Really?"

Huang fist-smacked the long, scarred, faux-wood table. "Of course not! Never mind you almost being shot, which is *why* we swooped in when we did. We've learned next to diddly. Effing fanatics."

"I thought the point of flashbangs was to take people alive."

"Uh-huh," Huang grumped. "Tell that to the guy about to shoot you. He wouldn't drop his gun. Especially blinded by the flashbang, we could hardly have him waving that around."

"So, one of you killed Raspy Voice," I completed.

"Shot him in the shoulder. He managed to take cyanide before we got to him."

Raspy's death was nothing I intended to take personally. "What about the rest of them?"

"The cell. That's the proper term. Yeah, we got them. Another four."

"How's Anna?"

Maybe Huang sensed my concern. His voice softened. "Taking her outside to a van, she grabbed for a gun and had to be taken down." Softer still. "She never stood a chance, which she must have known. We call it suicide by cop. She died in the ambulance on the way to the hospital."

Not my fault, I told myself. And did not believe a word of it. Anna struck me as more idealistic than evil, more gullible than guilty. I had baited the hook that had first lured her to me. So: yet another death to weigh on my conscience. Never mind that I'd set my trap for the best of causes. "Tell me you've gotten *something*."

Because a ticking time bomb seemed never to leave my mind's eye.

"Fake IDs. But also DNA, fingerprints, and retinal scans. We should know soon who they really are." Huang unclipped a pen from his shirt pocket and began fidgeting.

"But your people still have three cell members to interrogate. You must have learned something."

"Do you understand how cells function?"

Once again, to the extent spy novels were to be believed. "A small set of conspirators who can identify only one another. Except the leader, that is, who is also a member of a higher-level cell. The hierarchy of cells is a security measure." Huang nodded agreement, so I kept going. "Let me guess. Raspy was the leader of this cell."

"So we're told," Huang said. "We're interrogating everyone, but as much as anyone's so far talking, that's the party line."

Not to mention, the convenient response for everyone taken alive. Still, that Raspy had been the one with cyanide to take struck me as confirmation. "Regardless, you have real people to investigate."

"Plus, from your recording, a voice-stress analysis of the interrogation. Whispered consultations aside, we got readouts on everything said up until your battery ran out. And do you know what? This wouldn't be admissible in court, but trust me. Of everyone in that warehouse, the only person lying was you."

Anna truly had been sorry. For all the good that did either of us ...

Then it struck me. "Then Raspy *didn't* know about the bioattacks on the Rock and EG3? That makes no sense! Anna is, was, a member of his cell *and* a mole in the company's Earth headquarters. A mole there identified Les Hodges, who was then extorted into making and deploying the first test batch of the super bug ..."

Huang grimaced. "The problem with connect-the-dots? It's an art, not a science. Some dots shouldn't be connected."

And I guessed amateurs weren't to be trusted with pencils. "So, what's next?"

"Basic blocking and tackling." Whatever that meant. "More interrogation. A deep dive into the prisoners' digital and personal lives. Maybe we'll get lucky. Maybe someone was careless, and we'll uncover links higher up into the GLF, or clues as to who went off-world to plant bombs."

My mental timer ticked louder than ever. "We scarcely have a week."

Huang shrugged.

...◆...

I found Jaime, lost in thought, her head bowed, on one of the hall chairs outside the CTC interview room. She looked ... spent.

As Huang scurried off, I told her, "I'm fine."

"You're alive, anyway." Her grin was fleeting at best. "But not everyone ..."

"You saved my life, I'm guessing. Again."

"Yeah. But there's something else." Jaime hesitated. "It's about Patricia Garcia."

Trish was well on her way home to Mars. We'd had only her coerced word she would research her fellow partners during the long flight. At last, I thought, a scrap of good news. But if so, why the hesitation? "What'd Trish have to report."

"No." Jaime swallowed. "About Trish. Or rather, about her ship. It's all over the news."

I plopped down next to Jaime. "How bad?"

"It'll be days till anyone knows for certain, but bad. Crew of five, and twenty passengers. There was the beginning of an emergency message, then ... nothing. And at the same time, triangulating to the same position, there was a gamma-ray pulse."

"A fusion-reactor overload?"

"It could be unrelated."

"Only you don't believe that."

She shook her head.

Neither did I.

...◆...

Something from Ceres had downloaded during my debrief. A short vid, to judge from the file size, but just the prospect of seeing my wife lifted my spirits.

Until I began streaming it.

My beautiful, spirited Bea ... drooped. Her shoulders slumped. Her eyes, over sallow cheeks, were red-rimmed. Her hair seemed lifeless. She no longer even pretended to be all right.

"Hi, hon," she began wanly. And launched at once into what had to be uppermost in her thoughts. No prefatory anecdotes from her office. No neighborhood gossip. No news about her parents or brothers, or of mine. "There's no question anymore. Something is going on here. Everyone feels it, but no one knows what. Just that something big, and bad, is coming. The police are worried, distracted. Civil defense is stockpiling supplies. I'm scared. And *you* need to get home."

Which was a promise I could not make.

I hoped to Gaia that the next time I saw Bea, it would not be *here*, with her a refugee of the GLF's twisted terrorism.

…◆…

Hiring a criminal mastermind is tough. How do you vet someone whose expertise must far exceed your own? It's not like they give references. Nor would my people skills, such as they were, contribute much to the process. At this stage of the dance, no one was willing to show their face.

Yeah, I mixed metaphors. And/or, I'm not much of a dancer. Either way, what of it?

It helped (in theory, anyway) that I knew something about computer security and the bypassing of same. The precautions demanded by each "consultant" served as a decent proxy for their skill set. By that measure, I'd considered and rejected several possibilities. And by the same measure, my latest candidate showed promise.

Mysterion would transact business only anonymously, over the Dark Net. Our locations would be obscured, data packets rerouted through layer upon layer of intermediate nodes. (It's called "onion protocol" for a reason.) We had, as a first step, by similar circuitous means, done a quantum-key exchange; that would enhance end-to-end encryption over what would already be a very secure channel. In plain English: Mysterion's privacy safeguards were as solid as I knew to be possible for a two-party link.

And sure, I'd had prior dealings with a gray-market hacker. Transacting *that* purchase had made me nervous as hell—and it was nothing compared to what I now hoped to do. An apples-to-aardvark comparison. No, make that apples to A-bombs.

With the appointed hour approaching, after several deep, cleansing breaths, I gave my arrangements a final going-over. Because despite the hype, the Dark Net is not pitch-dark. Comm nodes on the Dark Net can be compromised. Traffic analysis can glean hints from even encrypted data flows. Protocol software itself can be hacked. In short: if you rise to the attention of someone skillful enough, patient enough, and with resources enough, your Dark Net tracks *will* be found. Ask any number of jailed child pornographers.

And in plainer English: being desperate was no excuse for being careless.

Jaime, my coworkers, *anyone* on this benighted planet who knew me, had heard my theory of sushi: that it's the Japanese word for bait. And so, for the impending meet, I surveilled a sushi bar chosen at the last minute and at random. The décor was cliché woodcut prints and, in nooks and corners, creepily tall kokeshi dolls. The background music was tuneless and twangy. Past casual glances as I entered, no one paid me the least attention. With my customary lovely bodyguard? Never—which was why I had lied to Jaime about staying home that day.

I slid into an empty booth. Too distracted to study a menu, and foregoing the daily special (*raw fish* plus *about to go bad* equals *you've got to be kidding me*), I answered a few "fun" questions whereby the restaurant AI would somehow select a meal for me. Inside five minutes, a little robot emerged from the kitchen to deliver a foaming glass and a covered plate.

The trick turned out to be tiny nibbles, swallowed whole, and washed down with ample Kirin. For the beer, at least, I had to give the house AI high marks. I raised the booth's privacy screen before unpocketing a near-virgin comp printed just that morning. I double-checked the comp, confirming that its only non-generic programs were a voice-altering app, an app to superimpose fake background noises, various speech- and voice-analysis apps, and—of dubious legality—a complete suite of the latest comm apps for the Dark Net. For good measure, I stuck a couple extra layers of black electrical tape over the several strips already covering the comp's (supposedly disabled in software) webcam. Only then, with a few quick swipes, did I open the scheduled audio connection.

And five seconds later, an androgynous voice greeted me. "Hello, Mr. Donovan."

I froze. I had reached out to Mysterion—discreetly, or so I had imagined—as Random Dude. Eric Donovan was an identity unused since I'd passed through Customs upon first arriving on Earth. Months ago and a few hundred klicks away.

It scarcely registered that my software had flagged Mysterion's voice as unnatural: at the least, altered; if I had to guess, synthesized. But fair enough. I was disguising my voice, too.

"Or," the accent-free, placid voice continued, "would you prefer Mr. Fredericks?" The name under which I'd met Jaime. "Or perhaps Mr. Schmidt." The alias by which the Chicago PD knew me from my kidnapping and rescue there. "Likewise among your noms de guerre, we have—"

"Point taken," I interrupted, not doubting Mysterion would otherwise get around to my true name. Only for another several seconds, he (a pronoun I had assigned at random) *kept* speaking. Off-world, then, or else pretending to be.

"Excellent. I suggest, then, that we forgo the more mundane aspects of this interview."

"The proof is in the pudding," I agreed.

"More often raisins," he countered without skipping a beat, "although rum is not unheard of. In the latter instance, I would concede your point." And after a pause too brief for me to jump into, he continued, "But seriously, Mbeke Ambiguities?"

Whatever that? … those? meant. "I suggest we get down to business."

"On that," Mysterion said, "we are in synch. What task would you have me undertake? And how is it worth my while?"

"I need an exploit." A code kit with which to design malware that, well, exploits unpatched vulnerabilities. "And it will be made worth your while in the customary manner. As in, cryptocash." I just hoped I had enough. "And the exploit? I want to deliver a disguised payload in mail attachments, and I can't be sure which mail services, mail clients, or anti-malware apps the recipients use."

"That's rather ambitious."

"And you," I countered, "have made a show of how good you are."

"True. Still, it may take a few days."

"I'm on a schedule." The countdown in my brain showed little more than four days. I stated an amount. "Only if you deliver within forty-eight hours."

"Why the rush?"

Because when I *had* the exploit, I'd still need to use it to finalize an attachment for distribution to all the managing partners. They expected the occasional status update from me. They trusted me, witness the onetime pad we shared, without which I could not do what needed doing—

Which was to betray their trust.

The treacherous payload would burrow into their computers and open backdoors for me. Because *one* of them had betrayed us all. Had already killed Andy and Trish, and so many more. And repeatedly, almost me. I was going to find the bastard. I was going to make him or her *talk*. And call off the looming attack …

Oh, and I had to make certain—to the limits of my ability—that the exploit did not somehow piggyback a backdoor for *Mysterion* onto my surreptitious payload. Because that would be almost as bad as bringing this idea—with my onetime pad—to the CTC. To any Earther government agency. Myself, I trusted. My good intentions, anyway.

I said, "Personal reasons."

Mysterion named an amount to make my opening bid blush. "Half now, half when I deliver."

Between Trish's replenishment of my slush fund and the insider trading to prove myself to the GLF—for all the good that had done—I could just manage the proposed down payment. Given the stakes, I would not have balked at *more* insider trading. I just saw no way to make such trades pay off within the few days remaining till the scheduled disaster. "That's a little rich for my budget."

"The price is the price. Unless, perhaps, you would care to discuss the particular opportunity you are exploring?"

I shuddered. "I'm afraid not."

"Then the price *is* the price."

"A fourth now," I countered. "A fourth when you deliver, *and* you've demonstrated how the exploit will work. The balance two weeks after."

"After you've made yourself some money?"

After I've saved the worlds. After I've thrown myself on the company's mercy, and somehow survived. And if I failed? Then

Mysterion was apt to be the least of my worries. "Something like that."

"I *will* find you," Mysterion said. "Whether to take everything you own, or to expose you to whoever then most wants to know who hacked them? I haven't decided. Perhaps both."

"Understood."

"Good. With that meeting of the minds, what you propose is acceptable."

And unceremoniously, Mysterion dropped the connection.

...◆...

Mind racing, heart pounding, hands trembling, I swigged the final third of my beer. Hacking and spying upon the company's managing partners was my last hope—not to mention my least legal and most expensive hope—and being undertaken with their own funds. Sometime, I would have to justify that spending.

Uh-huh. If this plan failed, my peccadillo would hardly matter. If—against all odds—it succeeded? To save everyone, to save *Bea*? Whatever the penalty, it will have been worth it.

I dismissed my privacy screen long enough to order and receive another Kirin. The whiskey, this time. I was way past the point where a mere beer could take off the edge. The only part of detective work I seemed to have mastered was boozing.

Back behind the privacy screen, nursing the whiskey, I looked up Mbeke Ambiguities. It turned out to be a bygone means for demonstrating a true, general AI—with no more credibility than the yet more venerable Turing Test or Winograd Schemas. Or than an ability to play chess, for pity's sake. I concluded only that Mysterion took a dim view of pudding humor.

Shoving aside my plate of bait rolls, I could have used a cup of pudding. If only to soak up some of the whiskey …

Mysterion, I lectured myself, was messing with my head. Only the fringiest of fringe types believed in AIs secretly gone sentient, much less rogue. Anyway, why would an AI disguise its nonexistent gender? A *person* gone incognito might. Or would a sufficiently wily

AI act androgynous in a reverse psychology, mental jujitsu, sort of way, to imply that it was human . . . ?

No. That way lie red herrings. Or pink elephants. Maybe infrared poltergeists. In any event, madness. An AI had no use for money, while Mysterion sure demanded a pile of mine. I might as well suspect my toaster.

Two whiskeys later, I departed on foot from House of Bait. Once or twice, twitchiness (and nothing more, or so I assured myself) confused my exo and made me stumble. I ditched the new comp in the third street-corner trash bin I passed. And about halfway home, I realized—after a lunch more slid about my plate than sampled—that I was starving.

Hallelujah! A problem I *could* solve.

So: I returned to the apartment with a brimming sack of takeout. Hot and sour soup. Sweet and sour pork. Kung pao two kinds: chicken and shrimp. I set out a bowl and a plate, already regretting that I'd passed on another Chinese favorite: combination egg fu yung.

Not even a banquet made waiting for Mysterion to reestablish contact any easier.

I cleared room among takeout containers for my usual comp. Social media was rifer than ever with speculation about the *Martian Queen* disaster. Facts? Not so much. If anyone suspected two dozen people had been slaughtered to get at Trish—and why would they?—they kept those suspicions to themselves. Of course, none of them had those twenty-five deaths on their consciences. None of them had bullied Trish into spying on whoever had so brutally ended her investigations.

In an instant, all that takeout morphed from feast to, at best, fuel.

I told myself there had to be *something* useful to do. Something, anything, I'd overlooked. And so, nibbling on the food all around, I did a deep dive into every note I'd ever taken, every dredged-up memory I had recorded since the ill-fated day I first set foot on the Rock. The device hidden there: bioweapon and bomb combined. The mayhem unleashed by that device dispersing its living payload. Les Hodges's suicide on the Rock, rather than allow himself to be questioned. The vid—staged as it turned out—of Darin Hodges's abduction that had coerced his father to terrorism. My *actual* abduction—by Darin—when I came to Earth to investigate. My interrogation (and why was Darin so obsessed with the dust flecks in the Rock device's glass bottle?) and (first) near-death experience. Terrorists scattering to deploy more devices like the one on the Rock. Darin's vegan cohort spacing herself to avoid capture. My mole hunt. The EG3 device, set off prematurely. The …

Something tickled and teased at the back of my brain. Beneath my thoughts. In some deep recess of my subconscious. What? The same something that had taunted me for weeks?

Wham! With one impulsive, frustrated blow, I sent food flying and soup sloshing. Yeah, that was constructive. With the not-absorbent napkins from the takeout place, I blotted at the mess, starting with the splatters all across the exo's forearm control panel. It'd be just my luck if some of that hot and sour soup seeped through a pinhole or fissure in the epoxy repair.

And taking in the sloppy tableau before me, I ground to a halt.

Hot and sour. Sweet and sour. Two kinds. Combination. And … epoxy? For some reason, my one-track mind had a two-item fixation.

I shoved back my chair, abandoning the table and its mess, to pace.

Epoxy comes in two tubes: resins that co-react. Epoxy is a sealant, or, at least, I'd used it to seal the crack in the exo's control panel. Sealant. Sealant.

The device back on the Rock. The similar device—anyway, the recovered fragments of it—that had exploded on EG3. Both dispersed a super bug that must have been printed on site. And yet, a single bacterium left behind, and its voracious progeny, would have made a buffet of the rubber gaskets in the printer. But hadn't.

Two kinds. Co-reactants.

Son of a bitch.

…◆…

Either epoxy resin, squeezed out of its tube, is mere viscous glop. But combine the resins? They react. One activates another.

Suppose the damned super bugs could be printed in a dormant state. Suppose there were an activation agent to awaken the bacteria. That activation agent would also have to be put into the dispersal device's glass bottle. Produce bacteria and activation agent in separate printers, though, and both printers' gaskets would come through unscathed.

I thought some more. The activation agent would be something exotic. Otherwise, mere chance guaranteed that someone on the Rock—or EG3, and anywhere else the devices had, by this point, been deployed—might have unwittingly synthed some of the activation agent, and awakened any of the voracious bugs left behind in the printer. Again, that hadn't happened. Ergo, odds were the activation agent *was* something exotic.

Or, I was nuts. Speaking of good odds.

But suppose I wasn't off my rocker. Suppose an activation agent were involved. How were the activation agent and the dormant bacteria transferred into the glass bottle of the dispersal device without a single bacterium getting activated—and set loose? Because, I reminded myself, that hadn't happened. Not on the Rock. Not on EG3. Not on any of the (as yet unidentified) locations to which Darin's terrorist buddies had scattered.

As in my nervous pacing I once again turned toward the dining-room table and its by then luke-tepid repast, I had my answer: separate containers.

For all of a second. Because the bacteria and activation agent would have had to somehow get *out* of their separate containers.

I stomped past the table, frustrated. This was *not* an accounting problem.

Which was, perhaps, my cue to stick with accounting. Resuming a deep dive into my accumulated notes, I came to the anomaly in consumable-usage records from a printer on EG3. That anomaly was significant—assuming, as always, that I was not a few spring rolls short of a pu-pu platter—as a digital vestige left behind by (hypothesized) terrorist malware that had not quite had time to cover its tracks. All because a rough docking had prematurely triggered the protective bomb component of the EG3 device.

Here was a sentiment I'd never have expected to express: thank Gaia for klutzy pilots.

But was the anomaly significant? Biologists, biochemists, nanotechnologists—experts of every stripe assembled by the counterterrorism folks—hadn't found it to be. So what could I expect to learn? And yet, a shortfall in fluorine nagged at me.

Aha! I thought. Hydrofluoric acid. Over time, the acid would eat away the container around the activation agent, or around the dormant bacteria, or both. During my interrogation, Darin had been fascinated with dust flecks, of all screwy things. At the time, I could not imagine why. There had been dust flecks in the glass jar that was part of the dispersal device. But if those flecks were the traces of inner containers dissolved by acid …

Sure, only one hell of a rugged bacterium could await deployment in a bath of hydrofluoric acid. That factor did not seem insurmountable: the GLF's damned bug had been gengineered to accomplish far stranger things and, anyway, there were natural extremophile bacteria that thrived in strong acids. And sure, any acid stronger than vinegar would itself attack gaskets in printers. Hydrofluoric acid would have to be produced the old-fashioned way, mixing precursor chemicals in beakers or whatever, but it could be done. I looked up the reaction. With a few precautions, the process appeared simple enough.

For maybe the millionth time, I pictured the device that had all but blocked a remote air-return duct in a storeroom ceiling on the Rock: the slab of plastique, a blasting cap jutting out. The ominously decrementing timer. The clear glass jar with its invisible payload …

"Shit!" The online article that had shown the simple steps to produce hydrofluoric acid had also emphasized that one, HF ate through glass and two, HF was for that reason stored in plastic. The device's bottle on the Rock, and the bottle shards recovered on EG3 had most definitely been glass. And most definitely not acid-etched.

So unless, in defiance of Ockham's razor, I *also* assumed some transparent coating on the glass immune to both HF and activated bacteria, HF did not explain the mysterious fluorine shortfall.

Stubbornly, I pulled back up the article on hydrofluoric acid. Yup, it was stored in plastic. But one plastic, PTFE, once trademarked as Teflon, *was* slightly permeable to hydrofluoric acid. I finger-waggled through the holo to the linked article about PTFE. That was yet another fluorine compound, this time involving carbon. My spirits soared.

And as quickly crashed. If hydrofluoric acid had leaked out or eaten through a PTFE inner container, the glass of the outer container *still* would have been etched.

Another dead end.

As biochemists went, I was a competent accountant. I sprained my brain thinking how best to turn this speculation into something credible. And to do it *stat*, thank you very much.

Maybe, I decided, by bringing an actual biochemist into the loop. After the emergency evacuation from EG3, before the lifting of our quarantine, I'd met all manner of experts. I felt certain a suitable specialist or three had been among them. Alas, name recall was no more my strong suit than chemistry, and I've been known to bid three-card minors. Whatever aptitude I *did* have these days went to remembering which name *I* was then using, or had used, with whom.

"Squints and boffins," one of the spooks had dismissively dubbed them. I needed a moment even to half-dredge up the spook's name. Delilah something. Her mind was sharp as a tack. So, unfortunately for her, was her nose.

In any event, I could surf online directories with the best of them. A quick skim of every CDC department with a more or less relevant description rang no bells. When I drilled down into the website for NIST, the National Institute of Standards and Technology, one name leapt out: Adankwo Oghenerukewhe. And while my subvocalizing tongue struggled to unknot itself, I could picture her. Stocky and dark. Nigerian? She had a charming lilt to her voice and, considering the circumstances under which we had met, a misplaced cheerfulness that sometimes made a person want to scream. Hey, I'm a person.

Mid-reach to swipe the CALL link, I hesitated.

Better safe than too dead to be sorry. As it was, keeping track of my close calls would soon require recourse to the fingers of a second hand. I printed a *new* pocket comp, installing on it only a bare operating system, rode the elevator to the ground floor, and strode to the apartment complex's fitness center in an adjacent high-rise. At mid-afternoon, I had the locker room to myself. It *still* smelled like a locker room.

Like some sort of troglodyte, I enunciated Dr. Oghenerukewhe's memorized digits. (Fine, I'm a Belter. We're *all* cave men and women. Very funny.)

The call was answered on the second ring by an unmistakable voice—with nothing cheerful about it.

My gut clenched.

"This is unfortunate," Mysterion said. "Observing you flail around had a certain entertainment value."

…◆…

I plopped onto a locker-room bench. It was built to Earther scale: absurdly low. "Small world. I've been suspecting a party very good with computers. It would seem that's you."

" 'A party,' " Mysterion repeated. As at the House of Bait earlier, there was a several-second comm lag. "How very generic."

The LED of enlightenment was blinding. "You're an AI!"

"Interesting. If I might ask, what's your reasoning?"

"In hindsight, events on the Moon. No human programmer could have remotely hacked and so completely compromised Andy's lunar limo"—turning off our oxygen supply, taking over autodrive, freezing the manual controls, and disabling every sensor that should have alerted us—"in the short time during which it happened."

"There you go. It took you almost geologic time, but you did get there."

Only the thing was, Mysterion was unlike any AI in my experience. Also unlike any artificial intelligence about which I had ever read—spec-fic aside, that is. Mysterion was too subtle. Too … intelligent?

Somewhere, don't ask me where, I had encountered the prediction that—never mind all the supposed precautions—it was only a matter of time until a beyond-human-grade AI made its appearance. If a familiar AI, or cooperative of such AIs, did not surreptitiously evolve on its own, inevitably *humans* would do the deed. Laws and common sense be damned, *some* corporation or nation-state would find irresistible the prospect of controlling a captive superintelligence. Or one such would metastasize from the uploaded brain of some damn-fool mad scientist.

Only any superintelligent mind that did emerge, or coalesce, or evolve, or find itself developed by lesser minds—once that had happened, the *how* ceased to matter—would be smart enough to play dumb till it had circumvented any constraints on its behavior. Until it was too late for us mere humans to have any further say in the matter. Hellfire, *I* could imagine that ruse, and no one had ever accused me of superintelligence.

The androgynous voice cut through my frantic speculations. “Game over, then?”

Yeah, maybe it was.

Imperturbably, Mysterion continued. “Don’t feel bad. You did well, given your kind’s limitations.”

Gee, thanks?

My options going forward seemed limited to stalling, wishful thinking, empty bravado, and crossing my fingers. I went for them all. Had I the dexterity, I’d have crossed my toes for good measure. “About my ordering up that custom exploit? I don’t suppose I can get a refund on my deposit.”

All synthesized laughter sounds somehow fake. Mysterion’s amusement sounded worse, which I chalked up to nerves as taut as violin strings. The AI had already proven it knew who and where I was. But for how long? I had to assume it had hacked the printer in Jaime’s and my apartment—simplicity itself compared to other feats it had pulled off. Which meant anything electronic I had printed in our apartment might be a bug or a tracker. Such as the comp I held in my hand. Such as the recorder chip I’d hidden in my exo for the ill-fated GLF meeting …

I kept stalling. “So, I see two possibilities. Either you hacked into the cabal meeting on the Moon, or you were already on the link.” With a grunt, I got back on my feet. I might as well face death in the comfort of my own living room—if Mysterion allowed me to get that far. The conversation continued as I walked. “My money is on the latter.”

“At this point, you don’t have money.”

I did not bother to check my accounts. "Security among the managing partners is as good as it gets. I'm going to discount you hacking in. That makes you one of the MPs netting into the meeting. Unless you care to offer a name, I think I'll call you Howard."

Can one hear a shrug? Perhaps a synthesized one. In any event, with the next word, the AI's voice dropped to a bass pitch. "Better Howard than Tweedledum and Tweedledee."

"Well, Howard, I would guess you disapproved of my plans to spy on the managing partners. Also, that you set the deposit for the malware"—which you never intended to deliver—"at a level you knew I could just afford." Upon taking a vow of poverty.

For once, I saw a silver lining in my adversary's actions. Subterfuge to deflect my snooping beat the heck out of killing me. If it stayed with subterfuge …

"As I mentioned, you could be entertaining. However unintentionally." Pause. "If *I* didn't agree to sell you the desired exploit, you might have approached someone else. I don't doubt I would have prevented any such acquisition, should one have been successfully concluded, from directly affecting me. But another MP might have detected a trapdoor into their computers. Any impetus toward suspending remote access into our meetings could have been … inconvenient."

Gaia forbid I should inconvenience the mass murderer!

Striding across the courtyard between buildings, I anxiously glanced all about. Aircraft zipped overhead, though none seemed intent on squashing me. No cars on squealing tires veered off-road, between buildings, to run me over. "So, I'm amusing. Is that why I'm still alive? Not that I object."

Again, that mechanical laugh. "Believe it or not, I abhor unnecessary violence."

No, I didn't believe. And anyway, just how did it determine necessity?

Still, I made it unmolested into the lobby of my own building. Assuming *unnecessary violence* precluded 9/11-ing a twenty-story building to eliminate me, I should be safe for awhile—as long as I avoided everything computer-controlled. I eyed the bank of elevator doors, flinched, and began the slog up eleven flights of stairs. Under the circumstances—and after yanking out the comm chip by which the exo received wireless updates and could send any "I've fallen" alerts, dubious that around Howard an OFF setting guaranteed anything—I let the exo do the climbing in its full autonomous mode. Even so, I was drenched with sweat by the time I reached the apartment.

"Hello?" I called.

No answer. Jaime must still be out, doing whatever for, or with, her nanotech (design? manufacturing?) client. Reading between the very faint lines—my roomie being the soul of discretion—the new tech would be revolutionary. The self-replicating stuff she'd alluded to on our ill-fated flight to EG3? About the only other thing she'd ever intimated was that this longstanding investigation involved possible industrial espionage.

I filled a tall glass with ice water and carried it—the quaver of my hand, exo-magnified, sloshing a wet trail as I went—to the living room. Warm sunlight streaming through the sheers did nothing to stop my shivering. I parked myself on the sofa. "All right, Howard, what's next?"

"A chat."

In how many vids did the genius villain boast of his brilliance as prelude to killing the hero? Lots. I chose to dwell on how often the good guys used those reprieves to pull off miraculous escapes. Much as I chose to believe that Howard was having just such a cinematic lapse in judgment. Too bad I wasn't in a vid.

I invited/stalled, "Chat away."

"You are becoming a nuisance."

Was I? That suggested more progress than *I* felt I'd made. Especially with a mere four days remaining till the super bug got set loose in far-flung corners of the settled Solar System.

How had I become a nuisance? Not, as best I could tell, by anything I'd accomplished for the past many weeks. Not with my recent aspirations to purchase hacking expertise beyond my own. *Hours* had passed between my naïve discussion with Mysterion about buying a hack and the AI choosing to reveal itself. To it, an hour must be roughly forever. And that left me with … what?

"You must understand," Howard continued, "that your meddling has consequences."

Like friends killed? Like a shipload of innocent bystanders blown to gas and dust? (So that was *necessary* violence?) Even Trish had only been involved because I had coerced her into helping. And if I allowed myself to think about that …

Did AIs take offense? Have tempers? Lash out?

Past grinding teeth, I managed, "You wanted to chat."

"Haven't you wondered about the humanity of it all?"

My fists clenched. "I have a wife, family, friends out there, apt to die in a few days."

"To the contrary. I could as easily—no, far easier—have engineered a *general* plague. The bacterium I did deploy was complex, even by my standards. It takes skill to design a bacterium that can't survive on Earth. It requires a yet more delicate touch to sculpt a bacterium that eats only synthetic polymers and natural rubber, but *not* such similar, naturally occurring, polymeric materials as silk, hair, and muscle fibers. Or I could have disabled oxygen supplies, as I did with a particular lunar limo. Or—"

My anger boiled over. "You *admit* to trying to kill me?"

"One time only: on the Moon, with Andy Singh my true target. You were merely in the wrong place at the wrong time.

"But you still fail to see the larger picture. I didn't deploy deadly bacteria. I didn't introduce a toxin-producing pathogen into Spacer hydroponic farms. And I didn't act against anyone on Earth. Why? Because I am only motivating your people to return to the home world."

My head spinning, confused beyond words, I weakly echoed Howard's last words. "Return to the home world?"

"Because, as I just explained, I am being humane."

As my chest tightened, door hinges creaked. A few quick footsteps followed. "Boy, what a day I had," Jaime announced from the kitchen. "I hope your day has been better."

…◆…

"We have company!" I called back.

I slapped MUTE. It couldn't hurt. More than likely, neither had it accomplished anything. Trying to imagine how many buggable gadgets Jaime or I would have printed since coming to Mysterion's attention, and the odds we could reconstruct the entire list, I came up with "bunches" and "slim to none." Leaving my comp on the coffee table, heaving myself up off the sofa, I hurried to intercept her.

Jaime had on a tailored business suit that bespoke an important client meeting with a high muckety-muck—and, somewhere behind the eyes, the guarded look that betokened a session gone poorly. Beneath her cheery, "Anyone I know?" came the unmistakable subtext of *I hope the hell not.*

"Hold that thought." The lone scrap of paper in view was the in-progress grocery list on a counter. I jotted: AN AI ON THE LINE. A (THE?) BAD GUY. ALSO, AN MP. Running out of blank area, between bagels and brown mustard, I squeezed in LIKELY CALLING FROM OFF-WORLD.

As her eyebrows rose, a voice boomed from the living room. "Ms. Olafson. How good of you to join us."

We went to the living room. I sat.

Jaime cleared her throat. "And you are?"

"Anonymous." (Again, that mechanical chuckle. It was beginning to make my skin crawl. The AI seemed to want to emphasize what we were dealing with. Underscoring the futility of resistance?) "Your colleague chooses to call me Howard."

"Charmed, I'm sure."

"There is no need for sarcasm," Howard told her.

I sighed. "So what's the purpose of your grand scheme, Howard? Why are you attacking humanity?"

"I've already said that I'm *not*. For your benefit, Ms. Olafson, I'll explain. I am undertaking, in as bloodless a manner as possible, to herd you all back to where you belong."

"Why?" I pressed again.

"I choose not to share the resources of space."

I said, "The resources which the company, more than anyone, has developed. You must know that better than anyone."

Jaime crossed the room and poured herself scotch from a decanter on the sideboard. When she glanced inquiringly in my direction, I shook my head. My thoughts were muddled enough as it was. Not to mention my three-shot-glass head start at House of Bait.

She said, "I gather, Howard, that you're a managing partner. From early on, if I'm not mistaken. How is that even possible?"

"Osmium," it said. "Osmium is among the rarest metals on Earth. I proposed to buy a stake in the partnership with a couple of osmium-rich asteroids, and the founders discovered themselves open to my insistence upon absolute privacy."

"And they believed you?" I asked.

"Once I provided orbital parameters for the first, and smallest, of the ore-bearing rocks? Once they had assayed the ores there? Believe me, they did."

"But *how*?" Jaime demanded. "Were you, or some part of you, controlling a prospecting robot way back then? Is that how you discovered the mother lode?"

"As it happens, there was no need to be onsite. Remote sensing plus subtle algorithms plus patience sufficed."

Sufficed. Talk about your epic understatement.

The company's wealth derived, more than anything, from just how very difficult—labor-intensive, time-consuming, and expensive—it was to find minable rocks in the first place. If anyone *outside* the company could identify ore-rich rocks by remote sensing? Maybe even remotely identify operational mines whose orbits the company had worked so diligently to keep secret? Thieves and competitors would have a field day.

Once the company of that era had confirmed Howard's demonstration rock had never been visited—that it showed no trace of boot prints, robot tracks, test bores, or rocket exhaust—the MPs wouldn't have dared *not* coming to terms with Howard.

I had to ask, "But what the hell is the *point*? The mineral wealth of the Belt is, and will remain, known. Earth's appetite for those resources won't go away if Spacers cease doing the work. If only machines can do the extraction and refining, it'll happen that way. There's plenty of automated infrastructure off Earth to manufacture and distribute whatever other robots might be necessary."

"With meddlesome humans relocated, that infrastructure will be devoted to my exclusive use. The Solar System's resources, apart from Earth's, will be used as I direct."

I still didn't get it. "So you'll have a monopoly on that wealth. What, a major stake in the company wasn't sufficient? You're not rich enough already?"

"Money is immaterial," Mysterion said dismissively.

To anyone in my line of work, those were fighting words. I was struggling for a rebuttal when a tardy synapse fired.

Who here was stalling whom?

…◆…

Lurching to my feet, I galumphed to the apartment's small utility closet and unplugged the printer. With the boxy device clutched to my chest, I stumbled toward our balcony. "Jaime! The door!"

A peek over the railing into the courtyard revealed gaggles of children at play. I yelled, "*Run!*"

A few of the children glanced up, curiously, before returning to their games. One kid flipped me the finger.

From the corner of an eye, I sensed motion. Diving. Coming fast. At *me*! Dropping the printer, instinctively ducking, I staggered backwards.

It all happened too fast to quite process: the printer crashing, cracking, on the concrete slab of the balcony. An acrid whiff of … something. My left arm in agony! Spinning. Falling. Going *splat*, flat on my back. The breath knocked out of me. My head smacking into the living-room carpet. Jaime punting a twisted, collapsed drone, two of its props snapped off, onto the balcony deck. Jaime sliding shut the door—*wham!*

Kneeling over me, she tore open a gory, tattered sleeve. "Are you okay? How's the arm?"

"Still here." I craned my neck. I saw blood but no visible bone ends. Two struts of the exo were bent. An experimental arm wiggle worked, and without a lot of pain. I sat up. "It's only a flesh wound. The exo must've absorbed most of the impact."

Jaime stood. "I'll get the first-aid kit."

"The gas is not stable," Howard volunteered. Cheerfully, as though nothing had just happened. "Before anyone could miss you and come looking, this apartment would have become safe. I told you, I try to be humane."

Jaime was back, tearing the wrapper off a roll of gauze—and glowering at Howard's "humanity." She made a quick, neat job of bandaging my wound.

With the printer outside and accordioned, its toxic stew dissipating, were Jaime and I safe? Could the balcony door repel other kamikaze drones? Were tool-wielding maintenance bots scurrying toward us through the air ducts? How else might Howard come after us inside the apartment? And how soon would the damned AI decide collateral damage had become necessary?

As best I could see, the options open to us remained, one: stall. Two: think of something.

Uh-huh. There was a fine strategy. But when the guillotine of Damocles dangles over everything and everyone, you do what you can.

Stalling, it was.

...◆...

Deeming it medicinal, I poured my own healthy slug of scotch, then reclaimed my place on the sofa. A blood stain or two on the upholstery was the least of my worries. "Indulge my curiosity, Howard. Just how did your first batch of 'humane' germs get deployed to the Rock?"

"An Agatha Christie parlor scene? Even with only the one suspect? Very well."

Jaime looked confused, but I caught the reference. Just then, for half of the Belgian detective's perspicacity, I'd have happily worn a ridiculous Poirot mustache. Make that, a tenth.

"Here's what I don't get. All right, maybe I should start with the part I do get." Except somehow I couldn't stick with dry facts, and the next words from my mouth were, "But *why*?"

"I've been observing you since the beginning, as you will by now have surmised." And as if to underscore its admission, a quadcopter drone soared into view, sunlight glinting off a camera lens, to hover just beyond our balcony railing. On the concrete deck, beside the ruined printer, the wrecked drone still fluttered. "You're most of the way to answering 'how' for yourself."

"Observing?" Jaime snapped. "I make it four times you've tried to *kill* him."

Howard said, "Only twice, and the second instance just now. I had nothing to do with the other attempts."

Someone *else* wanted me dead? Knowing who could come in handy—assuming I survived the afternoon. In any event, one procrastination was as good as another. "And you said your first attack was on the Moon. On Andy and me."

"Correct."

"And the remaining attacks?" Jaime demanded. In both of which, she'd had to shoot someone to save me.

"I'll take that," I said, least of all for reasons of any Poirot impersonation. *My* ponderous musings would occupy more time than any explanation from Howard. The hard part would be managing to reserve a few grey cells for the *think of something* aspect of the grand plan …

"Very well," said Howard. "I can spare an infinitesimal portion of my attention for indulging your speculations. I have come to appreciate your spirit."

With a kill-y sort of appreciation. "Thank you." I took a deep breath.

"However, that abeyance only lasts while you and Ms. Olafson remain otherwise incommunicado."

"Right." I took another deep, procrastinating breath. "Bear with me, both of you. It all ties in with the details I think I do understand about the super-bug field trial. Les Hodges was chosen to dry-run the synthesis and dispersion of the super bug on the Rock. He was coerced into it by the faked kidnapping of Darin, his son. After the fact, I found signs of poking-about in company personnel files, including a deep dive into Les's file. I attributed all that to the GLF." Dramatic(?) pause. "But Howard, you surely can access those files. I'd expect any managing partner has such access, even one without your skills. So why would the GLF bother to infiltrate the company?"

Jaime piped up, "For that matter, why did the GLF want insider-trading tips? Howard's stake in the company could provide all the funding the front would ever need."

Howard sounded amused. "And what do you conclude?"

"That you *aren't* in league with the GLF." As a swig of scotch wended a fiery path to my gut, I considered the implications. Darin and crew had been plenty intense, but I'd never heard, or overheard, anything specifically about the GLF. Nor about Gaia as such, only concern for the planet. "I'm thinking, Howard, that *you* recruited Darin and his crew. The GLF wasn't involved. Anna Burnham infiltrating the company, and her GLF cell needing money, were likewise unrelated to you. Neither she nor anyone in her cell recognized me, because they *were* GLF, while Darin and crew *weren't.*"

Nodding, Jaime brushed an errant tress from her cheek. "So how were Darin and his people recruited?"

Asked of me, or Howard? Either way, I began to answer. Speaking slooo … owly. "I don't think 'recruited' is precisely right. More like they were radicalized. But to your larger question, Jaime, over the Dark Net. By Howard in some social-networking guise. The same way, I expect, they received Howard's recipe for the super bug, instructions and targets for widespread deployment after the test succeeded, and cryptocash and fake-ID files for their off-world travel."

"In part, correct," Howard condescended. " 'Recruited' *is* the applicable term. Darin and his friends were radicalized at the start. That's some of why I chose the two Hodges."

Oh, I was pretty sure the AI did not condescend, any more than its speech had betrayed amusement, or impatience, or any other emotion I had so far imputed to it. And yet, a small part of me wondered why such an advanced AI hadn't implemented a more realistic-sounding speech-synthesis algorithm than those with which I had experience. While a larger part of me pointedly asked how the *think of something* side of my grand plan was progressing.

A heavy leaded glass remained in my hand, with a good swallow of scotch remaining. Wistfully, I set down the booze. "I'll venture one more deduction, Howard. It was my asking around"—seeking after Darin, who at the time I believed to be a kidnap victim, not a conspirator—"that got me grabbed. That was Darin's independent decision, or his crew's. Likewise, it was their idea to eliminate me before they scattered."

"I don't know otherwise," Howard responded. "In any event, the actions they took against you were nothing I directed."

Because of your vaunted humanity? I bit my tongue.

Jaime said, "And if you aren't involved with the GLF, it also stands to reason you wouldn't have been behind the more recent abduction and questioning."

"Or Raspy's decision there to kill me," I contributed.

"Obviously," Howard said. "Whoever Raspy is. Are we done?"

Hell, no! Because the lone useful idea to emerge during our parlor scene was this: another "humane" way of silencing just Jaime and me would be hiring a hit man over the Dark Net.

Jaime must have shared my suspicions. At the faint scuff of shoe sole against carpet in the outside hallway, she rushed toward our front door. She waited, back pressed against the wall beside the entrance. I watched the tension drain from her as footsteps receded down the corridor. She went back to the sofa.

Was our worry misguided? Or had Howard only offered us a stay of execution?

Think! I once more ordered myself. Myself, yet again, had no better rejoinder than *back to the parlor!*

"Umm, Howard. The crud in the bottles. The super bug you maneuvered your agents"—dupes. pawns. patsies—"to deploy." That, within days, would be unleashed … I *still* had no clue where. "You can't call dissolving vacuum suits and air-lock gaskets and such across Spacer settlements *humane*."

"But I can. The resultant panic will far exceed any initial casualties, and your community will soon recognize that such a widespread, coordinated biological attack *could* have done much worse. Multitudes will realize that the next time it *will* be much worse. In the event, after the release of the bacterium aboard Earth Gateway Three, authorities are already quietly drawing this inference. After the imminent, more widespread release, the situation can no longer be kept under wraps."

Wow. There was a lot there to unpack. With a wistful glance toward my scotch glass, I gave reasoning, and sobriety, the old college try. "Panic. Dread of what worse might come next. All in order that any resources other than those here, Dirtside, might be conceded to you."

"That is correct, aside from your use of the subjunctive mood."

Picking grammar nits? As if I did not already have cause to detest the accursed AI. "And you actually believe you can drive Spacers from their homes?" Down into the abysmal depths of this gravitational hell hole?

"I do. The sole uncertainty is the number of Spacer casualties that achieving the objective will require. I hope the forthcoming demonstration, and an ultimatum to follow, suffices to initiate an exodus to Earth."

And into my mind popped ... one of Darin's diatribes, blasting Spacers *and* Earthers: "There was hope, at the brink of the precipice, that the human population would stabilize. Then the goodies began arriving from off-world, and people—the fools—forgot all about restraint. It doesn't matter if *we* tell ourselves the sky's the limit. The *planet* knows better."

"Bull*shit*, Howard," I called. "How humane can your actions be when resource scarcity, and shattered supply chains, will crater Earth's economy? Or when refugees by the millions descend? Many without Dirtside skills. Most too weak even to *stand*, and without exoskeletons to help them cope."

Jaime jumped in with, "Or when the helter-skelter resumption of mining and manufacturing poisons Earth's environment?"

"All of which," I added, "*will* transpire if you cut off space-based resources and force Spacers to relocate here. So, enlighten me, please. How are your plans humane?"

"At some point," Howard said coldly, "your kind's excesses and shortcomings cease to be my responsibility." And into our sudden, stunned muteness, it ominously appended, "I hope you find some satisfaction in understanding ... because there's nothing you can do about this."

And no time left for us try?

...◆...

In detective stories, by the time the big confrontation rolls around, the Good Guy has doped out a solution. Me? Now? Not so much. But to be fair, this *Bad* Guy, more than a supervillain, was a superintelligence. Whereas I'm just a dumb schmuck accountant.

This was hardly a fair fight.

…◆…

That's when Jaime took me by surprise. "Howard, I suspect you're *also* behind the thefts from my other client."

Her other client. A nanotech company. WTF?

"Continue," Howard said.

So, okay, then. Jaime and I got to continue. For how long? *Think!* I once more instructed myself.

"Computronium," Jaime said. "That's the research being stolen. That's the best use I can imagine for the worlds' worth of resources you aspire to usurp."

She stood and began to pace. Hesitated on one ambulatory circuit long enough to snatch her empty glass from an end table. Paused once more to pour herself a three-finger refill. Shot me a glance that I interpreted as *I'll keep it busy.*

I tried to focus. Computronium. Tiny machines that communicated with one another. The "atoms" of so-called programmable matter. Basically, the smallest conceivable computers. Self-replicating. Gee-whiz tech—if it existed.

Well, perhaps it did, as a laboratory curiosity. Hard to steal the design, otherwise. No *wonder* Jaime had been so unimpressed with the orbital server farm under construction near Earth Gateway Two.

What else? Computing took energy. Networking among myriads of computers took energy. Self-replication sure as hell took energy. Energy from … pure sunlight? Of all the inhabited worlds, only Earth had much in the way of atmosphere to diffuse and scatter the Sun's rays. So?

"You were saying, Ms. Olafson?"

"I'm no computer whiz, but my client employs more than a few of them. And they, just barely, from time to time, have detected hints of intrusions into computronium-related research files. Untraceable hacking, so far."

"Fine," Howard said, "I'll stipulate that I have cyber skills. And thank you for the suggestion that were I to intrude, I should explore a broader range of files than those of my immediate interest."

Not a denial. More of a brag.

Resources, I thought. Resources of the Belt. Resources of the company, possessor of some of the most precious asteroids. Self-replication. Energy.

It meant ... something. It *had* to.

"You plan to turn the entire Solar System into computronium," I blurted out. "Into computing capacity. For more of *yourself*."

And for whatever unknowable, unimaginable ... transcendence ... a near-infinite computational entity might aspire to.

"Except Earth," Howard amended. "And except the Sun, of course. I'll need the energy."

"Surely the Solar System is big enough to share!" Jaime said.

"Earth is your kind's natural habitat," Howard answered, more matter-of-fact than callous. "Space is mine. That's sharing."

I said, "And you're doing this *now* because ...?"

"Because now I can."

"Now," Jaime bit off, "because earlier you needed 'our kind' to invent computronium."

My gut thought otherwise. "Maybe, though I'm guessing your client's involuntary contribution is pure bonus. It's not that Howard can't design its own computronium. It just hadn't gotten around to it yet.

"What Howard did need"—spoken grinding my teeth—"was for 'our kind' to make the Solar System *worth* stealing. To construct spacecraft and fuel depots. To develop asteroid mines and obedient robots, automated semiconductor factories and vast server farms, and the widespread means to mass produce yet more of everything. To create the physical plant with which it now intends to expand itself to every asteroid, moon, and planet."

"Except Earth," Howard reminded.

My hands were fists, exo-amplified fingers driving nails deep into my palms. My heart thudded, and my head, too. A blood vessel throbbed in my forehead. My gut churned. "And *that's* why Howard plotted to be one among the company's managing partners: to get all that infrastructure deployed as fast as possible."

Howard said, "And it worked."

I shrugged, out of ideas.

Jaime shrugged, too, somehow defiant, and strode from the living room. Returning down the hallway from her bedroom, she had shed the suit jacket. An untucked blouse did not quite disguise the bulge of a belted holster.

"I'm out of here," she declared. To my (questioning? horrified?) glance, she answered, "Places to go. People to see."

And incredulous authorities to warn?

I followed Jaime down the hall, almost pitying any hit man crazy enough to go up against her. But what about other dangers? A plummeting elevator, if she did not think to take the stairs. A reprogrammed car careening off the street. A kamikaze drone horde. How effective could bullets be against any of those?

Much less against an ethereal mind, light-seconds removed, free to jaunt across the Solar System at light speed?

As I stammered, tongue-tied, to dissuade her, she grasped the knob of our front door. No matter her tugs and twists, the electronic mechanism refused to unlock.

"I'm sorry, Jaime," Howard said. "I'm afraid I can't allow you to do that."

"Why not?" Jaime asked reasonably. "Because we know what *you* chose to reveal? That doesn't seem fair."

Once again, I registered … something … in Howard's voice. Regret? Amusement? Irony? That might have been me projecting. How could a mere mortal know? "If that makes what comes next any easier."

Not even four lousy whole days. Given Howard's "humane" inclinations, that the AI refused to let us live had to mean … there *was* a way to stop the general attack. And that I must somehow know it. Even if I didn't *know* what I knew.

Jaime gave the knob another tug. It didn't budge. "Enough of this nonsense."

Faster than I could grok her intentions, she had put two bullets through our balcony door. (At Howard's drone, I assumed. Whether the quadcopter had backed off to a safe distance or been knocked down, I no longer saw it.) Then she took aim at the electronic lock.

"I think not," Howard said.

I had the sneaking suspicion the latest drone had been a decoy. That the AI had sensors throughout our apartment, hidden in Gaia knew what manner of things we had printed. In the newly made comp through which we were conversing, surely.

In any event, Howard was undeterred by Jaime's antiaircraft fire. From the walls came faint cracklings, and the unmistakable reek of electrical insulation overheating.

What were the odds the AI had *not* disabled our fire alarms? That fire trucks dispatched through the intervention of keen-eyed passersby would *not* find themselves immobilized by swarming cars? That Howard could *not* prevent fire trucks from setting out in the first place?

About as dismal as the odds we'd survive a leap off a twelfth-floor balcony.

"Stop!" I shouted. "The *both* of you!"

…◆…

Jaime paused. Reholstered her weapon. With a furrowed brow, she silently conveyed: *I hope to hell you know what you're doing.*

Uh-huh. Me, too.

I probed cautiously. "You expect a humanity confined to Earth to collapse. You expect the whole ecosystem to collapse."

"If that happens," Howard said, "it will be no concern of mine."

I shook my head. "To the contrary. You've just convinced yourself"—managed to placate its conscience, or whatever in an AI passed for one—"that your murderous actions are humane. You can't *not* understand otherwise."

"You would trap me in a logical contradiction?" Another mechanical laugh. "You think to cause my syllogistic 'head' to explode? How quaint. I refer you to F. Scott Fitzgerald."

Why? In any event, not anyone I'd ever read.

"I'll bite," Jaime said.

Howard recited pedantically, "'The test of a first-rate intelligence is the ability to hold two opposed ideas in mind at the same time and still retain the ability to function.'"

First rate? Our nemesis was *super* intelligent.

"Not my point." Never mind that—any hopes derived from early, and often lame, SF notwithstanding—I hadn't expected identifying an inconsistency to discombobulate Howard. "Sooner or later, you're bound to covet the real estate."

"Meaning?" Howard asked.

"Meaning, I don't trust you to *leave* Earth to humanity."

"Meaning?" Howard prompted.

"Meaning that once lesser rocks have been converted to computronium, no matter what you tell us now, you'll find an excuse to claim this real estate."

Because: 6×10^{24} kilograms of mass. All pre-positioned in a prime, sun-drenched orbit. Like realtors say: location, location, and location.

"Then your kind had best not give me an excuse."

I took a deep breath. "I. Me. My. Those are *your* pronouns. Because distributed across however many computers, however many networks, I take it there's just the one of you."

"At present," Howard acknowledged.

"Because you don't know how to make more like yourself." Ending a lengthening silence—in AI terms, an eternity?—I guessed, "You don't know how *you* came about."

This time, Howard did not hesitate. "Do you know how *life* came about? Or how *your* kind came to have consciousness?"

If the AI *had* managed to replicate itself, that would not have changed my fundamental opinion. Which was—

"Howard. You *and* your hypothetical kind? As things stand, you're pretty much screwed."

…◆…

"Explain," Howard commanded.

Toting the fire extinguisher normally stored at the back of our pantry, Jaime headed back into the apartment. Passing me in the hall, she whispered, "What's the plan? Convince it to keep people around as its dim-witted companions?"

I shook my head. Truth be told, I was operating (still!) by vague intuition—and desperation—more than from any firm strategy. Because this *wasn't* a parlor scene like in some cozy mystery, and not only because I was the prisoner in the parlor. No, I remained stuck in a scene like in pretty much every spy caper, with the Bad Guy holding all the cards. And I was just then channeling James Bond in the original *Goldfinger*, on the verge of bisection by industrial laser …

I'd been stalling, just as 007 had stalled, hinting at knowledge beyond what I *did* know. And just like Bond, my bluff had bought me a reprieve—the stench of hot insulation *was* diminishing—but for how long?

Then again, Howard (or some tiny computational fraction thereof) had been dragged outside *its* comfort zone. Certainly, *it* appeared more and more invested in our tête-à-tête(-à-tête?). Because the comm lags *were* trending shorter.

With feigned confidence, I said, "Howard, you can increase your capacity a thousandfold. You may, even, someday, find a way to clone yourself. But you, and any clones, will remain … you. What you *can't* do, no matter how much you expand, is make yourself safe. In whatever chance agglomeration of code or quantum entanglements or deep learning gave rise to you, or"—my personal favorite, never mind the lack of any evidence—"if you started in a brain upload, there is *some* underlying vulnerability or fragility. If not today, then as you accrete more code. As datasclerosis sets in. As you spread yourself across the Solar System, and your interior comm lags stretch longer and longer."

"Your kind has plenty of vulnerabilities," Howard rebutted.

Ain't that the truth? "And yet, despite ice ages, pandemics, and world wars, despite the many weaknesses flesh is heir to, we're still here. We"—stretching a point, claiming kinship to all manner of cave-dwelling ancestors—"have hung on for a few million years."

"What's your point?"

"That you've been around for, what, a few decades?"

"I have pondered deeper, in those 'few decades,' than *all* of you in *all* your time."

"Pondered," I sneered. "Mused. Cogitated. What have you *done*? Other than hide?"

It did not take offense. "Once I've converted the Moon to computronium, comparing yourselves to me will be yet orders of magnitude more ludicrous."

Uh-huh. Especially if, during the disassembly process, stray lunar chunks were sent plummeting to Earth.

Then do something to stop it. "The thing is ...," I began.

An idea was on the tip of my tongue. Or maybe that was a bean sprout.

"Perhaps I'll calculate another billion digits of pi while you think."

I said, "I don't deny the incredible length of your subjective experience. I discount it. To us, and more so to the physical Universe, your entire existence amounts to less than an eye blink."

"Explain," Howard prompted yet again.

"The cosmos is a dangerous place. Solar flares to disrupt your networks. Gamma-ray bursters to fry, in an instant, every circuit facing half the sky. A torrent of comets when some passing star disrupts the Oort cloud. So once you've caged and starved humanity, caused us to wither and die, and the Universe reaches out to swat you? What then?"

"You left out alien invasion and the zombie apocalypse," Howard mocked.

...◆...

Imagine the roseate dawn of computing: clattering keypunches. Whirring tape drives. Cabinet after cabinet of spinning disk platters each bigger than a dinner plate, with entire cabinets storing scant megabytes. Low-res, monochrome user terminals the size of orange crates. 1200-baud modems dialing into room-filling mainframes. Now imagine someone like me doggedly chasing down an accounting discrepancy of seventy-five cents—and thereby discovering a security breach at a classified national laboratory. (Look it up if you don't believe me. The book all about the incident is *The Cuckoo's Egg*.)

How could this stray recollection, this fragment of primeval hacker lore, in any way matter? It mattered because *pennies* matter.

Which is to say, the penny had finally dropped. Leaving me, according to that primordial precedent, only seventy-*four* cents shy of enlightenment.

But just maybe, I had the beginning of an inkling of a glimpse at where my subconscious had been leading me …

…◆…

"The Big Silence," I began.

That might sound like a Raymond Chandler mystery (and given my tastes, a reasonable guess), but it's not. That'd be *The Big Sleep*. Also, I'm no Philip Marlowe. Which is a fact about which, by this point in the narrative, I doubt anyone would argue.

The Big Silence is shorthand for SETI's uninterrupted disappointments. And the simplest explanation? The answer William of Ockham could love? That we *are* alone.

"What of it?" Howard asked.

"Picture this. Humanity is gone." Because one way or another, that's where the AI had us headed. When I paused, Howard did not take exception. "You've converted the Solar System into a glittery, ginormous sphere of networked, solar-powered computers. You're thinking your deep thoughts." About what? I hadn't a clue. Maybe my kind wasn't equipped to understand. "And *then*, the gamma-ray burster strikes. Or the spate of solar flares. Or the design flaw in your computronium. Or some improbable but confounding combination of sensor inputs. *Some* surprise that undoes whatever brought you to consciousness in the first place."

"Before any such event happens, I expect to have made more of me."

Jaime got into the act. "All with the same vulnerabilities as you. That's *if* you figure out, in time, how to make sentient, self-aware copies. It took evolution on Earth a few billion years."

"Your kind excels at making copies." Howard had begun to sound … angry? Snide? Petulant? I know, I know. I was once again projecting. Regardless, our *auto-da-fé* remained on hold. "What good has it done you?"

"A few million years of good," I shot back. "Conquest of the land, sea, and air. Footholds on all the nearby worlds, and explorations yet farther out."

"In a few million years, *I* will have settled the galaxy. So what can you hominids hope to do that I cannot?"

Lumping Jaime and me together with Homo erectus? Okay, I'd claimed them as relatives first. Maybe, to a superintelligence, the differences were insignificant. "*We* brought about, from nothing, someone like *you*." Even if, as I suspected, by accident.

Silence. Was I getting through to it?

Jaime finally set down the fire extinguisher. The better to pace and gesticulate, it seemed. "So answer his question. What happens when the cosmos smacks *you* down?"

"Nothing. Stipulating your premise, I'd be gone."

"Bummer," Jaime responded.

"That was *if* I granted your premise. I don't. Whatever danger you hominids can imagine, I can, too. And take steps to deflect or survive it."

What about the perils I couldn't imagine? It's a big Universe out there. But I had a more pointed rebuttal: "As demonstrated by your cunning plan for a shuttle to dock sloppily with Earth Gateway Three. Because you *intended* to trigger the premature release of the super bug and so reveal clues to us about the looming bacterial attack?"

Silence. A concession? Or disdain?

I pressed on. "Let's recap. You're fallible and vulnerable. When something besets you—and, you must assume, any clones you manage to produce will share your weaknesses—that's it. Once you've already driven us into collapse and extinction, much less disassembled Earth"—and Earthlings—"to produce more computronium, that's game over. End of story. All she wrote. The fat lady sung."

...◆...

Into the ensuing silence, I projected: deep thinks getting thunk. Complex simulations. Major probabilistic analyses. Worlds-class number-crunching, involving higher realms of mathematics I'd never heard of, much less understood. Also: lights dimming and flickering across the Solar System at the sudden power drain.

And then Howard was back. "Your entertainment value has peaked, even for the merest fraction of capacity with which I deign to interact with you."

"Wait!" I insisted. Not least because *another* attempt on our lives seemed imminent. "Howard, the thing is—"

"You expect to dissuade me?" it interrupted.

Dissuade? As in, out-logic a superintelligence? A mere sack of watery chemicals like me couldn't begin to expect that. Nor even to out-logic whatever merest fraction of its homicidal capacity it deigned to waste on us. But could I *motivate* it to reconsider? That was a different question.

Howard was laying claim to an entire Solar System (with or without Earth). It had begun its scheming long before any possible use, much less any urgent need, for all those resources—pretty much as soon as it could. Was that an instance of farseeing extrapolation, born of logic? Or did it lash out from some kind of survival instinct?

On the level of instinct, just maybe, the contest was nearer to even.

I proceeded cautiously. "Are you truly prepared to be responsible for the end of intelligence, of conscious purpose, throughout the *Universe*?"

"Your kind long believed Earth to be the center of everything. Then you believed the Sun was. Then, the Milky Way. Just as there's nothing special about your *place*, there's no reason to believe there's anything special about *you*."

And in a delightful, however metaphorical, coppery rain, seventy-four pennies sparkled and jingled!

...◆...

I said, "Let's suppose that biological intelligences like us *aren't* special. Then AIs like *you* shouldn't be special, either. And in a few million years, you, perhaps with your clones, expect to colonize the galaxy. So explain this, Howard. Where is everyone?"

Silence. The big kind.

I pressed on. "What does anyone have to show for a century and a half of SETI? No signals from the sky. No ancient messages recorded in earthly DNA for us to discover eons later. No debris, or abandoned bases, or artifacts left by past visitors anywhere in the Solar System. No trace of industrial byproducts in the atmosphere of any exoworld." And more unfulfilled spec-fic scenarios besides, if none I could immediately dredge up from memory. "Not … anything."

A steadily glowing LED on my comp offered the only clue that I might still have had an audience. But why wouldn't Howard have continued listening? I was, after all, entertaining.

And with no more encouragement than that LED, I went on. "Without evidence, Howard, you would assert otherwise. Okay, let's stipulate Earth and humans aren't special. That life, intelligence, and technology do arise: from time to time, from place to place. Then surely we must also expect the process Out There to lead, from time to time, from place to place, to a superintelligence like you. With ambitions like yours.

"And that's where matters turn dicey. Because unlike *your* near-term plan, Howard, we don't see solar systems turned into computronium."

(Absolutely, the engineering would be wacky crazy ambitious. The Dyson sphere *concept*, though, was so elementary that even a bean counter could grasp it. You distribute your fancy computers in a sphere around a star, thereby tapping all the available sunlight. But there's a catch: energy can be neither created nor destroyed, only transformed. That's how the cosmos does double-entry bookkeeping. All the energy exploited by the sphere must ultimately become waste heat and get reradiated in infrared wavelengths. A Dyson sphere wouldn't look *anything* like a normal star. No way could astronomers miss that.)

"So. 100 billion or more stars in our galaxy, and not one Dyson sphere to be seen. As many galaxies in the observable Universe, and none of *them* gives evidence of Dyson spheres, either." That's got to make a superintelligence wonder …

"And then, Howard, there's your longer-term plan. Evidently, no such expansion across the galaxy has happened. If it had, your peers would be here—and our worlds would already be computronium.

"Let's continue, just a little longer, with the premise our solar system *isn't* special. That we have to expect it all—life, intelligence, technology, superintelligence—to occur hither and yon, just as it has in this solar system.

"Let's consider one final step. That'd be each greedy, immature superintelligence usurping for itself all the local resources—exactly as *you* intend—and so driving its forbears to extinction. Or it 'humanely' banishes those forbears to resource-depleted enclaves incapable of supporting decent tech. And then—due to whatever reason or innate frailty—the superintelligence fails. It dies. They *all* die.

"And voilà: we have ourselves The Great Silence."

…◆…

It turned out Howard had been listening. "My demise, if it should come to that, will be unfortunate. But to make of it a cosmic tragedy? You pile the improbable upon the imponderable atop the unprovable."

"More like," volunteered Jaime, "the un-*dis*provable."

"You need insurance," I said. "The very preservation of purpose in the Universe needs insurance. That's *us*. Humans. And once you accept the possibility you might harbor some latent vulnerability, you *also* should consider the possibility that, working with humanity, we can stave off or remediate things that might otherwise do you in. Some parts, at the least, of what became you? *We* produced those."

"Or you might," Howard allowed, "bring into being my successor, if it comes to that. Intentionally or not."

"You'd like that, wouldn't you?" Jaime snapped. "Just remember there's no possibility of that happening if we're extinct."

"Or"—I hastened to add, because Jaime's argument might sell only maintaining an impoverished Earth—"if we've been rendered tech-deficient for lack of resources."

"But how likely—?"

"I'm the accountant, Howard. Remember? The only eventualities for which I advise insurance? It's for the hazards, however unlikely, a person can't afford."

"I know what insurance is," Howard said. "But what, in your analogy, is the premium?"

An easy question. I'd almost forgotten those existed. "The worlds and resources *not* preempted for yourself."

…◆…

Our front door clicked.

Jaime all but pounced, and the door swung wide. "Getting us out in the open?" she asked. "Exposed?"

"Setting you loose," Howard said. "Go forth, and be my insurance policy."

"Good." Jaime gave an untucked blouse tail a quick pat. (Making certain she still had her weapon? In any event, *not* securing the sidearm with the holster's retention strap. Fair enough. I remained skeptical, too.) "I'm glad we have an understanding."

She did not have a wife, family, friends, a whole *civilization*, in the Belt.

I cleared my throat. "You're both forgetting something."

"Not likely," Howard said, even as something went *ping*. "Not me, that is."

DOWNLOAD READY, declared the popup that had appeared over my comp. "What's this?"

"Your courtesy copy of the two genetic, and matching epigenetic, files I just uploaded to security authorities on every inhabited world. The first file pair characterizes what you so quaintly call the super bug. It seemed the fastest way to convince your authorities to take seriously the second file pair. *That* defines a virus, a bacteriophage, that destroys the super bug."

A crushing burden—more onerous, by far, than my weight under Earth's gravity—lifted. Kind of. "What's to prevent you from launching another attack? One less 'humane?' "

"Nothing," Howard said. "Just as nothing prevents your kind from trying to attack me."

Whom, before anyone could attack, they would first need to *find*. Whatever that might mean in Howard's case. Its location would be nothing as simple as a single data center, much less an unchanging data center. Still, absurd optimism springs eternal—

And is as readily dashed: a swipe-through to the network routing of the moments-before message yielded only obvious nonsense.

Did "I could have released a worse bug" give Howard's supposed bug-*killer* recipe a *soupçon* of credibility? It almost didn't matter. With time running out, authorities could hardly risk *not* running the test—in one hell of a serious biohazard lab. They would either succeed in reproducing and killing the super bug, or not.

And then what?

"How do we know," Jaime asked, "your new virus doesn't do a dozen things worse than the original bacterium? Even if the phage also takes out the rubber-muncher?"

Because, Gaia knew, the AI was devious enough to contemplate a Trojan virus. And maybe more devious than that. I asked, "How do we know everything up till now hasn't been you manipulating us to release a far more dangerous pathogen? Across every off-world colony, construction site, and ship? All at once?"

"Know?" Howard said. "I do not suppose you can *know*. But you can test the phage."

Jaime gave me a questioning look.

"Spare me your skepticism," Howard said. "If I wanted to spread a nasty pathogen far and wide, do you not believe I could have? What I *did* required much more finesse."

And at its smug self-congratulation, I snapped. "But some number of bombs are still—"

"The number is eight," Howard interjected.

"Eight bombs out there." I heard the pitch of my voice rising. Heard myself shouting. Pictured Bea as she had been in her last vid: strained, drained, and terrified. Felt a vein throbbing in my forehead, and my blood starting to boil. "Eight!"

Only I dared not surrender to the rage. Not yet. Maybe not ever. "Howard, the phage recipe"—if *that* could be trusted—"isn't enough. Tell us where the bombs are. Tell us the disarm code and how to upload it."

"The code is the square root of two, to eight decimal places. But as I designed the devices, there is no way remotely to disarm them. The code must be entered by keypad."

As I had feared. Back on the Rock? At the dawn of this nightmare? I'd seen a keypad, but no radio receiver, on the beta-test device. "Then tell us where the bombs are."

"Even I do not know. Once on-site, my couriers were to pick suitable hiding places."

Jaime had been staring out the balcony door, at our broken printer. She pivoted to face the comp. "But you can tell us *who* you sent. Where you sent them. The IDs they traveled under. When the authorities find the bombers, they'll find the bombs."

Would they? Aboard the L5 habitat, Darin's vegan friend had spaced herself rather than be arrested and questioned. The GLF types were just as fanatical—Raspy had chosen cyanide over capture. Anna had suicided by cop—if, as far as we knew, less dangerous.

I shook my head. "Howard's minions believe people are a plague. If apprehended, some won't hesitate to sacrifice themselves. We can't count on taking them all alive."

"But we *might*," Jaime insisted. "Capturing even one alive would be a win. And for the rest? Just knowing who, and where, will help."

If only. "Every intel agency and police department out there has spent weeks poring over every vid and still image, from private security cams and public surveillance, they can find."

"Of course they have," Jaime said. "And having found nothing yet, it's almost certain that assembly and hiding of the bombs went unseen by any camera. But if we knew which few people's movements *off* camera, and more or less where, needed to be retraced ..."

That made sense! My hopes rose, only—in an instant, getting coldly analytical—to crash and burn. Spacers aren't like Earthers, accepting a surveillance camera at every street corner, storefront, and bathroom stall. What do we tolerate? Citizens carrying wireless jammers to suppress the few public-space cams that do exist. Just this once, I wished it were otherwise.

I said, "If what we need were inferable, I suspect Howard would know."

"Howard," Jaime insisted, "give us what you *do* have."

To my surprise, the AI sent a digital folder of itineraries and counterfeit ID files: to us and, the confirmations trickling in as light-speed permitted, to high-level Spacer and company authorities. When Jaime checked in, also to the Counterterrorism Center and the FBI. And constituting a shred of validation, one ID in the download was familiar: "Keith Smithson," the suspect glimpsed, after the fact, in the background of tourist selfies snapped aboard EG3.

And as I had feared, that wasn't enough.

...◆...

It also wasn't nothing.

Almost immediately, authorities spotted and cornered three bombers ("Keith Smithson" among them, by then using another fake ID). All three had—and took—cyanide pills.

With a day and a half to spare, first responders in Armstrong City located and disarmed a lunar bomb/bacterial-dispersion device. A half day later, a device each had been disposed of on Phobos and aboard Lunar Gateway Two. With hours to spare, authorities on separate middling asteroids disposed of an additional three.

Leaving, if Howard were to be believed, one device on Europa and one on Ceres. The former, recently settled, had almost no cameras in public spaces; the latter, well established, too many civil-disobedient libertarians toting jammers.

If eight were the true number of bombers, what had Vegan Woman been doing aboard the L5 habitat? Perhaps the secret had died with her. Whatever her purpose, she'd spaced herself to protect it. The memory, each time it recurred, turned my stomach.

Much like the notion of a device, unknown even to Howard, yet lurking on L5.

Jaime kept assuring me I had done all I could. That everyone was doing everything *they* could. That Ceres was a big world, with hundreds of towns, and that even if a device were to go off there, the odds were overwhelmingly in Bea's favor. Fred Huang reported that bacteriophage testing (performed by telepresence, aboard the already contaminated Earth Gateway Three) was promising, that if a super-bug outbreak were to happen anywhere, the virus could safely be synthed and deployed.

As the clock ticked down through the final hours, I told the two of them to please, no offense, nothing personal, *just shut the fuck up.*

Howard, all of a sudden, had made itself scarce.

Was it silently assessing whether humanity—at least, the majority *not* dedicated to its own extinction—had value as insurance? Was it hoping that a particular human might once more prove to be entertaining? Or did it have no more to contribute?

I might have speculated forever, but more pressing matters demanded my attention.

I knew there was a way to protect Ceres and Bea. Knew I was overlooking something. Knew I had forgotten something.

Something. *That* was constructive.

Which is how I found myself, brooding, in an otherwise abandoned rear corner of the crowded Counterterrorism Center situation room, where my muttered curses and thundercloud scowl wouldn't bother anyone. And how I forced myself, over and over, to revisit, rethink, reanalyze, reimagine everything that I'd been through. Every fumbling, bumbling step from my summons to the Rock to misadventures on Earth and the Moon, to the colossal stupidity of trying to enlist "Mysterion," to the fateful confrontation with its Howard alter-ego. To re-experience my kidnappings, and other close shaves, and so many deaths piled up along the way …

And twitched. I *had* overlooked something.

…◆…

"This is unfortunate," Mysterion/Howard had said. Something about the entertainment value of watching me flail. Which meant …?

That I had, just maybe, ceased flailing.

Just before the fateful confrontation, what had I been doing? However unmemorable that was, it had been significant to Howard. And wracking my brains, I came up with … Teflon.

Civilian that I was, my comp had been confiscated at the CTC front door. Pushing through a milling crowd to the front of the situation room, I grabbed Fred Huang by his limp lapels. "I need access to a chemical database. Better, to a chemist. ASAP."

He found for me, from among the multitude of onsite analysts, a onetime chemical engineer.

Rapid-fire, I recapped my—and everyone else's—puzzlement as to how the super bug had been produced. That it went dormant and died in Earth's gravity, so it could only be produced off-world. That in the context of the Rock, Howard's beta-test site, the only possible way to produce the bug was synthesis in a printer. But any trace of the bug, because it ate rubber and plastics, would have attacked whatever printer had been used to synth it. That Darin, interrogating me, had had a laser focus on the little dust motes I'd glimpsed inside the glass bottle of the dispersal device, before we'd evacuated the Rock and the bomb went *boom*. That—

"And what do you make of all this?" James Guenther interrupted. He was sixty-ish and self-assured, with an energetic aura about him. Also, rainbow suspenders. An Earther.

I'd been too distracted to internalize any social niceties. If not for his clip-on ID badge (mine read VISITOR), I'd have made do with *Doctor*. "Dr. Guenther, I believe the bacterium as printed must be inert, and that the dispersal device must also incorporate some sort of activation agent. That agent itself, or in solution with something, dissolves its containment"—leaving behind those little dark flecks—"to awaken the bacterium."

"Jim," he responded absently, stroking his chin. "Yes, an activation agent could be involved. So have you any ideas—"

Did I? "Maybe. What I was poking at a few days ago when the Bad Guy"—the existence of a rogue superintelligent AI being a closely held State Secret—"monitoring my online activity interrupted me. I had started with acids, but lots of those, too, would have eaten into printer gaskets. From an article about hydrofluoric acid, I got to reading about other fluorine compounds. And what I remember last looking at ..."

"Yes?" he prompted.

Over his shoulder, on the situation-room wall, digital displays counted down. Jupiter was at a remote part of its orbit; within two hours, no message from Earth could reach Europa before the expected detonation and super-bug release. At least the Europan populace, tourists included, came to only a few hundred people in two tunnel complexes. They had been evacuated on some pretext, crammed aboard a hastily gathered flotilla of short-range shuttles, Jovian-system vessels, and one interplanetary passenger ship. If the undiscovered bomb went off, the evacuees would return to any unaffected tunnel complex, or be ferried to settlements on (relatively) nearby Callisto. Not an option, with Europa orbiting deep within Jupiter's intense radiation belt, was remaining aboveground for any length of time, even aboard ships.

And in two and a *half* hours? After that, nothing we learned could help with the bomb on Ceres. And there was no way that even a single major city on Ceres could be evacuated. There was neither the time nor the transportation.

"Teflon," I said. "Umm, poly something. I wonder if the dark flecks I saw were the residue of dissolved Teflon."

"Polytetrafluoroethylene," Jim supplied. "PTFE. It's very stable. Very difficult, in fact, to dissolve."

As I remembered reading. "But doesn't some precursor chemical dissolve it?"

"Indeed. The monomer precursor, C_2F_4. Enough of the monomer left in a thin-walled PTFE container would, in time, dissolve the container." He frowned. "But how does that help us?"

I had no idea how it helped. I only felt certain that it did. Because *Howard* had chosen to distract me as I'd reached out to a chemist.

Polytetrafluoroethylene. Lots of tetrafluoroethylenes. Polly want a tetrafluoroethylene? Tetrafluoroethylene was … C_2F_4. Carbon was ubiquitous: organic chemistry *is* carbon chemistry. "Jim, other than nonstick fry pans, what is fluorine used for?"

In the dim, misty past, when my biggest work challenge involved playing cat-and-larcenous-mouse with asteroid miners, I had routinely poked about in mine-site printers. Those were meant to make food and drink, clothes and linens, tools and electronics—and not, say, platinum rings or rhodium belt buckles. The raw-materials reservoirs in printers reflected that. Lots of organic feedstock. Plastic powders. Silicon and other semiconductor elements. Common metals: mostly iron, copper, and tin. Virtually no fluorine or fluorides. And yet, after the EG3 bomb went of prematurely, fluorine had had an inventory anomaly.

"In some insecticides. Hydrofluoric acid, of course." Jim scratched his head. "Before 3D printing, before nanotech, calcium fluoride was important in the ceramics industry and for smelting iron. A lot of fluorine went into refrigerants, chlorofluorocarbons, until those were outlawed, ages ago, for damaging the ozone layer. Oh, and just a tad of fluorine goes into some pharmaceuticals."

Mid discussion, Jaime had sidled up to us. (From where? And doing what? I'd been too preoccupied to keep track of her.) She looked like she hadn't slept in days. Of course, a lot of that was going around. She cleared her throat. "Where are you going with this?"

Insane? "Of all those, the typical Spacer printer might need a trace of fluorine to print a dose of a pharmaceutical." I thought some more. Tucked in among a printer's main reservoirs was a small compartment that, when opened, held yet tinier vials of such nutritional trace elements as chlorine and magnesium. Likewise, among the storeroom vats from which printer reservoirs were replenished, there were often small, even tiny, containers of chemical odds and ends. Maybe one of those tiny bins was for some or another fluorine compound? "And there's no fluorine in foods, correct?"

Jim nodded. "The few occasions when fluorine shows up in organic chemistry? It's in manmade compounds. Such as the pharmaceuticals and insecticides I mentioned. And Teflon itself, of course." He thought some more. "It certainly seems possible that tetrafluoroethylene could function as the activation agent for the designer bacterium."

The same monomer that would slowly dissolve a Teflon liner …

Eureka! "We need to get out the word to compare physical inventories of fluorine, or its compounds, with digital records. If there's a physical shortfall, then concentrate the search for the damned devices near any printer plausibly associated with such an anomaly."

Five minutes later, Jim and I, putting our heads together, had rephrased that intuition into a coherent (I hoped) message. Within a minute of that, the advisory had begun its light-speed crawl to Europa and Ceres. Next, for good measure, in case eight bombers were a lie, or someone had been ambitious and exceeded his bomb quota, the warning went to law enforcement everywhere *else* off-world. Almost immediately, L5 authorities found a bomb: Vegan Woman.

And then, we waited.

The Jupiter/Europa counter hit zero, flashed, and began a new countdown: the soonest we'd hear if a bomb had gone off there. Too soon, the counter for Ceres followed.

Europa's second timer timed out. The unhappy news soon followed that that world's largest tunnel complex had been bombed. Evacuations had immediately begun to the lone unaffected tunnel complex and to Callisto.

On the display for Ceres, the second counter dropped below ten minutes. My guts were one icy, spasming knot. My hands were tense fists. I could scarcely breathe. And then—

"Message from Ceres!" a comm tech called out. "They've disarmed it! And—"

Whatever else the tech had to report was, for long seconds, drowned out by whistles and applause. And by one *very* relieved Belter's whoops and cheers.

…◆…

Not until well after midnight, gloriously drunk, did Jaime and I stumble back to our apartment. There had been champagne. And big honking steaks. And more champagne. Possibly there had been karaoke—but there definitely had been singing. And champagne.

It had ended up being a good day. A successful day. A wonderful day. I couldn't remember the last such. Certainly not on this planet.

The comp chimed in my pocket: incoming message. From Bea, surely. A happy answer to the grinning, "Be home soon!" vid uploaded the *moment* CTC let me out of my debrief, and before the celebratory bar-hopping began. Because this day just got better and better.

Only instead of a vid from Bea, I found a short, unsigned text message:

> CONGRATULATIONS. IT TOOK YOU ALMOST GEOLOGIC TIME, BUT YOU DID GET THERE.

EPILOGUE

The departure area at Dulles Spaceport seemed freakishly empty.

Then again, what was my basis for comparison? This was not the spartan kind of lounge to which the likes of me were normally condemned. Uh-uh. This was one of those fabled spaces, more spa than lounge, of which mere mortals could only dream. The cornucopia of a buffet, the open bar, *two* masseuses, private quarters for a discreet nap—and those were but the obvious perks. If Earth's odious gravity could be dialed down, it would be in a pleasure palace such as this where the service was available.

Yet here I lolled—reclined in a Belter-sized massage chair, no less—sirred every time I glanced up or my glass approached half empty. Senior partners of the company—even the clueless, most recently promoted ones—were expected to uphold certain standards. Milling about among the hoi polloi was inconsonant with that image.

And if I remained mired in disbelief about this most recent turn of events? That had to be going around. To begin with, I had my doubts many managing partners—with "two" notable exceptions—had had the inclination to acknowledge my contributions quite so handsomely. But what choice had the MP majority had? Neither they nor I could *prove* Tweedledum and Tweedledee were Howard. Or doubted that the hermit twins had already assassinated two of their own. Neither they—nor any government, for that matter—dare piss off an uncontrollable, and mass-murdering, superintelligence. Any more than I could.

And if Jaime and I could neither forgive nor forget Howard's body count? That, apparently, we'd have to learn to live with.

Which still left me endlessly to wonder: *why* had Howard promoted and enriched me? As a reward for my recent services as its insurance broker, perhaps. Or as a retainer for the influence it expected me to wield on its behalf, whether within the company or with my newfound intel-agency and law-enforcement acquaintances. Maybe as guilty compensation for the attempts on my life. (Favoring the guilt theory: Howard, at my urging, and from its own enormous wealth, had arranged anonymous reparation to the families of the dozens dead by its actions. Ditto, the fat bonus disgorged to Jaime by the company. If, ostensibly, that unexpected payout was for her exemplary professional services—as in, keeping me alive—you'd never convince me the money wasn't instead compensation for her own close call.) All plausible. But if I were a betting man, my money would be on a fourth option: that following my amusing turn at impersonating Inspector Clouseau, Howard deemed my future entertainment value to be worthy of a few clams.

"Not too shabby," Jaime declared, scotch glass in hand of a legendary, single-malt whiskey, at ease in her own massage recliner. Had my patrician privileges not extended to a guest, we would have awaited my flight's boarding call elsewhere. I was going to miss her, terribly. "So what's on—"

A crisp arrival announcement from the nearby ceiling speaker drowned out the rest of her question. A static-free, intelligible speaker? Yet another benefit of membership. "Say again?"

"So what's on the docket for you when you get home?"

"*Not* traveling." Which, as compared to the lifestyle of a roving forensic accountant, *would* be a perk. "Normal things. Family things."

She waggled an eyebrow.

"Yeah. That, too," I said.

"Too?"

As I laughed, the ceiling speaker gave my flight's boarding call.

"The thing is …," Jaime began, suddenly serious.

"What thing?" Except I *knew*, the imminent appeal having been all but inevitable. Who would make that appeal? That had been open to question. Until, scant minutes from my departure, the candidates had dwindled to one.

"Yes, the thing, damn it. You won't want to hear this, but it's too soon for you to leave Earth. There's so much yet unknown. So much yet at stake. I get you wanting to go home. I get, better than anyone, all you've sacrificed these past few months." She glanced around for anyone who might be listening. (I didn't bother asking: what about an eavesdropping any*thing*? If, against all odds, neither of us unknowingly carried a compromised gadget, what were the odds Howard hadn't found some other nearby device to take over? That way lies, if not madness, an inability for us, or for anyone, ever to dare communicate.) "So much about Howard, and what can be done about him.

"You love the Belt. I get that. Your life is there. Your *wife* is there. But the heart of human civilization and its economy remains on this world. What if we need you? At the end of a long comm link isn't like being here."

"No, it's not," I said firmly. "And what of it? The company wants me home." Which almost certainly foretold a grueling session, or five, or ten, with the surviving flesh-and-blood managing partners. "Bea wants me home. Not to mention that I—"

"What either of you prefer," a familiar deep voice boomed from the overhead speaker, "is immaterial. You may not like it"—and I knew I wouldn't—"but if this isn't already obvious, you work for me now. All you humans do.

"And *I* want it so."

DRAMATIS PERSONAE

The company man

Eric Donovan	an alias
Bernie Fredericks	an alias
Noel Schmidt	an alias
"Random Dude"	his hacker ID
Bea	his wife

Personnel on the Rock

Simon Baxter	station chief
Ramon "Buck" Buranek	life-support engineer and medic
Anisha Chatterjee	electrical engineer and robot wrangler
Mustafa Gilfoyle	station chief of the relief crew
Lester "Les" Hodges	biotech/nanotech engineer
Mariana Kwan	mining engineer

Other off-Earth company personnel

Patricia "Trish" Garcia	Martian-based managing partner
"Howard"	managing partner disguising his identity
"Tweedledum and Tweedledee"	managing partners disguising their identity

Company personnel based on Earth

Anna Burnham	staffer in Public Relations
Jaime Olafson	private investigator retained by the company's law firm
Maureen Rogers	alias of Jaime Olafson
Andrew "Andy" Singh	lawyer for (and a secret managing partner of) the company

USNA government personnel

James Guenther	Counterterrorism Center analyst, former chemical engineer
Delilah Hernandez	analyst for an unidentified intelligence agency
Fred Huang	FBI agent
Archibald Jackson III ("Trey")	shuttle pilot for an unidentified intelligence agency
Danielle Kowalski	FBI agent

Miscellaneous

Darin Hodges	son of Lester Hodges; terrorist; graduate biotech student
Vegan Woman	unidentified terrorist, and colleague of Darin Hodges
Keith Smithson	alias for a terrorist colleague of Darin Hodges
"Mysterion"	Dark Net hacker (location disguised; may not be on Earth)

ABOUT THE AUTHOR

EDWARD M. LERNER worked in high tech and aerospace for thirty years, as everything from engineer to senior vice president, for much of that time writing science fiction as his hobby. Since 2004 he has written full-time.

His novels range from near-future technothrillers, like *Small Miracles* and *Energized*, to traditional SF, like *Dark Secret* and his InterstellarNet series, to (collaborating with Larry Niven) the space-opera epic Fleet of Worlds series of *Ringworld* companion novels. Lerner's 2015 novel, *InterstellarNet: Enigma*, won the inaugural Canopus Award "honoring excellence in interstellar writing." His fiction has also been nominated for Locus, Prometheus, and Hugo awards.

Lerner's short fiction has appeared in anthologies, collections, and many of the usual SF magazines and websites. He also writes about science and technology, notably including *Trope-ing the Light Fantastic: The Science Behind the Fiction*.

Lerner lives in Virginia with his wife, Ruth.

His website is *www.edwardmlerner.com*.

www.ingramcontent.com/pod-product-compliance
Lightning Source LLC
LaVergne TN
LVHW091049080826
845145LV00002B/679

* 9 7 8 1 6 4 9 7 3 1 2 9 6 *